Two Can PLAY

A Conaire Gray Thriller

E. PAUL BERGERON

Cover Design & Formatting by Gray Publishing Services

ISBN 978-0996701327

1

Miguel Zapata pointed and said, "There. You see her? She is going to pull out."

Eduardo Fuentes swung the black Suburban into a U-turn in front of a Honda Civic and pulled into the parking space vacated by a minivan. Zapata rolled his window down and answered the chorus of blaring horns with a one-finger salute.

Pedestrians passing the vehicle waved their hands in front of their faces at the thick cloud of smoke drifting out from the open window. In answer to their gestures of disgust, Zapata flicked a cigarette butt out window and watched it drop to the sidewalk.

Zapata's fingertips beat a furious tattoo on the dashboard. He then reached over and shut off the engine, killing the cool air from the air conditioner.

"Hey, what you do that for?" said one of the men in rear seat. The man sitting next to him echoed the complaint.

"Shut the fuck up," Zapata ordered. "I need to think and not listen to you two."

He watched the door of the rust-colored stucco building across the street. A blue awning shaded several buckets of flowers sitting on the sidewalk in front the flower shop. Zapata ignored the question, swiveling the rear view mirror to watch for anything approaching from behind. "You sure the police will not give us trouble?"

Fuentes shook his head. "We will be okay if we do not stay too long."

Zapata glanced at his watch. If the police should ask them to step out of the car, what would they think seeing a thick-bodied Hispanic with a heavy mustache and wearing a silk shirt unbuttoned to mid-chest to reveal heavy strands of gold chain. The others in the car would draw no less attention. If they were in San Fernando or Pacoima, it would be different, but not Laguna Mesa, or up the coast a few miles in Newport Beach. He swore at himself for not wearing something less obvious, but how was he to know what these fucking Americanos wore.

Contrary to what the American press referred to as the Latino invasion, he saw few Latinos. *Fuck the Americans*. All he wanted to do was grab the woman and get back to Mexico where he felt safe. "You are sure this is where she is?"

"*Si*, I went in yesterday and bought flowers. She is there," the man seated behind him said.

"What about today?"

"I do not know. You want me to go in and buy more flowers?"

Zapata shook his head. If this were in Morelia, he would go in and take her, and no one would interfere. The police would simply shrug it off and ask for more money.

Fuentes rocked in the driver's seat and lit another cigarette while Zapata studied him. Zapata knew that his father, the legendary Don Emiliano Montoya, trusted Fuentes. When the assassin's bullet meant for Montoya killed the don's only daughter and her newborn son, it also killed Eduardo Fuentes' wife and child. From that day on, Eduardo Fuentes swore solemn allegiance to the drug baron.

Zapata reviewed the meetings he had had earlier in the day. The meetings went as expected. These people needed the money he brought, and his presence was enough to convince them of Don Emiliano's intentions. Why else would the big man send Miguel Zapata into the United States—where the police and judges could not be bought—and expose him to possible arrest if this was not of utmost importance to him.

Zapata moved his hand unconsciously to touch his shirt pocket, feeling the bulk of the small notebook that never left his possession and in which he recorded much needed information.

"Look at what is coming, Miguel. She is looking for you. I know this," one in the back seat said.

Zapata watched a young woman jogging toward them, holding the leash of a golden retriever, her blonde ponytail brushing her tanned shoulders. His eyes took in the long bare legs. American women are too skinny, he mused. Mexican women have more meat on their bodies, but this one he knew he would not turn away. "How much longer?" he asked.

Fuentes consulted his watch. "Soon, I think, unless she is not there."

"She must be there. We cannot wait another day. It is too dangerous.

Ten minutes later a young woman with shaggy brown hair came out of the flower shop wearing a red polo shirt with the store's name on the front. She danced down the steps, shouldering her bag as she spoke to a man sweeping the sidewalk in front of the small deli next door. He laughed at whatever she said and went back to work, but his eyes followed her swinging hips.

"Look, Miguel, that is her. You see? We told you she was there," the one sitting behind Fuentes said. "We should grab the bitch now. Why should we wait?"

Soon, Zapata thought. Soon it would be over, and they would be safely back in Mexico, at least as safe as being in another cartel's territory allowed them to be.

Zapata watched the woman until she turned up a side street.

"Is that where she lives, on that street?"

"It is a little way up. Maybe a couple of blocks, I think," said the one sitting behind Zapata.

Zapata reached back and grabbed the man by the shirt, pulling him forward until they were nose to nose. "You think, fuck head? You think maybe a couple of blocks? What do you think we have paid you this money for, to guess where the woman lives?"

"No, Miguel. It is where she lives. I promise."

Zapata nodded to Fuentes. "Drive down the street and let this one out, and then we will get something to eat while we wait."

Fuentes pulled into traffic and drove along Pacific Coast Highway until he found a spot to pull over.

Zapata motioned to the one behind him. "Walk back and watch her house. You have a phone. Do not use it unless she leaves the house. If she does, follow her. Do you understand this?"

"*Si*, Miguel, but what if she drives her car somewhere? What do I do?"

"Call me and run after her like your life depends on it, because it does. Now go."

2

Conaire Gray slipped the pack off his shoulders and propped it up against the sign that read "Bishop Pass, 11,980 feet." The climb up from the Pacific Crest Trail had taken him most of the morning and, standing among the rock and talus, he figured the six miles to the South Lake Trailhead would take another two and a half hours.

Two weeks before, Gray had hired an outfitter to set up a camp beside a small lake well off the trail that took northbound hikers from the Mexican border at Campo, California, 2,650 miles to Manning Park, British Columbia. Gray had promised himself the luxury of someday taking the four months or so to walk the trail. This ten-day trip, however, focused on the ten linen canvas panels nestled in the custom-built box strapped to the back of the Gregory Denali pack. When complete, the paintings would bring a minimum of $1,500 a piece after the gallery took its commission.

Gray made a mental note to send a tip along to the packer. The camp and supplies, in bear-proof containers, had made the ten days as enjoyable as Gray could expect, given the torment that sent him into the mountains to begin with. The one thing about these trips he could count on—the nightmares remained behind. On previous trips Gray had stretched the supplies to add an extra day or two, but he was anxious to return to his car and call Bethany, knowing she and her six-year-old daughter, Carlie Kate, would be waiting to hear from him.

From the high pass, the faint trail switch-backed down through the rocks to the parking lot four thousand feet below. Far to the east, across the arid Owens Valley, the White Mountains lay hot and dry in contrast to the often snow-capped Sierra Nevada Mountains. Spearhead and Long Lake lay below him, at the foot of massive Mount Agassiz. He shouldered his pack and began the descent.

Half an hour later he stopped, his eyes following the graceful glide of a raptor searching for food. The bird dropped quickly on a pile of rocks to Gray's right but veered off and rose again. Gray froze and remained motionless as he watched for the movement that had attracted the hunter. He saw the marmot perched atop a large boulder. He waited, the wind whipping the ends of his pack straps as he and the animal faced each other, motionless, until the large rodent slid between the rocks and disappeared. Gray grinned and continued on down.

His thoughts kept returning to the subject that he and Bethany had discussed before he left. Could they have a life together? He knew he could never tell her why her father had split them up eight years earlier. Even with the secrets he held, any life with Bethany and Carlie Kate would be more rewarding than the years he had spent alone.

The knee-crushing descent passed through the subalpine zone, marked by a scattering of Whitebark Pine and Sierra Juniper, all struggling to find subsistence in the thin soil. Below, a mountain meadow, still lush from the winter snow melt, fed a creek that flowed into South Lake at the trailhead.

The trail wound along the shoreline until its final descent to a parking lot filled with cars and campers belonging to fisherman and day hikers. Someone had parked a large motor home across five parking spots, a blue awning shading enough furniture for a small apartment. A cooking grill sat at the end of a collapsible table covered with condiments. Two people sat in canvas chairs watching a small television screen, a large cooler between them.

Gray crossed the parking lot and eased his pack onto the blacktop in the narrow space between the rear of the forty-footer and his two-year-old Jeep Wrangler. He shook his head, wondering why people drove their motel-on-wheels up to a place like this to watch television.

Gray watched as the man heaved himself out of his canvas folding chair and reached into the cooler. His hand came out holding two dripping cans, and he started toward the Jeep. Gray had seen the type at any number of trailheads: overweight, wearing baggy shorts and a Hawaiian-type shirt with white knee socks and lace-up shoes.

The man lumbered over and held out a can of beer. "How about a cold one. You look like you could use it."

"No, thanks," Gray said.

"Well, my bride of thirty years and I been here a couple of days. Wondered how come that car of yours was still here. You been up there?" the man said, pointing to the peaks in the distance.

Gray nodded while he continued to unstrap the paint box from his pack.

"Yes, sir," the man continued. "Been sitting here watching *I Love Lucy* films on our VCR. Sure wish this road went further up there. Those mountains sure look pretty." He pointed at the beaded headband Gray used to keep his long hair out of his eyes. "Say, you one of the local Indians hereabouts? Paiute, right?"

Gray placed the box in the Jeep and tossed in his hiking poles and pack. "No, afraid not."

The man's bride was attempting to push herself up and out of her camp chair. Finally succeeding, she shuffled over to join her husband. Gray fought the urge to tell the man why he didn't deserve the privilege of going up "there" as he put it. Besides, dropping this pair off at 11,000 feet would probably kill them.

As he drove away, he passed two more motor homes grinding up the narrow road to the trailhead parking lot, one oversize bus pulling a mid-sized SUV. Gray grinned, knowing the driver wouldn't find any place to park the vehicle, or turn around. He could picture the driver attempting to back down the narrow, curving road.

The temperature rose steadily as the road wound its way down into the Owens Valley. The little town of Bishop, California, consisted of about four thousand or so rednecks, out-of-work Paiute Indians, and retirees looking for a place to spend their remaining years. It served the thousands of Los Angeles citizens who drove up California's Highway 395 bound for Reno, Nevada, and Lake Tahoe. Others came to spend the night before hiking into the backcountry or trying their luck fishing the Owens River. In winter, skiers passed through the town heading for Mammoth and June Mountain, or farther north to Squaw Valley.

The traffic light at the corner of Line Street and Highway 395 gave Gray the opportunity to power up his phone. While he waited he watched a couple enter the Mountain Light Gallery, a gray-white building that exhibited the photography of Galen Rowell. Gray had a copy of Rowell's book, *In the Throne Room of the Mountain Gods,* a history of those who chose to risk their lives attempting to summit K2. On several trips Gray had stopped by the gallery to meet the man, but Rowell spent much of his time on assignments. Then, unfortunately, Rowell and his wife died when their plane went down attempting to land at the nearby airport.

The light changed and Gray pulled into a spot across from the old Bishop Grill. He picked up the phone and swore when he saw the power level was too low to make a call.

After plugging in his charger, Gray jogged across the street to the Mexican grill. A rusted-out red pickup sat at the curb in front of two planter boxes in need of water and a fire hydrant. Duct tape held one headlight casing in place and empty beer cans littered the bed of the truck.

3

The tree stood atop a narrow flat, nearly a mile away, alone and sinister looking in its isolation.

Emiliano Montoya, known as Don Emiliano to those who worked for him, stood in front of the bulletproof window of his expansive hacienda. He carefully peeled away the wrapping of a Piramides Añejados Cuban cigar and spoke to the man who had advised him for the last six years.

"Have you seen some of the things they are writing about us?" he said, pointing the cigar at the stack of newspapers on his desk.

"We are portrayed as animals by these crusading journalists, while they take the money from our hand that pays for their whores."

"Is there one in particular, Emiliano?"

"This one, from Morelia, speaks of the twelve people tortured and killed as being Federal Agents. They were Federal Police, and that is a big difference, and this story says nothing about how much money they took for their protection service. It only says we are to blame. Now they have created an excuse to arrest some people so the politicians can tell the Americans they are doing something about the trade in drugs, and hope the money keeps flowing into their pockets from both sides. If the Americans were not so hungry for these drugs, there would be no problem to solve."

Caesar Castillo sat across the desk from Montoya, his ever-present leather tablet open to record his orders. "It has always been this way. It will not change."

Montoya shook his head. "Has anybody ever figured out what the people would do without this trade? There would be a revolution without this money." He sat down and clipped the end off of the cigar. He glanced up at the clock again, noting only five minutes had passed since the last time he looked. "Did Miguel tell you what time he planned to act?"

"He said he would wait until darkness. Our man at the border is not on duty until midnight."

"Of course, I remember, but I like to hear it said again." Montoya carefully lit his cigar and placed the lighter beside the cut-glass ashtray. He took a deep breath and closed his eyes. He thought about all the planning and all the opposition Castillo had put forth, and Castillo's constant warning of the consequences of failure. Montoya had overruled his advisor. This meant too much to be put aside, and he had waited too long to get the revenge that consumed him. Now, if only Miguel would follow his orders, everything would go as planned. "Good, now are we finished?"

"Not quite. The priest is here again," Castillo said without looking up. "It is about the church in Aquililla. He said you had offered to replace the roof."

"Yes, I agreed to it. It is the church that Miguel's mother attends. Give him what he needs."

"There is one last thing. It is about the two whom we discovered passing information to the American DEA agent. What is it you want to do with them?"

Montoya stood and returned to the bulletproof window, his hands clasped behind his back. The wind rolled down the hill and swept the patio before curling in through the open French doors and ruffling the papers on the desk. "Have Miguel take care of it when he returns."

Castillo closed his tablet and rose.

"Do you know what day it is?" Montoya said.

"Is this a special day of some sort?"

"Yes," Montoya said. "It was eight years ago today it happened."

4

The Suburban inched its way up the narrow street.

"There," Miguel Zapata said, pointing to a figure standing behind a curbside tree, smoking a cigarette.

Eduardo Fuentes pulled to the curb and shut off the engine.

The man came out from the shadows and dropped his cigarette in the gutter. "That is the house, the one with the white fence," he said.

The house stood well back from the street on a well-maintained lot. A sprawling, weathered, clapboard house with large bay windows, surrounded by a thick belt of foliage.

"You are sure?" Zapata said.

"Yes, that is where she lives."

"And she is there now?"

The man nodded. "Yes, she has not left the house."

"There is something else?"

"Miguel, she is not alone."

"What do you mean she is not alone? Has someone come to see her?"

"No, it is not that. She went to another house and came out with a child, who is there with her now."

Zapata slammed his hand down on the dashboard. "You fucking idiots, you did not know about this child?" He turned to Fuentes. "Did you hear anything about the woman having a child?"

Fuentes shook his head but remained silent.

"Enough fucking talking. It is only one woman and a child," Zapata muttered. He motioned for Fuentes to pull forward.

Fuentes restarted the engine and allowed the Suburban coasted down the street to the white picket fence. The three men exited the car and eased the doors shut. Zapata whispered to his two henchmen, who moved into the shadows to watch. They had their orders. They would warn him if anyone approached.

Terra cotta pots containing blood-red geraniums lined an uneven walk of used brick while clutching bougainvillea vines claimed an arbor, their tissue-like petals blanketing the path. The air stirred with a fresh ocean breeze bringing the smell of the salt air to mingle with the garden foliage as Zapata and Fuentes men slipped through the gate and approached the house. Zapata put his hand on the doorknob, ready to throw his shoulder against it if was locked. The door opened without a sound and both men burst into the well-lit room.

The child saw them first. "Mommy, someone's here," she said, backing up while hugging a doll to her chest.

"Who is it, Carlie?" a woman's voice called out from another part of the house.

Before the child could answer, Fuentes picked her up off the floor.

The girl screamed.

"Carlie," a woman cried, rushing into the room with a wet towel slung over her shoulder.

Zapata stepped forward and pinned her arms to her sides.

"Leave her alone," the woman screamed, struggling to free herself. "What do you want?"

"Shut up, bitch, and we will not hurt her. Do not struggle or it will be worse for you," Zapata said.

"Mommy," the girl cried out again.

"What do you want? Tell me, but let her go. She's just a child," the woman cried. "You hurt her and so help me I'll kill you."

Zapata clamped his hand over her mouth and carried her toward the door.

"What about this one?" Fuentes asked of the girl struggling in his arms.

"How the fuck do I know? She wasn't supposed to be here. We want the woman. You will have to figure it out, but she can tell them who we are. Take her in the back and get rid of her."

The woman in Zapata's arms twisted her head back, freeing her mouth for an instant and bit down on Zapata's hand. He felt her teeth strike the bone at the base of his thumb.

"Fucking whore." He pulled his hand away and clutched it to his chest, blood soaking the front of his shirt.

With a twist the woman broke out of his grasp and sprinted toward the back of the house.

"Grab her before she can use a phone," Fuentes yelled.

For a moment Zapata forgot the pain in his hand and raced after the woman. She ran into a room at the end of the hall and threw herself across the bed, attempting to reach a phone on a bedside table.

Zapata leaped on the bed and grabbed the top of her tank top. He pulled her across the bed and flipped her over onto her back, ripping the thin material and the shear bra under it. The woman instinctively covered her breasts with both hands.

Zapata's breathing became heavy. For the moment he forgot the pain in his hand and reached across with his good hand to pull her arms away from her breasts. He squeezed one roughly, running his thumb over her nipple and wondering what his father would do with her. Still struggling, the woman vainly attempted to twist out of his grasp, but Zapata had pinned her legs between his knees. She jerked one leg free and brought it to her chest, then drove it upward into his face.

Zapata felt a tooth snap as her heel drove it into his lip. He cursed, stumbling back and releasing his grip on her legs. She lashed out again with both legs, this time hitting his injured hand.

"Fucking bitch," he screamed, leaning over to neutralize her legs and attempting to pin her flailing arms with his good hand. But she eluded him long enough to reach up and rake his cheek with her nails, leaving deep white furrows along the side of his face.

Jolted by the new source of pain, Zapata could think of nothing but retaliating. His hand felt as if it were on fire, his jaw throbbed, and blood dripped off his chin onto the covering of the bed. "Fucking whore, I will kill you, bitch," he swore, grabbing the fingers on one of her hands and bending them backward until he heard a series of cracks.

The woman's screams tore through the house. Realizing her cries might be heard by neighbors, Zapata clamped his injured hand over her mouth. This time her teeth bit into the already seeping wound, causing Zapata more pain than he had ever experienced. He could no longer remember why they wanted this woman, or what his father's orders were. He only knew he wanted to punish her. He slammed his fist into the side of her head repeatedly, until she lay motionless.

Fuentes rushed into the room, still struggling to control the hysterical girl under his arm. The girl cried out when she saw her mother lying on the bed with Zapata's blood streaking her breasts. Fuentes clamped a hand over the child's mouth. "Mother of God, Miguel. What has happened?"

Zapata cradled his injured arm to his body. "I hit her when she struck me. I think I hit her too hard and she might be dead."

Fuentes stared at the woman lying on the bed. "What will we tell Don Emiliano? It is no use taking a dead woman to him."

"It was not my fault. She attacked me and I lost my head. Look at what she has done to me."

"Miguel, we must go now. People may have heard. This is not Mexico where people forget what they hear. Someone will call the police, it is certain."

"We must give them something to follow," Zapata said. "That package in the car will give the police something to think about."

Zapata left Fuentes holding the child while he raced to the Suburban and removed a wrapped bundle from under the front seat. He glanced around the neighborhood, listening. The nearby houses remained quiet. There was a possibility they could get away before anyone reported the sounds. All he wanted to do was leave this place and find something to help with the pain. In Zapata's privileged life, he had not known times of such pain. Fuentes wrapped the girl in a blanket. He had found adhesive tape and covered her mouth to stifle her cries. "What are you doing?" Zapata wanted to know. "We cannot let her live."

"I cannot do it, Miguel. I think we should take her with us."

"You are a fool. She has seen us."

"Think about it, Miguel. If your head were clear you would understand. Your father sent us here to take this woman and bring her back to him, but she is dead and your father's plan will fail. This girl is the woman's daughter. Can she not take her place? Why do we not let your father decide this? Besides, Miguel, I cannot kill the child. You must understand this."

"Fuentes, we will talk of this later. Right now let us get the fuck out of here before it is too late." Zapata opened the package and spilt some of the white powder on the woman's face and placed the remainder on the bedside table. He found the bathroom and pulled two towels off the rack, wrapping one around his hand and holding the other to his face while Fuentes carried the girl out and put her into the back of the Suburban. Fuentes climbed in and released the brake, coasting the short distance down the street to Pacific Coast Highway.

Zapata glanced at the dashboard clock. In order to cross into Mexico without trouble they needed to be at the crossing at Tecate at exactly fifteen minutes after one. Zapata fingered his mother's Virgin of Guadalupe medal, wishing he had kept some of the powder to dull the pain.

5

Conaire Gray ordered a plate of enchiladas and refried beans along with a bottle of Pacifico beer. The waitress kept coming back to see if he needed anything else and seemed disappointed to find out he was not a new local.

Outside the restaurant he stood for a moment and breathed in the clean, high-desert air, while the craggy granite faces behind the town slowly disappeared in shadow. Gray hated to leave the sleepy little town nestled beneath the bulk of Mt. Tom and its thirteen thousand-foot companions, but special people were waiting. In other times he might have stayed, or driven north to hike into the Minarets, but not at that moment, not with the work ahead of him. The canvasses he had blocked in over the last ten days were far from gallery ready, and orders for his paintings left little time to wander the high country in search of peace.

The red pickup still sat by the curb as Gray made a U-turn and drove out of town. He rolled the windows down to let in the heavy scent of the desert sage growing in the arid fields.

Traffic was light, a few campers and an occasional big rig working the highway from L.A. to Reno. South of Bishop an array of radio towers, referred to by the locals as the "big ears," searched the heavens for answers. Further south a Tule elk herd grazed on a farmer's alfalfa field.

His cell phone showed sufficient charge but no signal, so he tossed it back on the seat. He knew they would be anxious to hear from him. He grinned. No one had worried about him for years.

A sign notified him the highway ahead narrowed to two lanes. Before pulling over he glanced in the mirror and saw a vehicle gaining rapidly, apparently hoping to pass before the lanes converged. A semi, followed by an SUV, approached from the opposite direction. Gray checked the mirror again. The same red pickup from town had closed to within inches of his rear bumper. Gray increased his speed but the pickup, its horn blaring, remained glued to the back of the Jeep. The oncoming semi swept passed and the pickup swung out into the far lane as the approaching SUV narrowed the distance. Gray quickly backed off the gas to allow the pickup room to pull into his lane. He caught a glimpse of an arm protruding from the open window, a beer can in the hand of a red-shirted passenger. For an instant the can seemed suspended in the air before smashing into the windshield of the Jeep. Gray hit the brakes and flipped on the wipers as the pickup veered back into his lane ahead of the on-rushing SUV, red-shirt extending his arm in a one-finger salute.

Gray swore, jamming the gas pedal to the floor. Up ahead the pickup pulled out again and swept past a lumbering motor home towing a compact car. Gray eased up on the gas as more traffic approached. He took a deep breath and followed behind the slow-moving motor home, letting the tension flow out of his body.

"Assholes," he muttered, questioning what it was he expected to do when he caught up with the pickup. As he thought about it, he admitted his options were pretty limited. He could try running them off the road; that would probably produce results since most assholes refused to wear seat belts as a sign of their superior knowledge and total disregard for the law. Or he could pull alongside the pickup and call them assholes, or have the satisfaction of returning their one-finger salute. All of which would gain him nothing except to escalate the situation. Only hours out of the mountains and he was already letting people get to him. He really needed to hear her voice.

A few miles below the little town of Independence, he passed the sign for the turnoff to Manzanar, the first of a dozen internment camps built to relocate Japanese Americans following the attack on Pearl Harbor. On a previous trip Gray took the turnoff and walked the grounds that had once held more than ten thousand people in small apartments surrounded by barbed wire and armed guards. Gray wondered if those interned had felt like Native Americans living on their reservations like citizens of a third-world country. Maybe the barbed wire was missing on the reservations, but he remembered times when he had felt as if it was there.

He pulled over at a rest stop and tried the phone again. This time he received a busy signal. He frowned.

The lights from an all-night gas station and mini-mart created a halo of yellow against the blackening sky. He pulled off the highway and parked beside the forward pump. A hand-lettered sign duct-taped to the pump directed him to pay inside. He pulled two twenties from his wallet and walked past an ice chest advertising bags of ice cubes. Faded advertisements for beer, snacks, and the availability of spending your food-stamp money on lotto tickets littered the dirty windows. No one had bothered to peel off the yellowing tape from past posters.

Gray noticed the red pickup parked on the unlit side of the mini-mart. He paused, his hand resting against the glass door. Should he get back in the Jeep and leave? He had enough gas to get to the next station. He shook his head. He wasn't looking for trouble and there was no reason why there would be any if he ignored them.

Inside, the store reminded him of a Vietnamese liquor store in Westminster. Aisles containing an assortment of motor oil and batteries, canned goods, dusty and long passed their expiration date, along with a few toiletries. End caps with bags of chips and peanuts. Coolers lined the back wall with cold drinks and beer, while on the counter boxes of lighters, jerky, and single shots of energy drinks left only enough room for the transaction of business, while overhead racks offered a wide selection of condoms for those on their way to the brothels of Carson City and Reno. A fluorescent light flickered at the rear of the store, illuminating boxes of goods stacked ceiling high.

Gray grimaced at the sharp smell of burnt coffee and overcooked hot dogs on the grill.

The red-shirted passenger from the pickup held a six-pack of beer out to the thin-faced Asian behind the counter. Gray noted the heavily tattooed arms and neck of the man who had tossed the beer can on the Jeep's windshield. Low-hanging jeans revealed red pimples on pale white skin.

In a mirror above the clerk's head, Gray watched the one he figured was the driver of the pickup. Pale faced, haunting, with shaggy black hair poking out from under an Oakland Raiders hat. Gray watched him stuff packages of snacks into his pockets, while the one at the counter blocked the clerk's view.

The clerk's eyes shifted to Gray.

Red-shirt followed his gaze and noticed Gray for the first time. He held the six-pack up in the air and grinned. His teeth weren't much cleaner than the rest of him. "Hey, chief, my last beer just up and fell out the window back a ways. This gook here wants to charge enough for this pack to support all his relatives. Think it's worth it?"

Gray ignored the taunt and walked toward the coolers for a bottle of water. It would have to do considering the state of the coffee. He unscrewed the top and took a drink.

The clerk shook his head at something red-shirt said, then replied, "You pay me seven dollar."

"Shit, I ain't paying seven dollars for this horse piss beer. How about you toss in a pack of smokes and we'll call it even."

"You pay seven dollar, no cigarettes." The clerk reached for the six-pack, but red-shirt grabbed his arm and twisted it to the side.

"Fact is, slant eyes, I might just take it on account of you being such a prick."

Gray wanted no part of what was escalating into a pissing contest. He tossed the money on the counter for the water and gas. "Punch in forty for gas on number four," he said.

Red-shirt swept the bills over to the clerk. "Do as the chief says, Charlie. Then you and me can discuss our problem."

Gray noted the store video camera above the cigarette rack. The lens hung by a wire, obviously out of commission. He wondered if red-shirt had noticed it. Below the camera the clerk did a nervous shuffle. Gray felt a sharp jolt against his shoulder.

"Why don't you get your ass out of here and pump your gas, chief. Me and this here oriental turd still have to come to an agreement," red-shirt snarled, his finger still embedded in Gray's shoulder.

Gray's eyes moved down to the finger, catching a glimpse of the outline of a gun beneath the man's T-shirt. Maybe the clerk had already seen it. It would account for the level of fear in his eyes. The clerk shook his head when he caught Gray's glance. It was obvious he didn't want to be left alone.

Ten days in the mountains and all Gray wanted to do was get gas and get back on the road. Two people were waiting to hear all he had to tell them of the beauty and magnificence of the most beautiful mountain range in the world. Two people who meant a new life for him, and possibly a future that so far had eluded him. He knew he should go out the door, pump his gas, and be back on the highway. The guy behind the counter took the job knowing there would probably be situations like this. All he had to do was nod his head, smile, bow if that's what he did, and let the assholes have their beer and pilfered smokes. Hell, what was the cost anyway, three or four dollars?

Red-shirt jabbed Gray in the shoulder again. "You hard of hearing, chief? Drag your tail and save yourself mucho grief."

Shit, he hated to be touched. And he hated even more being called chief. He knew he should have removed the beaded headband when he left the mountains, but he had grown used to it, and it kept his long hair out of his face. As far as he was concerned it had nothing to do with his heritage.

The driver of the pickup stood in front of a window watching the traffic on the highway. "Hey, man, we ain't got all night. Let's get out of here before somebody shows up."

"Your buddy's got the right idea," Gray said. "Why not pay the man. Hell, if you don't have the money, I'll pay for it. It's not worth somebody getting hurt over."

Red-shirt grinned. "Well now, chief, if you're willing to pay for the beer what else you willing to pay for?"

Gray pushed the hand off his shoulder. "I said the beer, nothing else."

Red-shirt's hand dropped to his side. He pulled up the T-shirt, exposing the gun tucked beneath his belt. "Fun's over. I ain't saying it again. Now beat it 'for you get yourself hurt."

Gray figured he should let the guy behind the counter make his own decisions. The problem was the one still burying his finger in Gray's shoulder while clutching the butt of the pistol with the other. He was the one who couldn't seem to let it go.

Gray took a step back from the pressure on his shoulder and rocked forward onto his toes, throwing a right cross to red-shirt's exposed chin. It rolled the man's eyes toward heaven. The man swayed a moment before slowly crumbling to his knees. A man willing to threaten with a gun deserves to suffer the consequences, Gray thought. He grabbed him by the back of the head and drove his knee into his jaw, hearing the bone snap. "Be awhile before you'll be able to call me chief again."

The driver let out a yell when he saw red-shirt crumple to the floor and charged up the aisle. Gray wasn't sure whether the driver was trying to leave in a hurry or coming at him. He figured it wasn't worth taking a chance. He grabbed the front of the man's shirt and used his momentum to throw him up against the hot-dog grill, sending it and its hot contents crashing to the floor. The driver howled in pain as his hands came in contact with the hot surface. He pushed himself to his feet and Gray hit him in the kidneys, causing him to drop his arms to protect his sides. Gray then chopped two rights to the jaw, sending him face first onto the floor, his lying across the other amongst the items littering the floor.

"Call the police and tell them you were about to be robbed," Gray said. He reached down and picked up the 9mm red-shirt had dropped.

Gray spun around and crouched as a door slammed shut in the rear of the store. The counter area was empty. He looked for the clerk, then realized the man had left. Gray raced to the back door and flung it open. A battered Toyota compact squirreled out of the parking lot onto the highway and headed south. He shook his head, figuring the man probably wouldn't stop until he was safe in the confines of Orange County's Little Saigon, then asked himself why in hell had he bothered to get involved? He should have followed his first instinct and left when he could. Any moment someone would pull into the gas station, and he would be answering a lot of questions. Well, he wasn't planning to stick around to find out. He ejected the magazine from the gun and wiped it off with the end of his shirt before tossing it to the back of the store. He did the same with the gun and dropped it beside the still inert bodies. "Sorry, assholes but you asked for it."

One of the men moaned as Gray pushed through the door and headed for the Jeep. To hell with the gas. He knew of a station farther down the highway.

Five miles south he picked up the cell phone and tried her number again. The phone was still busy. Bethany rarely talked on the phone for long periods of time. Something had to be wrong with the phone lines.

6

The Suburban pulled off the highway and onto the cracked asphalt of a deserted gas station. Fuentes parked between a battered dumpster and a fifteen-year-old Chevy sedan, and turned off the vehicle's lights. The waxing gibbous moon provided all the light they would need.

Zapata swore as he tried opening the car door with his swollen hand. "Fucking woman. If she was not already dead I would kill her for this."

Fuentes got out and opened the rear door to let the girl sit up. He checked his watch. "We must be on time, Miguel. It would not be good if we are late."

Miguel Zapata lit a cigarette and spoke to the other two men before they climbed into the sedan and drove off. He had to think about what to do about them, but not now. He hurt too much to think. "We have time. Tell her we will kill her like we did her mother if she makes a sound."

"I have done so already, but now we should go," Fuentes said. "As soon as we cross over we must call your father. He will be waiting to hear."

"This is a call I do not want to make, but maybe he will see the girl is better for him," Zapata said. Possibly he could claim this idea as his own.

Fuentes started the engine, turned the headlights on, and eased the Suburban back onto the highway. A few miles south, he turned off and followed the signs to the U.S.-Mexico border crossing at Tecate.

As they approached the brightly lit facility, Zapata asked,

"You know the one who will be here?"

"I know him."

"Do you see him?"

"That is him ahead. The one in the first lane."

The man had been well paid to keep their crossing a secret from anyone who might be interested, which meant any Federal Police captain anxious to get rich in a hurry.

Off to the side, two *Federales*, their sidearms hanging below large bellies, stood talking to a woman wearing a miniskirt that exposed her heavy thighs. No one paid any attention to the Suburban.

A thin-faced man wearing an ill-fitting uniform waved them forward and peered in Fuente's window. Zapata pointed his finger at him as if he had a gun. The agent nodded and waved them through.

Fuentes drove slowly down Tecate's main street, passing a well-lit bus station teeming with men and woman sitting beside what possessions they had brought with them, waiting for the morning bus that would take them east. Somewhere along the road they hoped to meet up with their *coyote*, who would take then to a point to cross into the U.S.—unless he robbed them first and left them in the killing heat of the desert.

"We must make the call soon," Fuentes said, rubbing his unshaven jaw. "I am afraid he will not take this news well. You know how he is if things do not go as he planned."

With an effort Zapata shook a cigarette out of its pack and used both hands to hold the lighter. "That fucking woman has caused us too much fucking trouble. She is dead, but we will be the ones to suffer. I will talk to Castillo. You drive the fucking car and let me handle my father."

Fuentes shrugged. "Just telling you, Miguel. You know how he is."

Zapata waited for Fuentes to say something more, but the man just stared at the road ahead. Would he back his story, Zapata wondered, or would he twist it to make it look like the woman's death was all Zapata's fault. Yet, maybe behind those movie-star looks of Fuentes he had a point, one Zapata could use. Maybe the girl was even better than having the woman.

"I know this without help from you, Eduardo," Zapata said. "I hope Castillo can give him good advice before he orders both of us shot."

The moonlight revealed a dirt pullout alongside the highway. Fuentes pulled in and parked in front of a pole shelter supporting a canopy of rotting boards. A wooden table sat behind a hand-lettered sign advertising clean used motor oil for those hoping to make it to the next town before their engines seized up. Beside the table a pair of five-gallon tins sat with a funnel and a kitchen strainer for filtering the oil.

Zapata got out of the SUV and searched the darkness. As far as he could tell they were alone. He reached for his cigarettes again and took a deep breath. He knew his father waited for his call. Out of habit he touched the pocket of his jacket. He felt nothing. His hand flew to the other pockets of his jacket, going back repeatedly to the pocket where the book was kept. All of his pockets were empty.

A cold flush of fear began at his head and swept down over his body. He stood rooted to the ground, his heart pounding, his hands still fluttering from one empty pocket to another. Mother of God, what would he do?

7

Gray continued south on Highway 395 toward Randsburg, still angry at himself for getting involved in a situation he had absolutely no business being in, but he hated people who disregarded the rights of others. He also hated those who flaunted the law when there was no one to stop them, and the two back at the mini-mart were guilty of both. Still, he shouldn't have done it. He had lowered himself to their level, and that's what really bothered him.

He sorted through the half dozen CDs lying on the passenger seat and chose one with a collection of Mozart piano concertos. He slipped it into the Jeep's CD player and turned the volume down low, wondering what old-time Jeep owners would think of the options available to current buyers.

Few cars drove this lonely section of highway at this time of night. He passed Johannesburg, population one hundred seventy and declining, then Red Mountain, a collection of rusted out mining equipment, pickups, boarded-up antique shops, gas stations, and dilapidated shacks. The only signs of life came from an occasional flicker of light peeking through the curtains of a house trailer long past its road usage stage. The clean sharp smell of the high desert died beneath one of decay and lost hopes.

The next place he could expect phone service would be somewhere close to Kramer Junction. He could call then; Bethany never went to bed before eleven. Or she might have left a message if she discovered her phone had been off the hook.

He thought about reporting the incident at the mini-mart, but then someone would want him to explain, and since there were two of them, and the clerk had done the disappearing act, whose word would they take? He had wiped off the gun and clip. Besides, he doubted the police would bother checking for fingerprints over two guys who probably wouldn't admit only one guy beat the crap out of them.

Before he left for the mountains, Bethany had asked him to think about their relationship. The question he faced was simple. Could he be a loving husband and good father for Carlie Kate, and how long would it last with the secrets he carried? Secrets that might destroy any hope of her ever getting back with her family, along with the secrets he swore never to divulge. Secrets, which could put all their lives in danger.

The warm desert air flowed through the open windows of the Jeep. Up ahead the lights of the gas stations and truck-stop cafes held back the night where Highway 58 cut across the high desert on its way to connect with Las Vegas-bound traffic. He pulled in between two compact cars in the parking lot of the Shuttle Café, remembering another time he sat in this same spot and watched the Space Shuttle Challenger silently glide overhead as it dropped out of the sky onto the runway at Edwards Air Force Base.

His phone beeped with a message, but it wasn't from Bethany as he hoped. The message came from Paco Juarez, the one person he could talk to about demons without violating any trusts or agreements. He didn't need to share the stories with Paco. Paco had been with him.

He dialed Bethany's number and got a busy signal again. He slipped the phone back in his pocket and went into the restaurant.

Back in the Jeep, Gray sipped coffee from a paper cup while listening to Juarez's message. Nothing of importance, only a reminder it was time for their usual two or three times a year lunch to update their lives. For a moment he thought about deleting the message and putting off returning the call, but then he got thinking. Juarez must have faced the same problem when he got married; what had he shared with his wife? Gray decided he would return the call later.

In the miles of stunted desert growth awash in dim moonlight, Gray reflected on how their paths had crossed. He and Juarez had found themselves the two outsiders in Marine Boot Camp. Indian blood ran through the veins of both. Juarez's father's family were *Raramuri* natives from northwestern Mexico, and Gray was one quarter Southern Piegan Blackfoot. This common bond kept them together through their training, and only when the Marines transferred Gray after the mission were they separated.

Traffic through Cajon Pass amounted to a steady stream of big rigs, with an occasional passenger car keeping to the outer lane of the long downgrade into San Bernardino.

At the bottom of the long grade, Interstate 15 cut through Norco and its overpowering odor of horse farms and feed lots. Gray rolled up the window and hit the return message number.

Juarez picked up the phone on the third ring.

"Paco, my friend, how you doing?"

"Doing well. Glad you found time to call. The last time it took you three months.

Gray grinned. "Thought you wanted to borrow money. Anyway there's something I need to talk about, but I'd rather not do it over the phone."

He waited a moment for Juarez to respond.

"Well, amigo, I suppose you can buy me lunch if it's that important," Juarez said.

"Why not, but my choice this time," Gray said, remembering the last time they met. Juarez took him to a taco wagon in Santa Ana that turned out to be a converted delivery van staying one step ahead of the state food inspectors.

"Why, you don't like our food?" Juarez said. "I can't understand. It has flavor; it has substance; everything a normal person would want. I don't know of any place serves reservation food, unless it's jerky to go. But, if you're paying, I'll eat anywhere you want."

"I know that. You've never turned down a free meal in your life. You still working at that place that tries rehabilitating wayward Mexicans?"

"This place you are referring to is called Taller San Jose, and they are not all Mexicans we help. They are from many countries. But before you ask, no, there are no Indians. We don't want none."

Gray grinned knowing the conversation was following the form developed over long periods of time. "Yeah, I'll bet, but you guys all look alike to me."

Juarez chuckled. "You Indians should talk. Where do you think you would be if we hadn't come up here and civilized you? Gave you all that religion, even if you didn't want it."

"Least we didn't have to crawl through sage brush someplace in Texas or Arizona to get here."

They kept up the insults until Gray was well down the 605 toward the Beach Cities and they agreed to meet at a place in Santa Ana. Gray figured Juarez would give him an unbiased opinion. It might not be what he wanted to hear but he would live with it.

With the issue temporarily resolved, Gray pushed aside what he couldn't do anything about and tried to focus on the work ahead. The last ten days only deepened his appreciation for the canvasses of Edgar Payne and other early California Impressionists who saw the savage beauty of the Sierra Nevada Mountains as their challenge. He faced the age-old problem that had confronted them. How does an artist capture the breath-taking power and beauty of these mountains and transfer it to a one-dimensional canvas? Payne had come close, as had Thomas Moran, and Bierstadt before him. Gray knew he still had miles to go before he could begin to equal their work, which reminded him that the Laguna Beach Art Museum planned to exhibit canvasses of Granville Redmond and Braun the following month. Very few opportunities came around for him to view the original works, and when they did he spent hours studying the pieces and wondering what the artists were thinking when they created them.

Pacific Coast Highway glistened with water from the runoff caused by the sprinkler systems beginning their nightly ritual with precious water brought half way down the state.

Only a few twenty-four-hour-a-day neon lights blinked in the cool night air. Gray turned up Bethany's street and drove past her house. A light over the front door lit the brick walkway. He thought about stopping but figured it would wait until morning. He drove to his house and parked in the garage. Before the door closed he saw a light flicker across the street as the curtains parted and his neighbor peered out through the opening. He shook his head wondering how the woman always managed to appear in front of her window when he drove up. He hadn't spoken to her since she made it clear she was always available, but Bethany and Carlie Kate's appearance seemed to have put a damper on her hopes. He slipped the backpack over his shoulder and unlocked the front door.

8

Miguel Zapata's mind fought with the pain in his hand and face while trying to recall the last time he had the book. He remembered reaching up and touching his pocket while sitting in the car in front of the flower shop. He figured it had fallen out while he struggled with the woman. He had to go back for it before the police discovered the woman's body.

Fuentes opened the car door, throwing a narrow band of light across the cracked asphalt. Zapata watched the girl climb out of the car and go into the bushes, glancing over her shoulder to be assured no one followed.

Zapata walked to the edge of the clearing and waited for a smoke-belching semi, bound for Tecate or Tijuana, to rattle past. They were waiting. He knew they must be told soon. Again his hand strayed to the empty pocket where the notebook should had been. He looked at his watch and decided there was still time to go back and find it. He took a deep breath and punched in the number.

Castillo answered on the second ring.

With as few words as possible, Zapata told him what had happened with the woman. Castillo said nothing. It took Zapata longer to tell him about the notebook. "It is important I go back now, before it is too late," he pleaded. "The information in it cannot be discovered by others. You know this. Make some excuse my father will believe."

A few minutes later Zapata pocketed the phone, picturing what was taking place in his father's office in Michoacán. Castillo had not questioned him; that would come later. Castillo placed him on hold for a moment, then asked who the two from Otay Mesa were that went with him. He said he would send them back right away. But Zapata knew Castillo would have them report to him if they found anything.

Zapata tried to clear his head. Would Castillo understand everything in the book? "Yes," Zapata muttered to himself. He was too smart not to. But what could Castillo do with this information? Would he want the pictures Zapata had taken, the time he caught Castillo and Maria Consuella, his stepmother, in bed, she moaning loud enough to wake Christ himself? There was no place other than outer space where Castillo would be safe if he and the woman were discovered by Emiliano Montoya. But if Castillo were to discover what was in the notebook, Zapata knew he faced the same fate. He also knew Castillo would have him killed if he knew where those pictures were.

"*Cabron*, I'm fucked no matter what happens," Zapata moaned as he walked back to the car.

Fuentes closed the car door behind the girl. "What are we to do with her?"

"He says the plane will be there in three hours. We have to go now. He said he will tell us what to do with her when we get there."

9

The morning sun crept down the wall of Gray's bedroom and across his face. Ten o'clock, he figured by the amount of light coming through the slit in the drapes. He rolled out of bed and stretched some of the soreness out of his muscles. No matter how much he trained, or hiked, some stiffness remained the first few mornings after a week of climbing trails or bushwhacking across mountain slopes in search of the perfect spot. He flexed his right fist, the one that broke the guy's jaw at the mini-mart, or was that his knee that did the damage. It would take a couple of days for the swelling to go down.

Gray picked up his cell phone and started punching in the number for the flower shop, still feeling a shadow of concern that Bethany had not called or left a message. He put the phone down after deciding to shower and shave first, then surprise her at work. If Dorothy could spare her for an hour, they could have lunch at the little restaurant that served all the organic foods Bethany loved.

A knock on the door came as he toweled off from the shower. He grabbed a robe, stopping briefly in the kitchen to pour himself a cup of coffee. The second knock sounded more like a flat-handed pounding.

Gray had kept the beautiful front door with the chipped glass panels that came with the house, installed at a time when people in Laguna Mesa didn't lock their doors at night, or install peepholes. He didn't see the sense of putting a heavy secure door on the front when there were a number of glass windows anyone could break if they really wanted in.

Two men stood on the brickwork beneath the wide overhang. Neither looked like they were soliciting souls for Jehovah's Witness or selling vacuum cleaners.

"Conaire Gray?" the larger of the two asked.

Gray nodded.

"Detective Mondavi, Laguna Mesa PD," he said, holding up his credentials. "Like to ask you a few questions. This is Detective Chavez."

Gray's eyes shifted from the one calling himself Mondavi to the slim Hispanic who pocketed his badge and stood off to one side, his suit jacket pulled back to reveal a holstered gun at his belt. He guessed Mondavi's height at a few inches over six feet and weighing a good two hundred fifty pounds, with the thick shoulders of a former athlete and olive complexion making Gray think Italian-American. The shaved head was offset by a large handlebar mustache.

Mondavi frowned. "Mind if we come in?"

Gray hesitated a moment before stepping aside to let both men enter. "Sure."

They walked to the center of the room and split up. The one who had introduced himself as Mondavi spoke. "Do you know a woman by the name of Bethany Taylor?"

A sudden chill enveloped Gray. "Bethany, of course. Why? What's this about?"

The other detective said. "When was the last time you saw her?"

Suddenly the unanswered phone calls took on a new meaning. "Why, what's happened to her?"

"Just answer the question," Chavez said,

"No, you tell me what the hell's going on. Where is she?"

Detective Mondavi said, "A woman was found dead in her home this morning. We believe it to be Bethany Taylor. We understand you knew her."

The room swayed as Gray rocked back and forth on his feet. He walked over to the fireplace and put his hand on the mantel to steady himself, then spun around. "What about the girl, her daughter? What about her?"

Mondavi shook his head. "At this time we don't know anything about the girl. We do need to know when you saw her last and where you were last night."

Out of the corner of his eye he saw Chavez move to one side out of his line of vision. Gray took a half step back. He did not like having people standing behind him. "To answer your question, I saw her ten days ago, the night before I left on a trip. We all had dinner together."

"These ten days you say you were away, did you speak with her at all?" Mondavi asked.

"No, I haven't spoken to her since I left. I tried calling her last night but there was no answer, then her phone was busy."

Detective Chavez strolled over to the other side of the room. "Where were you for this time," he said, turning back to face Gray.

Gray stared at him for a moment. "I was at a place called French Canyon."

"Where the fuck is French Canyon, somewhere in Canada?" Chavez said.

"It's in the John Muir Wilderness. Up in the Sierra, out of Bishop."

"When did you get back?" Mondavi asked.

"Last night. Actually about one this morning. Okay detective, now it's your turn. Tell me what happened."

"The woman we believe to be Bethany Taylor was murdered sometime last night. We're not sure of the exact time yet."

Gray couldn't believe it. Somehow there had to be a mistake. "But the girl. You're saying she wasn't there?"

Mondavi shook his head. "We have no information about her. We only found out about a daughter when he spoke with the woman's employer. She was the one who gave us your name."

Gray walked over to the fireplace, took a framed picture off the wall, and studied it a moment before handing it to Mondavi. "This is the girl and Bethany. I took it about a month ago. You need to be looking for her; she's only six."

Mondavi took the picture and passed it to Chavez. "You know if Ms. Taylor had anybody that might want to hurt her? The child's father, a boy friend?"

Gray shook his head. "No, Bethany and I have been seeing each other for the past six months, and she hadn't gone out with anyone for some time before that."

"What about the father? Is he from around here? Do you think he might have taken the child?"

Gray could see where Mondavi was going. "From what she told me, the child is from a brief marriage about six years ago. It lasted six months, and he left before she knew she was pregnant. She hadn't seen or heard from him since."

"Maybe the kid got scared and ran away. Could be she'll show up soon," Chavez said.

"If she did, she would have come here," Gray said. "She knows where I keep a house key."

"Look," Mondavi said. "We don't have much to go on yet. But don't get me wrong, the girl is a real concern. Fact is we have very little information about the woman. We thought you might be able to help us there."

Chavez walked over to the table where Gray had laid out the new painting panels and picked through them until he came to the one Gray had done for Carlie Kate. In two silent strides Gray was at Chavez's side, startling him. He took the panel from the detective's hands and placed it on an empty easel. "The paintings are still wet. Don't touch any of them."

Chavez said, "What, you think I was going to hurt it somehow? Maybe I want to buy it. I think my girlfriend might like it. How much is it?"

"You couldn't afford it, trust me," Gray said. "I wouldn't come into your home and walk around picking up things. You don't do it in mine. That badge of yours doesn't give you that authority unless you have a warrant. And that painting is not for sale."

"Look, Mr. Gray," Mondavi said. "Why don't you tell us what you can? For starters, what was your relationship with Ms. Davis?"

Gray stood staring at the tiny painting in his hands. "It was the best thing that's ever happened to me. In fact I was seriously thinking about asking her to marry me."

Mondavi nodded, his eyes searching the room before answering. "Sounds like this decision was a hard one to make. Care to elaborate."

Gray shook his head. "That has nothing to do with this. Let's leave it there."

Chavez spoke up. "What if we say it has?"

Gray turned slowly and focused on the skinny detective, then spoke to Mondavi. "I've answered your questions. Now, could you tell me what you can about who might have done this?"

Mondavi flipped his note pad closed and dropped it in his coat pocket. "As I said, it's early and we have very little to go on. After the coroner looks at the body and the forensic team has had a chance to go over the house, we'll have more. All I can tell you is we got a call from an early morning jogger who passed the house and saw the front door partially open. She said she called out and then peeked in the house and saw an overturned chair in the hall. When no one answered she phoned us."

No one spoke for some time, then Mondavi took a card from his pocket and handed it to Gray. "Look, why don't we get together again tomorrow. There are still a few things I'd like to ask but now might not be a good time."

Detective Chavez hunched his shoulders and shook his head. "I think we should take him in and see what he knows. If you ask me, he knows more than he's telling us. What about your hands, Mr. Gray. You mind telling us how they got scratched up so bad? Doubt you got them painting posies."

Gray had no intension of mentioning the previous night's episode at the mini-mart. "You ever climbed rocky mountain slopes, Detective? You ever bushwhacked through seldom used passes? If you had, your hands would look like mine."

Mondavi thanked him and said to Chavez. "I don't think Mr. Gray is going to tell us anymore today. I think tomorrow would be a good time for us to get back together," Mondavi said. "Give me a call and we can set up a time. Maybe I'll have more information by then."

Gray followed them to the door with Mondavi's card in his hand. The detectives' blue sedan sat at the curb. "Detective Mondavi," he said. "Carlie Kate, the girl. Find her. Find her soon and God help the ones who took her if anything has happened to her."

The big man hesitated for a moment and nodded slowly. "We'll do everything we can, I promise."

Gray knew he couldn't keep them from knowing the truth. They would find out eventually. "There's something else you need to know, Detective."

"Anything will help at this point."

"It won't help with her murder, at least I don't think it will, but it's something you should know about Bethany Taylor."

"What about her?"

"It's about who she was."

Mondavi looked puzzled. "I don't follow you."

"Before she was Bethany Taylor, her name was Bethany Davis."

"Okay, that's something we can look into. We'll see if that name brings up anything. Is there anything else?"

"It's not just a name, Detective, Bethany Davis was the daughter of Senator Jefferson Davis."

It took a moment for Mondavi to grasp the significance. He shook his head as if to clear it. "You don't mean Senator Davis of Arizona, do you?"

Gray nodded. "The one and only."

"Oh shit," Mondavi muttered. He turned to his partner. "Both of you, I want this information to remain between us only for now. At least until I can get a handle on it. You sure about this, Mr. Gray?"

"There's no doubt, but walk carefully with it, Detective.

Senator Davis hasn't heard from his daughter in seven or eight years. I believe he thinks she was already dead."

10

The phone rang as Gray watched the two detectives climb into their car, apparently disagreeing about the path the interview had taken. He closed the door and walked to the phone.

It was Dorothy, Bethany's employer at the flower shop.

"My God, Conaire, have you heard?" He could tell she was barely able to control herself.

"The police just left, Dorothy."

"I am so sorry, Conaire. I can't believe this happened in Laguna Mesa, and why? The police said they had no idea. And poor Carlie, what would they want with that child?"

Gray found himself shaken by the conversation. He didn't want to talk with anyone until he had time to think. "Listen, Dorothy, I can't talk right now. I'll stop by the shop later. Maybe we'll have some answers by then."

"All right, Conaire, but promise you'll call if you hear anything, please."

"I promise," he said. He hoped with everything in him that he would hear something soon and that the girl was okay.

He hung up the phone, feeling an enormous sense of emptiness. He couldn't believe Bethany was dead, and wondered if he hadn't left would she still be alive? It didn't make any sense. It wasn't as if she was struck by a car or some other logical explanation. Detective Mondavi had said nothing about whether he thought it was a home burglary that got out of hand. That he might be able to deal with. But what about the girl? He poured another cup of coffee and walked outside, pacing the width of his brick patio, while he rehashed everything the detectives had said. He stopped, rocking gently back and forth with his eyes closed, his thoughts tumbling inside his head but always returning to the same disturbing thought. What had they done with the girl?

Through the sliding door he could see the small painting he took from Chavez, propped up on an easel. He walked back inside and put it on the mantel to replace the photo he had given to the detective. He needed to talk to someone, but hurts and feelings were not things he had ever learned to share with others. The loneliness crept up over him, bringing with it all the bitter memories of the past.

The phone rang. He walked over and unplugged it, then realized it might be the detectives. He plugged it back into the socket, grabbed his coffee, and went outside to sit in a canvas lawn chair. Anyone seeing him would think he had fallen asleep, but Gray's eyes never closed, instead focusing on the shadows edging across the corner of his lawn. When they began moving up the decorative cinder block wall, he rose and walked into the house, pouring the remainder of his coffee in the sink.

The refrigerator yielded nothing, everything remotely perishable having been thrown out or dropped at the local food bank before he left. He closed the door and returned to the living room, where he studied the small canvas again. He had painted the delicate flowers while kneeling on the steep slope of a mountain, planning on giving it to Carlie Kate for her birthday. He could picture her studying it, her head cocked to one side like a perspective buyer. Then the questions would begin. Why had he chosen these particular flowers? What kind were they? Were they really this color?

On the mantel, the picture of his grandfather brought on a grin of remembrance that, for the moment, replaced the darkness. One afternoon he had picked the girl up at school and brought her home until Bethany got off work. They were planning on driving up the coast to a little restaurant on Lido Island for dinner. The girl had wandered around his studio while he worked until coming to a halt in front of the fireplace. He watched from another room as she tilted her head to one side, her hands clasped behind her back, and Gray knew questions were forming in her mind.

"He looks like an Indian," she said.

Gray walked up behind her and placed his hands on her shoulders. "That's because he is an Indian."

"Whoa," she said. "A real Indian. That's awesome."

It took a moment for the question he knew was coming.

"Does that make you an Indian?"

He picked up the picture and studied it. It had been taken a number of years back; his grandfather's long braided hair hung to his waist, held in place with a beaded head band much like the one Gray wore to keep his long hair in place. "I'm part Indian, about a quarter. Not like him though. My grandfather is a full-blood Piegan Blackfoot."

She had squeezed her face between her hands, her eyes staring at the photo. "Wait till I tell my friends my mom likes an Indian. Do you think I'll ever meet him?"

Gray had picked her up and hugged her. "Maybe someday," he said. He hadn't returned to the reservation in years; in fact he had tried to put those years behind him. He didn't like talking about his Indian heritage or about those he knew who still lived in semi-poverty; they embarrassed him. He hadn't talked to his grandfather for a couple of years either, their only communication a card he sent at Christmas.

Gray put the picture back on the mantel, picked up the writing pad from beside his phone, and began making notes. He knew the possibility that whoever had murdered Bethany had done the same with Carlie Kate, and there was always the chance they would never find her. But until they knew one way or another, he would never stop looking. He knew that those who would look had limited patience, and time would dilute their resolve, but patience he had, and as long as she was missing he would never give up looking.

11

S imone St. Pierre sat in a chair in her home office, her sandals
lying on the floor and her legs tucked under her. She pushed her
reading glasses up a fraction and reached for another folder from the
pile on the coffee table. A tuna-fish sandwich sat at her elbow, along
with a bottle of Evian water and her cell phone.

The folder in her hand reflected her notes for the Saturday
morning meeting with the senator. It contained much of the current
happenings in the state, as well as upcoming events and bills the
senator would face in Washington. She and Steve Barnet, her

assistant, had already discussed it, but she liked to review it in case anything had been left out.

She tossed the folder on the coffee table and stretched her legs. As chief-of-staff for Senator Thomas Jefferson Davis, Simone spoke with the Washington office daily. It was an unusual arrangement, but she was not the only chief-of-staff to remain in the home state. When she heard of an Idaho senator who preferred his COS to remain in the state, she put together a proposal to do the same. The senator agreed, and it solved a couple of problems. The overly cramped office space allotted to a junior senator was not what Simone had expected when she agreed to the senator's request that she take over the duties as his COS, and the only apartment she could find came furnished in early frontier American. As Simone had related to a college girlfriend over lunch, the entire apartment could fit into the bedroom of her previous home, and no matter how much she wanted the job she had no intensions of living, or working, in a broom-closet atmosphere.

A far greater concern for Simone that made the move to the Arizona office prudent was the senator himself. A strikingly handsome man, whose years in the military had endowed him with an aura of leadership and ability, caused many to speculate on his availability, since he seldom appeared in Washington accompanied by his wife. Consequently, the Capital media spent countless idle hours discussing the possibility of a relationship between the senator and his beautiful chief of staff. When the rumors first began to circulate, Simone sat down with Susanna Davis, the senator's wife, and discussed ways of combating the rumors. The idea of working out of the Phoenix office solved the problem. It was a simple case of out of sight, out of mind, as far as the rumormongers were concerned. Once or twice a year Simone would schedule special charity appearances where the Senator and Mrs. Davis would appear, always in his home state. Susanna Davis's only trip to Washington was to be at his side when the senator accepted his initial appointment.

Simone reached for another folder, noting the chipped polish on her toenails. Not good, she thought, not with her date with Sergio tomorrow night. If she was lucky she could squeeze in for an early morning appointment and get a pedicure. She arched her back and stretched her arms over her head. "Oh God," she groaned. "What do I do about him?"

They had met at a political gathering put on by friends of the senator to raise money for the upcoming campaign. Sergio had subscribed a generous donation, although after they began seeing each other she wondered about his lack of political leanings. One thing she could never have seen herself doing was dating a handsome South American playboy, but here she was.

He had introduced himself as Sergio Collor de Mello, and in case she wasn't into South American politics, his cousin had been president of Brazil for two years, until forced out of office on corruption charges, something they had never been able to prove, according to Sergio.

After their initial meeting, they ran into each other on several occasions and began dating. It was not what most people would consider normal dating. Not when their dates included flying to San

Francisco for dinner, or Santa Fe for the symphony, or Belize to spend the weekend on a hundred-foot yacht and swim along the second longest coral reef in the world. But it was fun, and not complicated. Their time together helped relieve the pressures and frustrations brought on by handling the affairs of a United States senator.

And the sex was good; not spectacular, but good enough to take the edge off. One of her friends defined it as maintenance sex. But it left Simone little time for herself. She knew she needed to address the problem in the near future because it wasn't love. She wondered if she would ever meet someone she could fall in love with, someone to share her passions and dreams. She thought she had, once, but that early episode turned into something that still haunted her.

12

Gray rolled over in bed and checked the time on the bedside clock. It read 4:45. He figured he had slept a total of three hours. Anymore than that was out of the question. He swung his legs out of the bed and made his way to the kitchen. He looked in the refrigerator but found nothing but a half empty carton of orange juice. After checking the expiration date to be sure it wasn't too far past its prime, he opened it and filled a glass, carrying it back to the bedroom. He pulled on a pair of jogging shorts and his shoes, emptied the glass of juice, and hit the button on the coffee pot on the way out the door.

One block up his street ended in a cul-de-sac at the base of a shrub-covered hill. Gray crossed the sidewalk and picked up the narrow-use trail leading up the side of the hill to a fire break. Kids had created the trail by pushing their dirt bikes up it so they could ride the dirt road that led to the radio tower on the peak above.

Gray took the faint trail at a fast walk, using it as a warm-up before hitting the road and settling into a slow jog until he felt the leg muscles beginning to loosen up after the climb out of the mountains. The incline pulled on his legs as he churned away at the rutted track, sweat running down his face and soaking the neckline of his shirt. A mile later he stood beside the cyclone fence enclosing the tower and its maintenance shed. Empty soda and beer cans littered the grass where dirt bikers had spent time before beginning the run to the bottom. He watched a helicopter a mile off the coast settle on the lighted deck of an oil platform.

Gray started back down, figuring it would still be too early to call Mondavi, but mentally cataloging the questions the detective had not answered in their first meeting.

Half an hour later Gray poured himself a cup of coffee, moving from room to room with a deepening sense of frustration. He tried focusing on what needed done in order to pass the time, then sorted through the dirty clothes from his pack.

With time to kill, Gray carried his coffee into his studio. Everything remained as he had left it: the coffee cans filled with an assortment of brushes on the table beside his easel, a fresh palette pad alongside half a dozen palette knives, and unfinished canvasses leaning against the far wall. Gray chose the three pieces he felt were as complete as they would ever be and signed them. He needed to stop at the gallery and drop them off now that they had ample time to dry, then see Dorothy at the flower shop—not a visit he was looking forward to.

A wave of emotion enveloped him when he saw the package sitting on the side table. The package, wrapped in pink and yellow paper depicting a family of penguins, was another birthday present for Carlie Kate. Her own paint box, complete with a few tubes of primary colors and paint brushes. Gray had chosen to teach her to use gauche, a water-based oil paint he felt would be healthier than breathing pure turpentine fumes. Even the odorless turpentine he used left a lingering smell.

The pile of equipment from the trip still sat beside the empty pack. He pushed it to the side and called Paco Juarez instead.

Juarez was no stranger to the loss of those close to him. A number of his own family in Mexico had died, the result of families settling perceived insults, or drug-related deaths. Years before Juarez had left Mexico and made his way across the border to enlist in the U.S. Marine Corps in order to escape the wrath of a local drug lord. The drug lord had taken offense when Juarez killed one of his runners and gave the money to the families murdered by the man.

Juarez answered the call and Gray told him what had happened.

"Maybe we should talk about this," Juarez said.

"I could use someone to listen. Sorry it's you I'm calling, but you've been there before. You know the feeling."

Gray waited for Juarez to respond.

"It's okay, I would need someone to talk to if it were me. Whenever you want, okay? She was something special. I thought she was the best thing that had happened to you since you know when. You know, like my Maria. I think I would have gone over to the other side without her."

Gray knew what Juarez meant. The man lived in an area of Santa Ana saturated in the drug culture and anyone with Juarez's training and ability could have run the whole area if he wanted to. Instead, Juarez had met Maria and opened his own private investigating service and became involved with the non-profit group Taller San Jose, teaching Hispanic dropouts a trade.

They agreed to meet the next day and talk about Gray's situation.

With time to kill, and nothing in the house to eat, Gray drove down to Pacific Coast Highway and to a little place the locals liked for breakfast and the tourists hadn't found. He picked up the local paper and found the story on the front page. Nothing in it gave him any more information other than speculation by the reporter, who mentioned robbery, drugs, revenge, and everything else she could think of that gave her more words under her byline.

Detective Mondavi phoned as Gray was paying for breakfast. They made arrangements to meet at one o'clock.

As he worked his way through the morning traffic on Pacific Coast Highway, Gray kept thinking about the girl and where she might be. He couldn't bring himself to believe that whoever had killed Bethany had done the same to the girl. If not, why would they have taken her with them? He knew there was always hope. He also knew that every time the phone rang he would expect bad news.

At a stoplight a woman stood on the center divider facing oncoming traffic. She wore a faded Dodger baseball hat and a long-sleeve plaid shirt, with only two functioning buttons, over a once white T-shirt. Her torn jeans revealed more skin than local decency laws allowed. Chipped red toenails protruded from toeless black tennis shoes. The hand-lettered sign hanging around her neck read, "WILL WORK FOR FUD." At her feet a little girl played happily with a headless doll. Gray rolled down his window and handed her a twenty-dollar bill. It wasn't the first time she had collected from him. She smiled and said, "God bless." Most of her front teeth were missing. He wondered how many drivers had offered her work.

Gray pulled to the curb in front of the gallery as the owner, Richland Waterman, unlocked the front door. Waterman stood watching as Gray removed the canvasses from the back of the Jeep and carried them up the steps. Although in his seventies, he wore a blonde wig fashioned in an eighties style, making him look like a born-again hippie out of Haight Asbury. His flowered silk shirt hung open at the neck to reveal strands of gold chains, and his stylish jeans and patent-leather shoes completed what he considered West Coast chic.

But Gray had to admit most of what he knew about Impressionism came from Waterman's knowledge of the art form, from the Hudson River School up to what Eastern snobs referred to in a derogatory manner as that Eucalyptus School of Art practiced in California.

Waterman held the door open for Gray, who placed the canvasses against a wall. Normally the gallery owner would rush to see what his prize artist had brought.

"Conaire, sweetheart, I must ask," Waterman said, wringing his hands. "The young woman I read about in this morning's paper. Tell me that wasn't the same delightful lady who caused such a scene here some months ago?"

Gray could only nod, remembering the moment he had entered the gallery months before following Waterman's phone call that someone he supposedly knew wanted to see him and wouldn't leave until she did. Gray had driven over, upset at being pulled away from the easel, and saw her standing off to the side, a small painting clutched to her breast. On a chair against the wall a young girl sat, swinging her legs while holding a yellow and black stuffed penguin in her lap. Then the woman turned around and saw him. Gray shook his head to chase away the vision.

"Oh my God, oh my God," Waterman exclaimed. "And that precocious child, tell me they've found her and she is All right."

Gray shook his head. "Nothing yet, and I know about as much as you do."

Waterman closed the door and turned the closed sign back toward the street. "Do you know what that little person said to me that day? She said I looked like one of her dolls that she played with when she was a child. When she was a child. I couldn't believe what I was hearing. I was at a loss for words, and you know me, I'm never at a loss. But can you imagine, me, looking like a doll. Oh my God, what would my friends say about that."

"Sounds like something she would say," Gray whispered.

"I don't know what to say, Conaire," the old man said. "It's inconceivable something like this could happen in our town."

"Listen, Richland, I brought these pieces in to give you something to show. You'll have to take care of the framing. I don't know when I'll be able to get back to work."

Waterman put a hand on Gray's arm. "Never worry yourself, Conaire. I'll make do with what I have, but I'm sure you brought work back from your trip. I have a place to put unfinished work, and people love to see something the artist is still working on."

"I might, but right now I'm concentrating on not going out of my mind."

"We'll do fine with what we have. In fact I've been thinking about it, and I believe this would be an excellent time to raise the prices. Supply and demand you know and, let's face it, the demand is high and your supply is going to be lower for a while."

"You do whatever you think best, as long as people don't think I'm holding work back to raise the prices," Gray said. Whenever Waterman sold a painting, he deposited the money directly into Gray's bank account, and over the years the amount grew as Gray's work created more and more interest.

"When things return to normal, if they ever will," Waterman said, "I would like to discuss a very promising proposal I received from a major gallery in New York. Seems they are being asked why they have none of your work to show. Interesting, isn't it?"

While Waterman relived the conversation with the east coast gallery, Gray studied a gold-framed painting displayed in the most prominent position in the gallery but out of sight to street traffic. "I see you managed to talk that woman out of her Guy Rose. I hope you don't sell it for a while. I'd love to study it."

"It's from his blue period. If someone wants to purchase it I'll tell them they will have to wait to take it home," Waterman said.

Gray left the gallery and checked for messages. He had one from Dorothy wanting to know if there was any news and when did he plan to come by the flower shop.

Fifteen minutes later Gray parked the Jeep in front of a bistro catering to the crowds and walked across the highway to the rust-colored stucco building. None of the usual array of fresh flowers were displayed on the sidewalk in front of the store. Dorothy lived in a little apartment above the shop. She met him at the door.

"Conaire," she said, throwing her arms around his shoulders and burying her face in his shirt. "I don't know what to say. I can't believe it. This doesn't happen here. It happens in other places, but not here. Is there any news about Carlie Kate? Why would they take her and do this to Bethany?"

Gray held her a moment, then gently pushed her away to arm's length. "We're all asking the same questions. I have an appointment with the detective at one o'clock. Maybe he'll have more information by then."

"They came to the door, those two detectives, and started asking questions before they even told me what had happened. I told them everything I could and then they asked about other people who knew her. Of course, your name was the first I gave them. I didn't know if you were back yet, although Bethany was so excited thinking you were coming back last night. She couldn't wait, and Carlie Kate was on pins and needles waiting to see what you brought her."

"I kept getting a busy signal when I called. I thought she had probably forgotten to end her last call."

"She and Carlie spent the night here a couple of times while you were away. I keep thinking she would still be alive if she had stayed last   night."

Gray knew Bethany had thought of Dorothy as a mother figure who treated Carlie Kate like a grandparent would.

Dorothy walked to the back of the store and picked up a package. "I bought this hat for Carlie. It was her newest thing you know, wearing funny hate. She said she really looked *tres chic* in them," she said with a bitter smile. "Now where do you suppose she got that?"

Gray smiled. "I think I mentioned something along those lines about her mother. She obviously picked up on it."

"You know when those detectives were here I told them about a big black car parked across the street."

"What about it?"

"Well, it seemed rather odd. The windows were down just enough to let the smoke out. It looked like there were people in the back, too. You don't normally see a lot of people smoking in a car, not anymore anyway. Then the detectives came back a couple of hours later and started asking more questions about you."

"What kind of questions?"

"They wanted to know how you and Bethany got along, and if she ever mentioned anything about you and Carlie Kate. The big detective, he didn't say much. It was the other one, the skinny Hispanic. Something about that man makes my skin crawl. I told them I never heard anything but good things about you. I hope I didn't say anything out of place, Conaire."

"Don't worry, it's the kind of thing the police do. They have to start somewhere." Gray made a mental note to ask Mondavi what it was about.

He left Dorothy standing at the door of the flower shop. He was early for his appointment, but there wasn't enough time to do anything else and possibly Mondavi would be free.

13

Miguel Zapata sat outside the open door to his father's office and watched as Caesar Castillo waited for Emiliano Montoya to speak. Zapata fumed. He knew they were deliberately keeping him out of the discussion.

Castillo rose and came to the door. He motioned to Zapata. "Come in and sit. Your father will speak to you when we are finished."

Zapata hated being treated like a fucking child. He slumped into a seat beside Castillo.

Montoya brushed an ash off the front of his blue silk shirt and addressed Castillo. "As I see it, we have a number of problems to deal with. The first will be up to you to get answers. I assume we have someone up there we can use?"

"Not in this place exactly, but there is someone close by, in San Diego," Castillo said.

"Is he in a position to help?" Montoya inquired, toying with his lighter.

"Yes. If nothing else he can discover if they have anything. He will need to develop a story of some type to cover his interest."

"Contact him immediately. We must know everything as soon as possible. What they have, what they suspect, everything. Now the child. How old is she?"

"She told Fuentes she is six."

Zapata watched his father mull over what Castillo had said. "I believe she can be as persuasive as her mother would have been, in fact more so. Have Fuentes take pictures of her."

"I will see to it."

Zapata paid little attention to what they were talking about. The only thing he was interested in was what the two sent back to the house had found.

Montoya tapped the top of his desk with his lighter. Miguel Zapata felt his father's eyes boring into him.

Then Montoya spoke to Castillo again. "As soon as he has the pictures, have Fuentes take them to Tucson with the instructions and send them like we planned. Be sure he understands he must take every precaution that nothing can be traced back to us. The package must be delivered to the senator tomorrow morning. Also, when you speak with this person in San Diego, I want everything he can give me on what the police found in this place where she lived. We will need to have someone closer to this investigation, perhaps in the police department of this city. Money will be whatever is necessary. Do this immediately."

Castillo tilted his head in acknowledgement and walked outside to make the call.

Miguel Zapata tilted his head to watch Castillo, who gestured up to the sky as he talked into his phone, his voice coming across the distance, angry, threatening, and then conciliatory. Castillo was a master of convincing argument, but could he be trusted? And what had he told Montoya about the book?

Castillo pocketed the phone and returned. He eased himself into the chair and nodded. "It is done. This man will make inquiries at once."

"You emphasized the importance of this matter?" Montoya asked.

"Yes, he understands the information is of great value to you."

"Good." Montoya shifted in his seat and relit his cigar. "Have you heard from the two you sent back?"

Castillo studied his notes. "They could not enter the house. By the time they returned, it was already morning and there were people on the street. Someone would have seen them if they had remained."

Montoya remained silent, then said. "Miguel you are certain this is where you lost this thing?"

Zapata shrugged. They had already discussed this until he was tired of it. "It must be there. There is no other place for it to be."

"Then we must assume the police have discovered it," his father said. "And if they are any good at their job it will certainly lead them directly to us. And that means to me, Miguel. Is that not so?"

Zapata fought to control his temper. "That is why you should have allowed me to return instead of sending those fucking idiots."

Castillo pulled a sheet of paper out of a folder and placed it on the desk in front of Montoya. "I had Miguel write down what he could remember he has put in this book. It would depend on who finds it. This place, Laguna Mesa, has only a few policemen who would investigate such a matter as this. It would seem that much of what they investigate are relatively minor matters. So there is a chance the information will be of little value. Miguel has told me there are some addresses that are incomplete, phone numbers, names of those who are of assistance to us, a few locations that would be difficult to pinpoint. However, in my opinion, the longer it remains in someone's possession the more damage it could incur. Someone who would have a certain amount of knowledge about us could add these things up and destroy much of what we have put together."

Zapata knew Castillo was not telling the whole truth. There were addresses in the United States where Zapata had stored large amounts of cash. Phones numbers of prominent officials in Mexico, as well as the things even Castillo had no knowledge of. Zapata knew his survival depended on the book being destroyed.

Still ignoring him, Montoya said to Castillo, "Every effort must be made to discover its whereabouts. I will leave this in your hands.

Do whatever is necessary. Now, there is this problem of the woman's death. It will not take long for her identity to become known. The senator must know that this child's life depends on absolute silence. If he puts this into the hands of the police or the FBI, or anyone, all traces of her will disappear. He must understand we will know if he has been in contact with anyone."

"It is all in the letter. We can only hope he believes the child is his daughter's. Otherwise, everything must be erased." Castillo rocked back in his chair and met Montoya's gaze. "If not, there will be serious repercussions that I doubt even our highly paid politicians can cover up."

Zapata waited for his father's response.

"We will have to wait and see what transpires. There is little else we can do." Montoya said. "If everything goes as planned, this will be over in a matter of days, and I will have the information I need."

Zapata watched Castillo gather up his notes and leave. He slumped further in his chair, his arm hanging over the back. What could his father do to him anyway?

Emiliano Montoya crushed out a half-finished cigar in the ashtray and brush his hands. "I will be brief, Miguel. Your actions have jeopardized my plans and my entire organization. If the information your stupidity has forced you to record in this book is understood by those who might find it, many good people could be exposed. Some I will have to have killed."

"I should not have listened to you," Zapata said. "I should have gone back for it. Then you would not have this opportunity to lecture me again."

Montero's hand slammed onto the top of his desk. "Shut up. You will listen to me now, and then I do not want to see your face until I call for you. Take this with you when you leave. If it were not for your mother, I would have had you disposed of already. Do not say a word. Nod your head if you understand."

Miguel Zapata leapt up from his chair and threw it across the room. He leaned over the desk, wanting to reach over it and crush his father's head. He shivered when he realized his father showed no fear. He spun around and strolled out of the room.

14

Conaire Gray parked the Jeep in a visitor's spot in front of the Laguna Mesa Police Department. Two patrol cars occupied the adjacent slots. As he got out of the car, a new Range Rover equipped with a rhino grill pulled into a disabled parking slot and a middle-aged man in jogging shorts and polo shirt got out. He waved to a nearby officer and strode into the building. Gray glanced in the car window and saw the blue pass hanging from the rear-view mirror. As Gray passed the officer, he pointed at the car and got a shrug in return. *So much for Laguna Mesa's finest,* he thought.

The white stucco building with red-tile roof housed all of the city's government offices. Huge eucalyptus trees shaded the front walkway, and only the seven-foot wire fence topped with razor wire surrounding the police parking area distinguished it from the library across the street.

Gray pushed through the door and entered a small office that had several desks behind a waist-high counter. A woman in uniform glanced at him and finished her conversation with another office employee before approaching the counter.

"I have an appointment with Detective Mondavi," Gray said.

The woman glanced at a computer monitor on the counter and looked up at the clock. "Your appointment is for one. You're early."

"I know. I was hoping he might be available."

She left and returned a moment later. "Detective Mondavi says he'll see you now."

Gray followed her directions to Mondavi's office. Two desks sat back to back in the middle of the small room. Chavez leaned back in his chair, his feet propped up on the top of his desk.

Mondavi sat in his shirtsleeves, his shaved head gleaming in the well-lit office, a computer on a narrow table behind him. He rose and held out his hand. "Why don't you sit down? You know Detective Chavez."

Gray sat in the metal chair beside Mondavi's desk. "Is there any word on the girl?"

Mondavi shook his head. "Nothing yet. We put out an Amber Alert this morning, and I've had people interviewing the neighbors, but so far there's been no response."

Gray felt Chavez's presence behind him. "There has to be a reason for this to have happened. I was hoping you had something. Do you know yet whether it might have been a robbery that got out of hand? But then why take the girl?"

Mondavi shook his head. "Like I said, we don't know yet."

Gray studied the man across from him. He watched his face for any telltale sign. "Was she raped?"

"I can't go into any details. I can tell you the coroner doesn't believe she was."

"Have you contacted the Col— er…Senator Davis?"

Mondavi narrowed his eyes at Gray's stutter before replying. "Yes. The senator was somewhat confused, like you said. He believed she was already dead. I'm not sure he doesn't think this might be a cruel hoax. He said he would send someone immediately. He did request that, until the identity is confirmed one way or the other, we keep this strictly between ourselves. I'm already getting inquiries from the local press, but there isn't much they can do except ask."

Mondavi took a file folder off a pile on his desk and opened it. "There are a couple of things we'd like to clear up. But first, I ran a check on you. Also pulled what was available of your military record. Impressive. I'm surprised you didn't remain in the Corps."

Gray focused on Mondavi and waited for him to continue.

Mondavi glanced back at the sheet of paper in the folder. "A couple of things you can clarify for me. Would you go over your whereabouts for that night again? Everything you can think of that could be important. You know, times, places, people who might have seen you."

"Why? Am I a suspect?"

Mondavi leaned back in his chair. "Mr. Gray, we do this with everyone who was close to the victim, especially when we have so little else to go on. Do you have a problem with it?"

"I don't have a problem with you doing your job, Detective. I have a problem with seeing two of you wasting time on asking me questions when whoever did this is out there somewhere, and you haven't found the girl."

Behind him Chavez snorted. "Well, maybe we're not wasting our time. We usually find that most victims are killed by someone they know, and I'll tell you what, boyfriends are at the top of the list."

Gray turned in his chair and stared at the skinny detective.

Mondavi said, "I can tell you we're not wasting our time. You may think so, but that's not the case. We start by eliminating all the people she knew, and you and the lady from the flower shop are the ones she knew best. We hope you can tell us something that might not seem important to you but could be to us. You understand what I'm getting at?"

Gray settled back in the chair and waited for Mondavi to continue. He knew they would play out their game one way or the other, and the sooner he could convince them to look elsewhere the better.

"Okay," Mondavi continued. "I have the information you gave us yesterday. So, why don't you start from the beginning again. Start by telling us everything you can remember since the last time you saw Ms. Davis."

"Eleven days ago we had dinner together. I was leaving the next morning for this trip to the mountains to do some work."

Mondavi interrupted. "Where did you have dinner?"

"There's a little fish place down the coast a ways, in Dana Point. The Fish Shop I think they call it. We ate there."

"The girl go with you?"

"Always."

"Okay, so the next morning you drive up to the mountains. Go on."

Gray described the arrangements he had made with the packer who set up his camp and admitted he had not seen the man, or anyone else for that matter, during the ten days. Not until he came down to the parking lot and spoke with the motor home couple. Mondavi made a note, saying he might have an Inyo County sheriff's deputy run up to the trailhead and speak to the guy if he was still there.

"I had dinner in Bishop. She waitress was kind of friendly; she might remember me," Gray finished.

Mondavi glanced at his notes. "Any receipts?"

"No, I paid cash."

"What about gas, no receipts either?"

Gray shrugged.

Chavez dropped his feet to the floor and interjected. "You mean you keep nothing, not even for tax purposes? Seems those are legitimate expenses if you make your living selling pictures?"

"I don't carry credit cards when I go," Gray said. "It was only a meal that I paid cash for. I record my mileage and take an allowance for that. No receipts."

Gray flexed his fist and saw Mondavi study the scabs on the cuts on his knuckles.

"Looks like you banged up that hand pretty good. You said you got that from climbing over rocks or something?"

A half hour later Gray finished giving the detective everything he could remember about the altercation at the mini-mart, including a description of the car the clerk left in. Mondavi turned the page on his pad and sat back again. Gray tilted his head to check on Chavez, who sat impassively twirling a coin between his fingers.

Mondavi pushed his notes aside. "We've talked to the lady Ms. Davis worked for, but she couldn't help us with any background. How long was it you said you knew Ms. Davis?"

Gray stared at Mondavi, wondering how much to tell him. He figured when they spoke with Davis they would find out anyway so there was no use being vague. "We first met about nine years ago, but lost contact for a long time. We met again six months ago."

"But in the last six months you became close, is that correct?"

Gray had no intention of going into their earlier relationship. "Yes."

"All right, let me give you one piece of information and see if you can help me. We found drugs on Ms. Davis, and on her bedside table. We won't know for a while whether she had any in her system. Do you know if she was into any kind of drugs?"

For a moment Gray thought about what Mondavi was saying Years ago, maybe, but he would bet his life on her being clean now. He shook his head. "No way. If she took drugs, someone forced them down her. Bethany told me she had a problem years ago, until she discovered she was pregnant. She told me she had been sober since that day and I believed her."

Chavez's feet hit the floor. "It might explain everything, you know. Drug dealer not getting paid decides to make an example out of her. Takes the girl because she knows who he is. Makes sense."

"I said there's no way she was taking anything. I would have known if she was."

"What about you. Maybe you're not as clean as you make out to be. You willing to take a test?" Chavez said.

Gray felt his temper edging into the danger zone. He took a deep breath and ignored Chavez's remark. He spoke to Mondavi instead. "You checked me out and you found nothing because there's nothing to find. Bethany loved her daughter more than anything in the world. She would never do something to hurt her."

Chavez stood and moved around Gray's chair and leaned against the wall beside Gray. "And how much did you love her daughter?"

Gray turned and stared at Chavez. Nothing in his expression alarmed the detective. "What exactly do you mean by that, Detective?"

Chavez held his arms apart and shrugged. "Well, you know, the old woman at the posy shop said you often picked the girl up from school and took her home. You had a lot of free time with her. Cute little girl wearing short dresses. Things can happen."

Mondavi opened his mouth to speak but it was too late. Gray sprung from the chair, wrapping his hand around Chavez's tie and lifting him up onto his toes. Chavez grasped at Gray's hands, attempting to break the strangle hold.

"Hold it," Mondavi yelled, reaching for Gray but Gray spun Chavez away from the wall and turned Chavez's back to Mondavi.

"Stay where you are, Detective. I can snap the neck of this piece of shit before you take another step, and I haven't yet decided whether it's worth it or not."

Chavez's toes danced on the floor as he struggled to break free from Gray's hand.

Mondavi stepped back and held up his hands. "Okay, I think he got the message. Now let him go and we'll talk this over."

Gray released the gasping detective and shoved him in the direction of his chair.

Mondavi exhaled slowly and signaled Chavez to sit down. "You have to remember something here. Part of our job is to ask questions you may not like. What Detective Chavez was referring to happens a lot in this type of case. Apparently he didn't do his job and read your military record or he might have been a little more cautious about his approach.

"Detective, I made this appointment to come here and speak with you. You didn't have to come looking for me. I came to offer my help in whatever way I could. Like I said at the beginning of this meeting, I can't understand all the time you're wasting, when there's a little girl out there who needs found."

"Look, Mr. Gray, this is all part of the job and we don't consider interviewing people who knew the victim as wasting our time, so why don't you let me finish asking the questions and get this over with."

Gray turned his chair to the side so he could watch Chavez. The man busied himself at his desk as if nothing had happened, but Gray knew he had made an enemy out of the detective. Once again his temper had overridden common sense.

"Can you think of anyone who might have had a problem with Ms. Davis, maybe from her past?" Mondavi asked.

"No, I can't."

"How about someone else, besides you? She may have told about being Senator Davis's daughter."

"As far as I know she told no one. It was a part of her past she tried to bury."

Mondavi fiddled with the pen on his desk. "You might wonder why I ask, but when we deal with high-profile people, we need to look at all possibilities, and Senator Davis is definitely high profile. He is also someone who, like it or not, has enemies because of his politics."

The phone on Mondavi's desk rang. He hit the hold button and turned his attention back to Gray. "Any ideas along those lines?"

"None. I don't follow politics and she never mentioned anything to me. But I do have a couple of questions of my own. Could you tell me if there was any indication there might have been more than one person involved?"

"Possibly, but we can't be sure," Mondavi said.

"Was there a struggle of any kind or did whoever did it just walk in and kill her?"

Mondavi nodded. "She put up a fight, if that's what you wanted to know."

Gray thought about her trying to fight off her attacker and probably fearing the worst for Carlie Kate. Yes, he could see her giving her life for the girl. "The woman at the flower shop said she saw a car parked across the street that looked out of place."

"Yes, she mentioned that. Detective Chavez will be talking to the other shop owners to see if they saw anything. Now, is there anything else?"

"Just one thing," Gray said. "There are some things in her house I would like to pick up. When can I get in?"

"I'll let you know," Mondavi said, rising from his desk.

"We may want to talk to you again. I wouldn't want to have to go looking for you," Chavez said, a thin grin creasing his still-red face.

Gray looked at Chavez and nodded his head slightly. "If I wanted to disappear, Detective, you could look all you want. You'd never find me."

15

For the sixth day in a row Phoenix baked in triple-digit numbers. Simone St. Pierre backed her car out of the garage and flicked the air conditioner on to the highest setting. The summer months were brutal; five out of the twelve months of the year people spent most of their time in semi-comfort in air-conditioned homes, cars, and offices. At least once a month Simone fled the city to spend a weekend encamped in a mountain lodge outside of Flagstaff, savoring the time away from people and the heat.

She powered up her cell phone and saw she had received three calls from Senator Davis's home phone. Being the senator's chief of staff, she swore, realizing she had unplugged her phone when she returned from the previous night's concert. It was not uncommon for him to leave messages, but three missed calls in such short order struck a note of concern.

Early Saturday morning traffic was light as she drove the ten miles to the senator's sprawling Southwest-style ranch house. When Arizona's senior senator had died, the governor appointed Jefferson Davis to fill the vacant seat. Davis was about to run on his own, and, with his strong position on border enforcement, a balanced budget, and a strong military, he was a certainty to win a six-year term. Simone planned to see that his campaign encountered as few bumps as possible.

Fifteen minutes later she passed through the open gate in the seven-foot stucco wall surrounding the estate and drove through twin rows of palm trees to the front of the house.

She parked in front of the house and walked up the steps. Mariano, who had worked in Susanna Davis's household for years, opened the door before she reached it.

"Thank you, Mariano," Simone said, stepping into the cool air in the oversize entry. She had dressed in her usual Saturday morning summer wear, a stylish Diane von Furstenberg blouse over knee-length shorts and sandals.

The elderly Hispanic glanced at her attire, then said, "He is waiting outside." He led her across the tiled floor and onto an outside patio that had a sweeping view of the hostile peaks in the Tonto National Forest.

"Good morning, Senator," she said. She dropped her thin leather briefcase beside a chair and took her usual glass of iced tea from Mariano.

Senator Jefferson Davis stood with his back to her, looking out across the barren landscape and fields of cactus.

It concerned her when he didn't return her greeting. "I'm sorry I didn't pick up your messages last night. I had my phone turned off at the concert and forgot to turn it back on. I hope whatever it was could wait until this morning. I have my brief on the upcoming Senate bill and everything I could gather on a possible opponent. You won't believe who is considering a challenge."

Jefferson Davis turned slowly, without his usual pleasant greeting, and shook his head. "There was nothing you could have done last night that couldn't wait. It was something I needed to share. You're usually the first person I share with, besides Susanna, of course."

Simone noted the absence of the senator's usual bearing. He looked older. "What is it, Senator? Is it about the upcoming election, or something that happened in Washington?"

"No, nothing like that. It's about Bethany."

"Your daughter?"

"Yes," he said, pausing for a moment before continuing. "Last night I received a call. In fact, Susanna handed me the phone when I arrived from the airport and said there was a police detective from California on the line. Naturally I was curious so I took the call. This detective, Mondavi I think he said his name was, from a small town called Laguna Mesa in Southern California. He said a woman by the name of Bethany Taylor was murdered and some fellow she had been seeing informed him that her real name was Bethany Davis, and she was our daughter."

"My God," Simone said, shaking her head. "Did he say whether they had anything that could identify her?"

The senator shook his head. "No, that's all he had."

Another thought struck her. "Is there any reason to suspect it might be a story this woman made up? You know, something to gain some kind of stature with this boyfriend? People make up stories all the time."

The senator ran his hand over his jaw and walked to the edge of the patio. A warm breeze brought the scent of the desert across the dry expanse and rustled the palm fronds.

"Yes, I've considered the possibility. But, her name, her age, and the description the detective gave me fits her. I can't ignore it. I would never forgive myself if I did nothing and later found out it was Bethany."

Simone waited, sensing there was something the senator was not telling her.

"The detective said the woman had a daughter, about six years old, but that she was missing. Do you realize what it would mean if it's true?"

Simone let out her breath slowly. "It would mean you and Mrs. Davis have a granddaughter. Do you think she would have kept something like this a secret?"

"I can't imagine her doing this to her mother, but you have to understand the situation. Bethany felt she could no longer live with us after something I had done came to light. I said things I should never have said, and she in turn said some things her mother and I felt were equally inexcusable, and she left. And that was the last time we saw her."

"Have you told Mrs. Davis about the girl?"

The senator paused as if weighing his answer, then said, "I told Susanna about the woman they think might be Bethany, but not about the girl. I've decided to wait until we're positive one way or another. I don't think Susanna could take it, finding out Bethany was dead and there is the possibility of a granddaughter who can't be found."

Simone knew few details about Bethany's disappearance. The senator had hired a private investigation firm, out of Kansas City, to search for her. In fact it was one of the topics she had intended to bring up at this morning's meeting. She had the agency's latest report and invoice in her briefcase. The reports were brief summaries of the leads they had run down, none of which mentioned California. The one time she questioned their progress, the senator said it helped his wife knowing someone was still looking for her.

"Changing her name made the search almost impossible, especially if she never used credit cards. I wonder how she was able to do it?"

"You know, come to think of it, some months after she left we heard a rumor that she had married, but nothing came of it. Which makes you wonder, if she did marry, where is her husband now?"

"That's a good point. Did the detective mention anything about a husband?" Simone said.

"No. He did say something about a friend, or a boyfriend, but he didn't specify."

Simone took her planner out of her briefcase. It was obvious the senator wanted her to do some follow up. "All right, Senator, what would you like me to do?"

"This morning I tracked down a dentist we used before we moved here. I want you to fly out to California in the morning. Make arrangements for where you'll be staying and I'll have this dentist send her records Next Day Air. You can give them to this detective when you see him. Bethany also had a distinct birthmark on her left hand, at the base of the thumb. It looked like a rash." The senator picked up a framed photo from a side table. "Here's the last picture we have of her. I ask that you bring it back."

Simone's mind went into damage control. They had planned to go into full campaign mode in a couple of weeks, but with this situation unresolved a lot of things would need to be changed. She reached for her calendar and quickly glanced over the items and his appearances for the next couple of days.

"Will you be going back to Washington Sunday night?"

"At present I'm planning on it. I don't want to interrupt my schedule until we know something for certain. There is one other thing the detective asked about. He said preliminary investigations indicated the woman might have taken drugs before the attack, which could mean the murder was drug related."

"All right, Senator, as soon as I get home and see what flights are available I'll call this Detective Mondavi and arrange for a meet. Oh, one other thing we should be ready for. When the media gets a hold of this, they'll go berserk. It'll be the big issue for days unless Canada decides to invade New Hampshire. I don't suppose you have any friends in Canada who owe you a favor?" she said, smiling thinly to hide her wrongly placed sense of humor.

The senator chose not to comment. "Detective Mondavi agreed to keep this an issue involving a woman by the name of Bethany Taylor until we find out if this is our Bethany or someone else. We'll decide how to handle it after you see him."

Simone put away her note pad and stood. "If that's all, senator, I'll fax these notes on that Senate bill to Steve and he can review them with you Monday morning."

"Thank you. As soon as you know where you'll be staying call Mariano here and he'll see those dental records are at your hotel when you get there."

I'll call as soon as I know anything. There's always a chance this is not her."

Senator Davis nodded solemnly. "Yes, there is that possibility, but there are too many things pointing to it being Bethany. And, Simone, if it is her, find out all you can about the child. I'd appreciate that."

The temperature had already passed through the century mark as Simone walked to her car. Hopefully, California temperatures would be more reasonable than Phoenix in July.

16

Gray studied the canvasses sitting on the rack along the wall of his well-lit studio, a steaming cup of coffee clasped in his hands. He had told Waterman not to expect anything else for a while, but Gray knew work was the only way to dispel the grief. At 2:00 A.M., realizing sleep wasn't possible, he had come to the studio.

He stripped off the top sheet of his palette pad and rummaged through the rolled-up tubes of paint, setting aside the ones he needed. A half tube of Thalo Red Rose and another of Cadmium Yellow Pale alongside what was left of Thalo Blue. He squeezed out the paint in a triangular pattern on the palette paper and added the other combinations of violets, greens, and blues. Using a palette knife, he began blending the rest of the colors he would need. To the mixtures he carefully added a small amount of poppy seed oil, and oil of cloves, to prolong the drying time of the paint. Then, from the coffee can filled with an assortment of sables and bristle brushes, he chose four flat bristles and laid them on the table.

With his preparations complete, he picked up a linen panel that he had begun of a lake nestled beneath a twelve thousand-foot ridge that led to a craggy peak. Scattered pines grew up through the cracks in the rocky landscape surrounding the blue lake. In the foreground, Gray carefully added dabs of lavender to a base of green foliage representing a cluster of sky pilots and the deep yellow of daisy-like alpine gold flowers found only at these high altitudes.

Hours later he realized the light in the studio had changed with the morning sunlight. A small battery-operated clock on the windowsill read 9:00. He stood back from the painting and studied it before placing it on the rack to dry. Signing it would wait until he viewed it again in morning light. Sometimes the process went on for a week of more before the piece satisfied him.

When he walked into the kitchen for a coffee refill, he remembered he was supposed to meet Juarez for lunch. He put his cup in the sink and headed for the shower.

A typical Laguna Mesa summer day meant a sunny sky with temperatures in the mid-seventies and out-of-town tourists clogging the streets. Halfway down his block a woman dressed in baggy white slacks and a long-sleeve shirt stood before her easel, painting a knurled oak tree, her floppy straw hat adorned with flowers from a curb-side plant. She had been painting the same scene all summer and never seemed to have gone beyond the blocking in of her colors.

Once through the congestion in downtown Laguna Beach, Gray turned off Pacific Coast Highway and followed Laguna Canyon Road until it joined up with Highway 133, which cut across the freeway intersection commonly referred to as the "Y" and often the scene of historic traffic jams. He headed north on Interstate 5 until Santa Ana Drive and made his way over to the park at the Civic Center.

Gray spotted the food wagon parked by the curb fronting the park. He pulled the Jeep into an empty space behind an ageing Chevy with two flat tires. Juarez waved from among a small crowd of gangbangers.

Juarez met him halfway and embraced him. "How you doing, Shadow?"

A thin smile creased Gray's face at the use of a name he hadn't heard in years. "Could be better."

"Yeah, I know what you mean. Any news on the girl?"

Gray shook his head. "Nothing yet. They claim they're working on it, but so far nothing on who killed Bethany, either."

Juarez motioned to one of the heavily tattooed gangbangers who studied Gray's Jeep like someone imagining what it might look like without wheels.

The squat Hispanic ambled over, making sure it looked like it was his idea. "You know about me, right?" Juarez said. "You know who I am and you know what would happen if you were to do something I wouldn't like? Well, this guy here," Juarez pointed at

Gray. "He's worse than me, if you can imagine something that bad. You understand?"

Gray watched the shaved head nod once and saw the change in the gangbanger's eyes. Then a wide grin revealed three gold teeth and two empty spaces. "*Si,* Juarez. Would I mess with you or any of your friends? You know me better than that."

"Good," Juarez said and pointed at Gray's Jeep. "Now that car there is like my very own, you understand? Nobody touches it, okay?"

The shaved head bobbed again, then he motioned to the others to join him and they moved into the shade of a root-bound tree and squatted in the dirt.

"How long did it take you to train them?"

"Despite how they look, they're not hard core, yet. No hard time; no long-range plans though. Doesn't pay. Every once in a while one of them comes into our place and tries another way. Some are worth trying to save, but others," he said, shrugging his shoulders, "not worth the effort. They'll be dead before they're old enough to vote. Some say that's a good thing. They may sway some election someday."

The park served the neighborhood of small, single-family dwellings built around the end of the last European war. Most hadn't been painted since they were built and sported front lawns of weeds, garbage, and, if there was still room, the empty hulk of a car stored on blocks and waiting for wheels. Occasionally someone tried to grow geraniums in empty coffee cans placed on the front doorstep, the cans also serving as ashtrays. The only common denominator was the iron security shutters bolted to stucco walls.

"You're buying lunch, right?" Juarez asked.

Gray grinned. "We agreed it was my choice this time. Now you bring me to a classy place like this and then you want me to pay. I hope I brought enough money."

This time Juarez chuckled. "Wouldn't do to pull out a credit card here. They use those to open locked doors."

Under the awning a sweating cook scraped grease off the grill and slapped on a meat patty, then flipped two others and added slices of cheese. Juarez spoke to the woman standing behind a fold-up table, a change machine strapped to her ample waist. He ordered four pork tacos and a couple of Cokes and dropped the money on the table.

With their tacos wrapped in wax paper, Gray and Juarez found an empty bench and sat down.

Juarez finally broke the silence. "You tell them who she was?"

"Figured they would find out sooner or later so might as well come from me."

"Man, would I like to see the Colonel's face when he finds out. Especially if he discovers you're involved."

Gray wadded up the taco wrapper and tossed it toward an overflowing trashcan. It bounced off the heap of trash and landed on the ground amid accumulated food containers, napkins, and disposable diapers.

"Doesn't it though. Makes you wonder if it was planned that way," Gray said. "But look, Paco, about this talk with the police. I may need your help. I'm not sure yet, but I don't like the way they're looking at this with Bethany, and especially Carlie Kate. One of them would rather spend his time trying to find a way to put me in the middle of it instead of looking for whoever did it."

Juarez licked his fingers before replying. "And I suppose you sat there and didn't say anything?"

"You know me. I think I might have overreacted."

Juarez leaned forward and studied something behind Gray. "Want to talk about it?" he said.

Gray stood up and casually walked to the trash container, dropping the second wrapper in the pile of clutter. "They asked me some questions I didn't like, about the girl."

"About you and the girl?"

"Yeah, you know what kind of questions."

"I can imagine. I'd be more surprised if they hadn't. Might be a little early in their investigation, but they were bound to sooner or later, especially when they have so little to go on."

Gray's attention was elsewhere. "You know the new group gathering under the trees over there? They seem pretty interested in us."

Juarez nodded. "That's Pacheco and his posse. Runs this end of town."

Gray glanced back at those assigned to watch his car. They had also noticed the new group and appeared nervous. "This Pacheco fellow know you?"

"He knows me; might not like me, but he knows who I am. If they come over, let me handle it. Meanwhile, tell me what happened when they put those questions to you. You say you overreacted."

"It was just the one. This Detective Mondavi, the one in charge, he did most of the talking. He was okay. The other one was a Mex like you. I didn't like where he was going with some of his questions. I suppose I shouldn't have grabbed him."

"Might have gotten yourself shot. Was me I probably would have shot you," Juarez said. "Look, my friend, we've been through a lot together, more than most. I know you. I know you wouldn't do these things, but they don't, so play it cool for a bit. Let me see what I can find out."

"I know what you're saying, but while they chase after something to pin on me they're not looking for her."

Juarez held his hand up. "I think Pacheco wants to know why we're here in his backyard and not looking scared. Makes him nervous when people aren't frightened by him."

The one called Pacheco moved out from under the trees and headed across the park, followed closely by four others. Two wore wife-beater T-shirts under long-sleeve shirts buttoned at the neck and half way down the front. Pacheco's face bore the marks of a variety of tattoo artists' work and the arms of all four displayed gang insignia. They spread out and came to a halt about ten feet away, giving Juarez and Gray their practiced mean look.

"Pacheco," Juarez said.

"I have not seen you here before, but I know you, Juarez. The other one here I don't know him."

Gray's eyes locked onto Pacheco's, neither breaking off. Gray could tell the man was having a hard time keeping his eyes focused. Few would dare challenge the man in his territory, and Gray knew he was taking a chance, but they used to say that Gray could outstare an owl, and Pacheco's irritation soon became obvious.

"He's a friend of mine," Juarez said.

"I don't like him. Why is he here?"

Juarez shrugged. "From what I hear there are a lot of people you don't like Pacheco, and he's here because I asked him to be here."

Pacheco grinned at the obvious challenge. "This is my turf, Juarez, and I will let you come here, sometimes, if I feel like it, but he goes," Pacheco said, jabbing his finger at Gray. "Or I will take it as disrespect and you know about that, Juarez. You understand?"

Gray felt the tension edge higher. He kept his eyes on the one called Pacheco but felt the presence of the others. He knew they were readying themselves in case Pacheco called on them.

"Would not want you to get angry and do something that would not be good for you, Pacheco," Juarez said. "You might be surprised at what would happen."

Pacheco shifted his eyes from Juarez to Gray and back to Juarez. Gray knew the man was looking for a way out. The odds were too much in his favor to have this confrontation. Gray knew Pacheco was figuring there was something there he couldn't see.

"What the fuck you doing here anyways? You come from the other part of town?"

"We came for the tacos," Gray said. "We heard they were the best around."

"Well, eat your fucking tacos and beat it," Pacheco said, turning slowly around and swaggering back the way they had come. He motioned to the group gathered around Gray's Jeep, and they quickly moved off in the other direction.

"Nice neighborhood, and so much for their guard duties," Gray said.

"It was not always like this. Some of these old people have lived here most of their lives, and they will tell you what it was like years ago. They raised families here. The children went to school. They sat on the grass on their lawns and had a picnic, or talked to their neighbors and did it all without ever hearing gun shots. Now they can't leave. They can't sell their homes. They stay inside and only come out when they have to. Usually in the morning when the drug dealers are sleeping."

"What happened?"

"What happens to all these older places? Many of these people have no papers, so they can't go to the police. Pacheco put together an organization that moves drugs around the area. He takes his orders from others, who take their orders from the ones who have the money and supply the drugs, the cartels. Don't sell him short. He was in a good mood today."

"Then why did you push him?" Gray asked.

"He knows why. He's been moving north, up into a part of the city where there are still lawns to sit on. I was sending him a message."

Gray grunted. "Wish you had told me I was part of it."

"Well," Juarez said with a wry grin, "I didn't think he would be around today. I figured someone would tell him I came. This way was better."

While Juarez talked Gray felt the tension slowly release its grip. He hadn't noticed his increased level of awareness until that moment. Everything around him had suddenly sharpened with the escalation of the confrontation. The odors emanating from the food wagon, the voices of the children in the playground at the far end of the park, the flicker of sudden movement at the edge of his sight line, all brought to near critical mass. "Glad he took your message in stride. I wasn't sure where you were going with it."

Juarez chuckled. "You've mellowed. Time was you would have torn his head off for less."

"You, too, but times change, and so do people. Maybe we're both getting old."

Juarez seemed to think his answer through. "No, just learning to live with scum because the alternative is something society frowns on."

Gray watched Pacheco and his group pick up stray followers, including a couple of heavily metaled girls who looked to be in their early teens. They surrounded two graffiti-covered park benches and flopped down, attempting to transmit their fear-creating vibes back to Gray and Juarez.

"Think we should hang around awhile, you know, just to piss them off some more?" Gray asked.

Juarez shook his head as they walked toward the cars. "About this thing with Bethany. I'll see what I can learn that maybe they're not telling you. And don't do anything stupid, you know, with the cop. That's not the way you used to operate."

Gray unlocked the Jeep. "I don't like it, Paco. I don't like the way this makes me feel. I thought I'd left it all behind me. You know what I mean. It's been, what seven, eight years. I don't want to go there again. It's not who I am now."

Juarez nodded in understanding. "It's always there whether you like it or not. It's what they made us, and both of us had it in our blood to begin with. They recognized what they had and took advantage of it."

Gray turned away in frustration, but Juarez wouldn't let it go. "You can't run and hide from what you are. I know you've tried."

Over the top of the Jeep, Gray watched the watchers, aware of the conflict coursing through his body. "I'm not going back, Paco. It might happen again. I won't let it."

17

The dirt-stained stucco house sat at the end of a rutted road, surrounded by sun baked weeds. The smells from the town drifted up the slope to meet two men sitting in plastic chairs on either side of the green door, shaded by two ponderous trees casting shade across the front of the house. A Mercedes SUV sat within the shade, and on the other side of the house a mud-spattered Chevy Suburban with battered front fenders was parked beside what remained of a Ford pickup. The Suburban bore Texas plates. Both men wore white straw hats and rayon polo shirts, and sported multiple gold chains around their necks. One cradled an AK-47 across his lap as if it were Madonna herself. A Remington 870 pump shotgun rested against the wall in reach of the other.

Inside the house Miguel Zapata believed he was close to death. He stumbled out of the bedroom and slumped down in a chair at a table littered with empty tequila bottles. The pain in his face and hand brought back the reality of the last twenty-four hours. He swept the litter off the table to create space to lay his head down and groaned. But the memory of the night before drilled through the pain in his head and fought off every attempt to erase it. He lifted his head slowly and pressed it between his hands, hoping to stop the heavy pounding behind his eyes. On the table his Colt .45 automatic lay beside the chipped mirror used to create the furrows of pleasure to help him forget the disasters of his trip north.

The pistol, taken off the body of a drug dealer who thought he could bypass Zapata and the cartel and deal directly with his contacts in the north, sold for close to $10,000. Colt had the pistol's barrel engraved with the words *"El Presidente,"* and fitted it with pure ivory grips. Zapata picked it up, ran his fingers along the barrel, and laid the cold steel against his cheek.

A groan from the bedroom made him lift his head. The naked woman lying among the stained sheets on the king-size bed rolled onto her stomach. Her long black hair lay in sweat-induced tangles across the pillow and partially covered a large tattoo of a marijuana leaf adorning one shoulder. An image of the Virgin of Guadalupe decorated the other shoulder. The room itself had been created by tearing out walls to make room for the oversized bed, with no thought as to whether the walls held the roof in place. The local villagers had bets on how long before the house collapsed, many hoping its current occupant was inside when it did. A poster of Jesse Malverde that Zapata had picked from the outlaw's shrine hung taped to the wall above the bed.

He gripped his head between his hands, trying to remember what it was that seemed so important when he woke up. The book. It sent a chill through his body when he thought of the information it contained. He knew his father would do everything possible to discover where it might be, that he could count on. But if his father read what was in it, Miguel knew his own life would be worthless.

He had not told Castillo everything. He never did. Castillo turned his words around when he related information to Don Emiliano to make Miguel look incompetent. He knew that one day he would have to kill Castillo before the Colonel had him killed.

Behind him, the sound of heavy breathing caused him to turn his head slowly. Two young girls lay entwined on the couch, their thick bodies clad only in bikini panties. He tried remembering where they had come from. Then it began coming back, the three women in bed with him, the tequila, and the girls taking turns attempting to arouse him, without success. The laughter still rang in his ears and the image of them doing each other instead. He could not allow them to get the chance to talk about last night.

A thin layer of white powder dusted the broken mirror lying on the edge of the table. Miguel Zapata ran his finger over it and brought it up to his nose, drawing in deeply. He waited, but nothing happened. Cursing he threw the mirror at the couch and stumbled to the door.

The guard leaped to his feet. "*Si*, Miguel."

Miguel pointed at the squirming bodies. "Get rid of them."

The thin-faced guard glanced over Miguel's shoulder and shrugged. "What should I do with them?"

It hurt his head when he spoke. "I do not give a shit what you do with them. Fuck them, shoot them, sell them, whatever you want to do, but take them far away and do it now."

A car pulled in behind the Chevy and Castillo stepped out.

Miguel began to shut the door of the house.

"Miguel, we must talk."

Then he remembered what it was he had forgotten. "Did you send them back?"

Castillo shook his head. "Do you not remember? They could not search the house, but your father has authorized me to send others to look."

Zapata knew Castillo would send those in his own payroll, which meant they would report everything back to him only. "And what will you tell them to do with it if they find it?"

Castillo ordered the guard at the door to leave and took his seat. "Sit down, Miguel. I know what you're thinking. You tell me if there is another way. If whoever I send finds it, we must be sure it is destroyed or it will destroy us both."

"You do not want to have it sent back?" Zapata knew he would need to destroy it before Castillo saw it.

"No, that is too dangerous. It would pass through too many hands before we gained control. If it is there, they will find it."

"It must be there. There is nowhere else," Zapata said. "Is that all you have?"

Castillo brushed away the flies that had gathered around his face. "No, there is another problem we must talk about." He reached down and picked up a package of cigarettes the guard had left behind.

"What do you mean, another problem?"

"It is your DNA that you left on the woman and in her house."

Miguel Zapata turned and went back into the house as the guard carried the last of the women out and dumped her in the back of the Suburban. He needed a drink. His hand throbbed; his face ached where the American woman's fingernails had carved furrows in his cheek. He called over his shoulder. "Is this not something that can wait?"

"I suppose it can wait, but I think you should know about it. It could make the problem with your little book of little consequence."

Zapata carried the bottle of tequila out with him and sat across from Castillo. "What is this consequence shit? And this DNA? I did not fuck her. How could I leave anything on her?"

"Miguel, if your head was not up your ass you would know what I am talking about. You are not a stupid man. Where do you think the skin from your face is? Under her fingernails. Fuentes said there was blood all over her and her bed from your hand."

"So? They find this skin and this blood, so what? I am down here in Morelia. What can they do?"

Castillo lit another cigarette. "You will not like what I say. I did some checking. You remember that time in San Diego, with that woman, the one who filed those charges against you?"

"The bitch deserved what she got. We should not have paid her that money," Zapata said.

"Miguel, I do not want to discuss this episode again. There were three witnesses who swore you raped the woman and then beat her. It cost your father much money and favors to have it taken care of. He paid for the woman's hospital bills as well as enough money to have her drop the charges."

"So fucking what?"

"Do you remember them taking these samples from you? It is customary on felony charges to do so."

Zapata laughed. "As you say, I am not stupid. When the charges were dropped the samples were thrown out. It is the law. I read this."

Castillo nodded.

"What, I am wrong in this?" Zapata asked.

"On request of your council, this is so. Unfortunately no such request was made. I would assume your DNA is still in their computers."

Miguel Zapata felt the hole getting larger. He wished his head were clearer so he could piece together what it all meant. "So, what does all this mean?

"It means, Miguel, that when they run those tests, and sooner or later they will, your name will appear on their screen, and they will know who murdered the senator's daughter."

"Fuck. I'm fucked."

"No, Miguel, when that happens we are all fucked, your father included."

18

Gray leaned on the railing of the Huntington State Beach Pier and stared out over the choppy waters of the Pacific. A three-foot swell hosted a band of surfers waiting to catch a last wave before darkness made the concrete pillars of the pier loom deadly in shadow.

He watched the lines of local fishermen rise and fall, their bobbers undulating in the current. In the last hour only one added a fish to his five-gallon plastic paint can beside his chair.

This was the last place he expected to be. He had spent many hours here with Bethany and Carlie Kate, walking along the beach walk, dodging bikes and skateboarders and trying to walk three abreast while holding hands. Or taking off their shoes to run down the sand as the water receded, daring the next wave to catch them. The beach trips always ended with lunch at Ruby's, the hamburger place at the end of the pier. The first time Gray had told Carlie Kate about the first End of the Pier Café, and how a great storm surge years before dumped the iconic restaurant, along with most of the pier itself, into a raging ocean. But Surf City without a pier could not compete with Santa Cruz's for the name, so the pier was rebuilt. Now the surrounding beach and business establishments hosted a variety of surfing competitions, volleyball tournaments, and for a while paintball play wars, until it was determined the cleanup effort didn't warrant the income, paintball aficionados not being big spenders.

Half an hour later Gray drove south through Newport Beach, past the arched entrance to the Pelican Hills Resort, unable to accept the lack of information about the girl. Images of her bruised and battered body lying in some grave or being abused by her kidnapper haunted him.

He tore his thoughts away from an imagination out of control and back to reality. Would Davis come himself to pick up Bethany's body, or would he send someone? Gray figured someone would be sent. He made a note to ask Mondavi.

But what if Davis came? Would he confront the man? Would he tell him how happy they had been, and how things might have been different if Davis had not interfered? Again he felt the bitterness well up inside him. He pushed the thought away, remembering the hours and days he and Bethany had together that could never be taken away. He knew Bethany would have wanted him to let it go.

Gray turned off Pacific Coast Highway onto the short street leading up to Bethany's cottage. Three blocks up he pulled to the curb and shut off the engine. Mondavi said he would call when they were through with the house, but Gray wasn't going to hold his breath waiting for the call.

The white wooden gate beneath the arbor was unlatched. Someone had placed a small bouquet of flowers on the brick path beside the gate. He had forgot to ask Dorothy about Carlie's kitten and figured it might still be in the house hiding in some dark corner.

The front door stood slightly ajar, which caused him to wonder if the police had forgotten to lock up after finishing their investigation.

A flash of movement at his feet startled him. He stepped back quickly as Carlie's black kitten streaked past him into the house.

Well, screw them, Gray muttered to himself. If they have a problem with it they should have locked the door. He ignored the sign about imminent arrest, ducked under the yellow tape, and pushed the door open. He called out to the kitten, figuring it probably hadn't eaten in a couple of days. Gray had little experience with cats but enough to know they seldom came when called.

He stepped into the living room where they had all sat watching TV and flipped on the light switch, afraid to go any further, not knowing what he might see. He noticed the overturned end table with the broken lamp on the floor, alongside Carlie's school books and Bethany's glasses. He knew he was breaking the rules entering the house. It always bothered him when he did. He shook his head and pushed the feelings aside, surveying the room and seeing the spots on the carpet. The irregular brown stains led back toward the hall. Someone had circled them with a white substance, then he wondered what he might find where Bethany's body was found. Would he see a white outline, like he'd seen on TV? He paused at the head of the hall, not certain he wanted to continue.

Gray heard a scraping or scratching sound somewhere down the hall. He stood motionless, his head tilted to one side, listening. He moved down the hall toward the kitchen, passing Carlie's room. Bethany's bedroom was across the hall from the kitchen.

Halfway down the hall Gray slowed again, sensing something different, other than the noise a kitten would make. Was what he heard only the sounds of any normal house, sounds that are present every hour of the day and night? Gray's senses were honed on the reservation, when Grandfather had taught him how to listen for the sound of water rushing over rocks and nature in motion. At that moment these senses told him something that did not belong occupied a portion of the house. He knew whatever it was would know he had entered the house; he had announced his presence. Grandfather said such feelings, as sounds, were the actions of the dead returning to remind you of your existence.

He moved with caution, his breathing controlled. If someone was in the house, they had to be in Bethany's room or the kitchen. The refracted light from the front room cast ghostly images on the white walls of the hall. He paused again.

From the kitchen came a crash. Gray froze.

The kitten emerged and voiced its displeasure at not finding its dinner.

Gray spoke to the black ball of fur and reached down to pick it up, figuring he would take it home and feed it until he could decide what to do with it.

The blow brought a searing flash of pain and intense heat to the back of his head. He staggered, sinking to his knees, his shoulder smacking into the wall before his elbows hit the floor. He rolled over, his hands clutching the back of his head, and caught a glimpse of an upraised arm. Instinctively he kicked his legs out to protect himself as the arm crashed down toward his face. The second blow glanced off the side of his face and tore at his ear, but his assailant's downward motion had exposed his groin. Gray brought a knee up as hard as he could and felt the contact. It brought a groan of pain as his assailant momentarily doubled up, giving Gray a chance to roll over onto his side and attempt to regain his feet. The movement brought on a wave of nausea and dizziness. Gray pulled his knees in and started to rise as the assailant's arm rose and swept down again. For a second it seemed poised above his head. In the dim light he made out a series of tattoos that extended from the wrist up the entire arm. He raised his hands to protect his face when his head exploded again. He rolled over onto his back, catching the image of a second attacker before he passed out.

19

Simone St. Pierre pushed the silk sheets aside and rose from the bed as quietly as possible. The scent of the night's love making clung to her body but a shower would have to wait until she was back in her condo. She had made it a point from the beginning that they did not use her place for overnight stays, or any visits for that matter, preferring the suite Sergio used on the top floor of a Phoenix five-star hotel.

The bedside clock read 5:21. Silently she gathered up her clothes and slipped into the bathroom, closing the door before turning on the light. She dressed quickly, hoping to slip out of the room without waking Sergio. Her plane for California was scheduled to leave in about four and a half hours. It gave her enough time to go back to her place, shower, and pack a bag for the short trip. She hoped the time away would offer an opportunity to think over a number of things, this relationship for starters, and about this new concern. What if she brought back the news to the senator and his wife that their daughter had been murdered, and there was the possibility of a six-year-old granddaughter who was missing? Would it destroy the senator's desire to seek a full term in the Senate? And where would that leave her if he chose not to run?

The light on the bedside table greeted her when she emerged from the bathroom fully dressed, except for her shoes.

"Simone, you are leaving this early. I had hoped we might share breakfast before you left," Sergio Collor de Mello said from the bed.

Simone smiled. "I didn't want to disturb you. I have a lot to do before I leave."

"Yes, true, you are going to California this morning."

"Yes, I told you about it last night."

At dinner she had told him about going to California for a couple of days, and he had wanted to know why. That brought on an argument and his concern there was someone else in her life. In the end she related the facts about the senator's daughter after eliciting a solemn promise to say nothing to anyone.

Simone dropped her watch into her purse and walked over to the bed. "I'll call as soon as I'm back," she said, leaning over to kiss his cheek.

"No. Call me as soon as you have spoken to this detective person and tell me what he has said."

She smiled and ran her fingers over his shoulder. He could be like a pouting child if he was deprived of something he wanted, a sure sign of unearned wealth. "Will you still be here, in Phoenix I mean?"

He swung his legs over onto the floor, covering himself as he did so. "I will wait for your call, yes?"

"I said I would." She wondered what part of their conversation he hadn't heard.

Monday morning traffic began to build as she turned onto Highway 101 and drove north, letting her emotions step down after leaving his room. Her plan to avoid a confrontation by slipping out before he woke was meant to put their relationship back in focus.

Simone pulled off 101 and drove into a Starbucks in a small strip mall, parking alongside a compact car bearing a Domino's Piazza sign on its roof. She took a moment to push her hair into some semblance of order, aware that her clothing hardly resembled everyday wear, especially at that time of the morning. Luckily, only two people waited in line ahead of her. She smiled at the young barista and ordered a non-fat vanilla latte with an extra pump. Then, in a moment of weakness, she added a crusted cinnamon roll. She promised herself she would add more miles to her workouts when she got back from California, then remembered the article she read about the beach walk along Huntington State Beach and made a note to throw her running gear into her travel bag.

The gates to the condominium complex swung open as soon as the night guard recognized her car. She smiled to acknowledge his salute and drove over to her parking slot.

At the door to her unit, Simone opened the mail slot and grasped the handful of assorted envelopes and magazines. She tucked the mail under her chin and, with her heels dangling from the hand that held the latte, Simone balanced her purse on her knee and searched for her keys. She managed to open her door and stumble into the entryway before her purse and the mail hit the floor simultaneously.

A wrinkled, pale-blue envelope stuck out from beneath a fitness magazine, a return address handwritten on the corner of the envelope. Her friends sent e-mails if they had anything to say that couldn't be said on the phone. She couldn't even remember the last name someone had written her a letter. She frowned and plucked it out of the pile.

The red stamp below her name and address read simply "*Par Avion*." She read the return address. It had come from a street in the fourth *arrondisement* in Paris. Simone couldn't breathe. She dropped the latte and sunk to her knees, her hands shaking as she studied the envelope, afraid to open it. How could he have found her? It wasn't possible, her past no longer mattered. It was another time, another life.

Simone bit her lip and sobbed.

20

To Gray it felt as if a blacksmith had set up shop inside his head. He brought his hands up and felt the wetness in his hair. He opened his eyes to a flickering light doing a ghostly dance on the walls. He took a deep breath before attempting to evaluate his condition. Then he smelled the smoke as a wave of hot air washed over him. He rose to his knees but was forced to drop back to the floor and take short shallow breaths between the fits of coughing. The heat intensified.

He lay below the layer of smoke, fighting to control his breathing and gather his thoughts. He shook his head, which only brought on a new wave of dizziness. The sound of the fire grew louder, the rush of hot air tingling the skin on his arms and neck. He must move, but in which direction, since he wasn't sure where he was? He needed to concentrate or die in the next few minutes. He remembered being in the hallway when someone hit him the first time. Was he still in the hall? He felt the carpet beneath him, then reached out with both arms and touched the walls on either side. But where exactly in the hall? He pulled himself forward on his elbows, keeping his face as close to the floor as possible.

The smoke thickened, swirling over his head and causing a racking cough. He opened his eyes for a moment and suffered a blinding burning sensation. Gray pulled himself forward on his elbows another few feet, feeling the walls on both sides until his left hand felt the opening. He swung his arm back and forth, then reached as far inside as he could. It had to be a doorway, but which one and where did it lead? The bathroom, a closet? He tried to remember the layout of the house, the doorway being on his left. Either he had crawled down the hall and this led into Bethany's bedroom, or when he went down from the blow he fell facing the way he had entered the house. If he had, then this led into Carlie Kate's room. He knew he had little time left, as the acidic smoke continued to thicken.

A crash from somewhere behind him caused a wave of hot air to sweep over his back. If this was Bethany's room, he would have little chance to make it through her furniture and find the window. Knowing the pain it would bring, he opened his eyes for a second. Flickering light ahead of him meant the fire raced toward him from both directions. He would never make it, even if he stood up and tried to charge out through the front door. Only Carlie's room offered an opportunity to escape.

With his head as close to the floor as possible, Gray crawled through the opening, visualizing the girl's bed directly opposite the door and beneath the window. His hand swept around to his right, remembering Carlie's dresser against the wall by the door. When his hand contacted the bureau he knew he still had a chance.

Through the pounding in his head he fought to remember his training and override the panic. He pulled himself forward toward the bed that sat below the window, a locked window. He had only one chance. One shot at survival.

Gray's leading hand felt the cloth of the bedspread that hung to the floor. Carlie had insisted on it. She hid everything under the bed instead of putting it away where it belonged and thought her mother didn't know. His hand touched something solid behind the bedspread. With every breath he took in more smoke and less life-giving oxygen. Time had run out. He envisioned taking one more breath as close to the floor as he could, then making his attempt. As he started to pull his hand away from whatever it was under the bed he realized he had touched the old wooden paint box, the one he had given Carlie. Buried deep in his subconscious were lessons of past training. When in any situation where he did not have the tools or weapons he needed, use what is available.

Gray grasped the box in both hands and pulled it out from beneath the bed. Once he committed to the move he couldn't go back. Only one chance to make it out before he succumbed to the smoke. No more time to think. If he figured it right the window would be directly in front and above him. If not, he would crash into the wall and there would be no second chance.

Gray gathered himself and pushed up off the floor. He fought the pain in his chest but knew he could not take another breath. One step up onto the bed with the paint box held up in front of him as a battering ram, his lungs on fire, he hurled himself blindly at the wall above the bed.

The sharp edge of the wooden box shattered the glass ahead of him, pushing the jagged shards through the mesh of the window screen and tearing away the thin aluminum channeling that held the screen in place. Gray felt the searing burn as the razor edges of the glass lanced his arms and face before he felt himself falling through the opening onto the pruned hedge beneath the window. He hit the lawn with his shoulder, his knees coming up to strike him in the stomach and drive out whatever wind he had left. He lay on the grass, his mouth yawning, gasping for air until finally his muscles relaxed enough to allow the first breath of semi-fresh air to enter his lungs.

As Gray pulled himself across the lawn and away from the falling embers, he heard the sirens cease. A big red engine with flashing lights rumbled to a stop across the street. A moment later a spotlight found him lying alongside the bushes on the far side of the lawn. As he tried to rise a hand pushed him back onto the grass.

"Hold it there, sir. We'll have someone look at you first. Can you tell me if anyone else was in the house?"

Gray could only shake his head. Whoever had hit him would have been long gone. He touched his face with his fingertips, coming away with bits of skin mixed with blood.

A sea of flashing lights filled the street as another fire engine arrived, competing with Laguna Mesa patrol cars for parking space. Gray heard orders and instructions shouted as a paramedic unit pulled into a spot vacated by an unneeded patrol car. On another rig a team of fire fighters worked in unison to extract and attach a hose, while others hauled the nozzle end over the downed picket fence and began wetting down a neighbor's shake roof.

A hand reached touched his arm and a female voice close to his ear said, "I need to take a look at you."

Gray turned his head and saw her nametag, which read "Wilson." She wore the blue uniform and badge of a paramedic unit.

"Can you stand and walk with me? We'll be out of their way and we can talk."

Still dazed, Gray nodded and, with her help, he struggled to his feet, then allowed her to lead him across the lawn to where her partner was setting out their first-aid supplies. The partner handed her a mask attached to a small tank.

She had Gray sit down, then eased the mask over his head. "It may hurt a little, but it will help you breath."

Gray felt immediate relief as the oxygen began replacing the remaining smoke in his lungs. Two police officers stood a few feet away, their hands resting on their equipment belts. She told them they would have to wait until she finished. Gray could tell they didn't like the idea. He thanked her with a nod.

She smiled. "Love to tell them to wait their turn. Dents their ego. They always feel like they can butt in anytime."

For a moment her hands busied themselves in his hair as she gently probed the large bump from whatever his attacker hit him with. "You won't need stitches, but it will need to be cleaned up," she said. "But first I want to take a look at the rest of you."

She began cutting away at the sleeves of his shirt and gently lifting the material off his arms. "From what I can see you were pretty lucky getting out of there with as little damage as you have."

Gray pulled the mask down. "For a while I had my doubts."

"Bet you did. Lucky for you that window wasn't double paned or barred like some of them around here."

"Wouldn't be talking with you if it were," Gray said.

She cut away what was left of his shirt and began wiping the blood off of his arms and face. She dropped the bloody gauze in a pile on the grass and went back to the truck for another handful. Gray watched the two cops study her and grin. He couldn't hear what she said to them, but they both laughed. He had to admit they had great taste. She certainly didn't look the type of woman who wanted to be a paramedic, unless as an actress in a movie.

"You know them?" Gray asked her.

"Yeah, Carson and Gomez. Known them since high school. They haven't changed."

Gray grunted as she touched a particularly sore spot. "Wouldn't figure you to have this kind of a job."

She pulled away, her eyes wide. "Oh, you're qualified to say what I should be doing? Keep it up and I'll put you in the same category as those two."

"Sorry, I'm sure you hear it enough already."

"Apology accepted," she said with a grin. "By the way, I need your name and address for my report."

She wrapped a blanket around his bare shoulders, then Gray gave her the information and watched as she began putting away her equipment. She paused, a frown on her face.

"This is the house where the woman was murdered the other night, isn't it?"

Gray nodded.

"Did you know her?"

"We were friends. More than friends, actually."

"I'm sorry, I didn't realize."

"It's all right," Gray said. He touched the growing bump on the back of his head, thinking about how long ago it seemed they were all together.

"Well, I can't keep them away from you forever. I did my best and, for what it's worth, I think you might need a haircut. That fire didn't do much for your hair style."

Gray fingered the ends of his hair. "You think so?"

"Yeah, either that or expect a whole lot of bad hair days ahead." She pushed a loose strand of light tawny hair over her ear and gave him a sad smile. "Okay, guys, he's all yours. Don't stress him out or you'll answer to me, you hear?"

Both nodded their heads before walking the short distance to stand on either side of him. Gray wondered if they expected him to try to escape.

The one called Gomez took the lead. "Mind telling us why you were in the house?"

Gray told them about the kitten and the open door and filled them in on his being attacked. One asked the questions while the other took notes.

"What did these attackers look like?"

"I didn't see them. I only saw one of them for a second before the other must have hit me."

Gomez said something to his partner, then spoke to Gray. "We've had a couple of house burglaries like this lately. Guys breaking into empty houses and looking for a place to camp for a few days. No fires though. Could be you knocked something over and started the fire."

"You think a fire coming from two directions could be accidental? Maybe you should wait and talk to your fire chief first. If it was set on purpose, he'll know."

They didn't look like they appreciated his opinion so Gray figured to shut up and let them finish. All he wanted to do was to go home and take something for his headache.

Gomez shook his head. "With all that smoke, you were probably confused. We'll ask around the neighborhood and see if anyone saw anything suspicious. Too bad though. Pretty little house. Always liked it."

The streams of water attacking the blaze were beginning to knock down the flames, though it was obvious the house would not be saved.

"You sure you don't want us to drop you over at emergency?"

"I'll be fine."

"Okay, but you're to call Detective Chavez in the morning, first thing. He and Detective Mondavi would have come tonight, but they're both out of the area. Detective Chavez made it a point to make sure you understood."

"Chavez? How..."

"We already called this in, and when he heard your name..."

Gray waved him off and slipped the blanket off his shoulders. "You tell Chavez he knows where he can find me."

Gomez looked hurt. "Might be better if you called him."

Gray had always hated the smugness and superior attitude that seemed to come with a badge and gun. He couldn't resist a parting shot. "Schedule's pretty tight tomorrow. You tell Chavez to call for an appointment."

A yellow-clad fireman walked over holding the wooden paint box. "Want this as a souvenir? I don't suppose it's much good now. Pretty busted up."

"Matter of fact I do," Gray said.

The bottom corner of the box had cracked open from striking the window, jamming the paint drawer. Gray tried to pull it open but gave up. Since it was something of Carlie's, he decided to take it with him.

As he headed for the Jeep he passed by the woman named Wilson loading her equipment into paramedic truck. "Thanks again."

She smiled. "No problem. My job."

Then something dawned on him. "Any chance you might have seen a little kitten running loose? I doubt it made it out of the house, but you can always hope I guess?"

"Little black thing, white socks."

"Yeah, where did you see him?"

"Hang on a minute." She pushed her case into the truck and ran over toward the hedge. A minute later she came back with Carlie's kitten in her arms. "This the one?"

"That's him," he said, taking the cat in his hands.

"Glad I could help but it's a she, not a him."

"Probably means trouble ahead but thanks for everything," he said. He nestled the kitten in one arm and picked up the paint box.

"Anytime," she said, then laid her fingers on his arm. "Listen, I know this is not a good time for you, but if you ever want to sit and talk to someone, you know, or have a cup of coffee, you can find me at the station, okay?"

"That's nice. Maybe sometime I'll need someone to talk to."

21

Simone St. Pierre dropped her laptop into her bag and peered out the window as the plane lost altitude and crossed over the range of mountains east of Orange County, California. Stacked up against the western slope of the mountains a blanket of gray haze thinned as the jet descended toward the runway at John Wayne Airport.

The plane banked, bringing into view the protruding hump of Santa Catalina Island, twenty-six miles west of the California coastline. Earlier the pilot had mentioned that the current temperature at the airport was a comfortable seventy-six degrees.

Simone wondered how people could not want to live in one of the small towns along the coast with weather like that.

Forty minutes later, her long blonde hair fastened back in a ponytail, Simone drove the convertible Volvo C70 rental onto MacArthur Boulevard and headed toward the ocean. Detective Mondavi had agreed to meet with her that afternoon. Since plans often change, she had made reservations for two nights at the Ritz Carleton in Laguna Niguel.

The hotel sat on a cliff above the ocean, its curving patio restaurant offering million-dollar views, while below the restaurant's tiled terrace the Pacific Ocean washed across manicured sand. When she checked in, the smiling receptionist handed her a UPS Overnight envelope, along with her room key. She tipped the bell captain and had her bags delivered to her room, then found an empty table at the poolside restaurant. When her Seafood Louie salad arrived she put away her notes and breathed in the cool salt air. From one hundred and five degrees in Phoenix the thirty-some degree change in temperature couldn't be described as anything but blissful.

Summer tourist traffic through Laguna Beach crawled, making her thirty minutes late. Simone parked the car and hurried into the station, hoping her tardiness would be overlooked.

Detective Mondavi's six-foot four-inch frame towered over her. She appraised him quickly, from the open-neck white shirt to the pressed trousers and polished shoes.

"Ms. St. Pierre, I presume. I'm Detective Sam Mondavi."

"Thank you for waiting. I had no idea traffic would be so horrendous," Simone said.

He grinned. "Summer traffic can be a bit of an ordeal. But we're a tourist town. We have to live with it."

Simone felt more at ease than she expected. "Mondavi, interesting name. Any relation to the wine Mondavis?"

"None that I'm aware of. I don't believe the ones you're referring to come from Little Italy in Chicago. However, I have to admit that travelling through the Napa and Sonoma area in Northern California I have no trouble getting a good seat at any restaurant. Then someone always throws a monkey wrench into it and asks which side of the warring Mondavis I belong to."

Simone followed him down the hall to a small office.

"This is Detective Chavez. He's working this case with me."

Simone held out her hand to the thin Hispanic man whose eyes quickly dropped to her breasts. She held onto his hand longer than normal until his eyes made their way back to meet hers.

She took the metal chair Mondavi offered and sat down, placing her briefcase at her feet. "Detective, before we begin I want you to understand the position Senator Davis and his wife are in. Their daughter disappeared over seven years ago. Other than unsubstantiated rumors, they have had no contact with her since. For a number of years the senator has retained the services of a discreet private investigation firm in Kansas City, but until your call there has been no trace of Bethany Davis.

Mondavi leaned his elbows on the desk and folded his hands together. "I understand, Ms. St. Pierre, but all of that is immaterial until we're certain the body we have is that of Ms. Davis."

"Of course," Simone said. She reached down and took the file from her briefcase. "I have a photo taken a number of years ago and the senator had these dental charts sent to me this morning."

She slid the folder across the desk to Mondavi, who flipped open the cover. He studied it for a moment and handed it across the desk to Chavez.

"Bethany Davis also had a birthmark on her left hand. Sort of a rash at the base of her thumb."

Simone saw the look Mondavi and Chavez exchanged.

"We'll need to have forensics look at these dental charts, before we are certain, but, I'm sorry to say, Ms. St. Pierre, this photo, and the birthmark you mentioned, match the body we have."

Simone settled herself in her chair and took a deep breath. All along she had hoped this was a wild goose chase, for the senator's sake and, she had to admit, for her own. This news would definitely put a hold on all the current plans for the campaign.

"Very well, Detective. We'll assume that the woman is Bethany Davis. I'll need to call the senator immediately, but I know he'll have questions, and I imagine he'll contact the appropriate people to have her body sent back to Phoenix once you release it."

Mondavi said nothing for a moment. She could feel the other one still staring at her profile and turned away from his line of sight. Let him imagine the rest, she thought.

"As soon as the coroner confirms the identity we'll let you know," Mondavi said.

"The senator will want to know what you have. You can imagine what they'll be going through when they know for sure it is her. What about the child you spoke of? Is there anything I can tell them about her?"

Mondavi leaned back in his chair and clenched his jaw. "Nothing so far. It's a strange case. Not the type of homicide we normally encounter, but it's still early."

"What's your best guess, Detective, for the murder and kidnapping?"

"This type of homicide can often be the case of one parent taking a child and in the process killing the opposing parent, but until we have information on who the child's father might be we have very little to go on."

"Pardon me," Simone said, holding up her hand. "I know I may come across as blunt—" She heard Chavez snicker at the remark but decided not to respond. "I wouldn't imagine you have many murders in this town. How much experience do you have in this type of crime?"

Mondavi put the photo in the envelope with the charts before answering. "Actually, I do. I worked homicides with the Los Angeles Police Department for a number of years, and before that the gang units, which you can imagine produced a few."

"I'm sorry, Detective, but I had to be sure. One of the first questions the senator will ask is what I thought about your ability to handle this case. I needed to be sure."

"I understand."

Simone took a pad and pen from her handbag. "Can you tell me what you know so far? The senator said nothing about how she died. Was she shot, strangled, what?"

"As I was saying, the majority of cases like this involve some type of family dispute. Robbery, home invasion gone sour, rape, drugs, things like that have to be considered. Ms. Davis was severely beaten, but as far as we can tell there is no indication of robbery, and she doesn't appear to have been raped. The missing child could indicate a pedophile, but I doubt it."

Simone glanced at her notes. "You asked the senator about drugs, why?"

She noted Mondavi's hesitation and wondered if they were telling her everything.

"Let me say this. Drugs were found in her mouth and on her face, but until the autopsy report comes back we can't say for certain whether she had ingested them or whether they were placed on her for a reason. The people who we spoke to were adamant about her not using drugs. It could be someone placed them on her to lead us in that direction."

"You mean a misdirection attempt?"

The question seemed to take Mondavi by surprise. He nodded. "Yes, something like that. Like I said there apparently was a struggle and Ms. Davis suffered physical abuse, which resulted in her death."

She glanced at her notes. "You indicated to the senator that you interviewed the boyfriend. Did he give you anything you could use?"

"No, he seems to have been out of town when it happened. We'll follow up to be sure but I wouldn't hold out any hope of it leading anywhere."

Chavez said, "There's always the possibility though."

Simone shifted her chair away from the desk. "What do you mean, Detective? Do you know something you're not saying?"

"You know how it is," Chavez said. "Wouldn't be the first time a boyfriend played daddy with a little girl and got caught. Answers a lot of questions when you think about it."

Mondavi cleared his throat. "I don't often make a mistake when I talk to people about whether they're lying or not. This guy she was going out with doesn't come across like someone who might do what Detective Chavez is referring to. I could be wrong, but his reaction to that suggestion was rather impressive." Mondavi chuckled. "Damn near assaulted Detective Chavez right here in the office."

She watched Chavez squirm in his chair and wondered just what had occurred. "So you've pretty much ruled him out then?"

Chavez interjected quickly. "Not really. I would say he's still a person of interest. He was the boyfriend and his story hasn't been fully checked out yet. Says he was somewhere up in the mountains where nobody saw him. That kind of story leaves a lot of holes."

Mondavi nodded in agreement. "Everybody acquainted with her still is at this point."

"Some years ago the senator received information about her possibly being married. It turned out to be a rumor, or that's what those who said they checked it out thought."

"I'd like to hear whatever you have on that because none of the people we've talked to have ever heard her talk about a husband," Chavez said. "I'll bet we put pressure on this guy she was living with, he'll know about it."

"Living with?" Simone questioned. "Did this boyfriend live with her?"

"No, I think Detective Chavez meant something else," Mondavi said. "They both had their own homes."

She wondered how much effort these detectives would put into finding holes in the boyfriend's story. Probably most of his time she figured.

"Getting back to what you were saying," Mondavi continued. "It doesn't have to be a past husband. There is a biological father out there somewhere, and if he discovered he had a daughter that might explain a lot. It's definitely a possibility."

Simone slipped her pad into her briefcase and stood. "There is another possibility we haven't discussed. If others had discovered her relationship to the senator, could this be a kidnapping gone bad? It's not generally known, but Mrs. Davis comes from a very wealthy family."

"And they took the child instead?" Mondavi questioned. "It's an avenue we'll need to consider, although kidnapping in these parts has gone out of style. Since you brought it up, has the senator heard something I should know about?"

Simone shook her head. "No, but until we know for sure that it isn't, we would like to keep everything out of the news. Is that possible?"

"As you said, this is a very small force here in Laguna Mesa. I think I can guarantee to keep a lid on it for a few days." Mondavi paused long enough to catch Chavez's eye. "After that I can't promise."

22

Conaire Gray heard the doorbell as he struggled with the simple act of dressing. A second series of rings followed, only seconds before an authoritative knocking threatened to disable the door itself. Gray slipped on a robe and answered the door as Detective Chavez was about to knock again. A young Laguna Mesa police officer stood off to the side as a backup.

Chavez held his badge. "You were told to call me, were you not?"

Gray recognized the young cop, the one called Gomez, who questioned him after the fire. Gray took a moment, then acknowledged Chavez's question with a slight nod.

Chavez gathered himself before speaking. "It would be easier to talk inside. We need to know about the fire."

Gray let them in rather than argue and saw his neighbor watching from behind her curtains as he closed the door. He couldn't be sure, but he thought he detected a smile on her face.

"Where's Detective Mondavi?" Gray wanted to know.

"Busy. He said to tell you, you should have reported like we asked."

"I'll bet he did. So what is it you want to know that I didn't tell him already?" Gray said, pointing to the young cop.

"We want to know what you were doing in the house when you shouldn't have been there. Detective Mondavi told you he'd let you know when you could go in. We still considered it a crime scene. But you couldn't wait. What was so important you had to cross the line and go in?"

"Like I told the officer, I remembered the kitten the little girl cared for and I saw that the door was open, so I went in to look for the cat. I couldn't see what harm that could do."

Chavez smiled. "I checked with the last officer at the house. He's positive the door was locked when he left. Do you want to rethink that?"

"Look," Gray said patiently. "When I went to the door it was partly open. Have you considered the fact that whoever attacked me in the house might have opened it, or is that too much to ask?" Gray knew he could only push Chavez so far before he reacted, but it seemed he was still looking for an excuse to implicate him.

Chavez stared at Gray. "That's your story, but personally I don't believe it. I think you went back to the house to burn it down and get rid of any evidence you left behind. Makes sense to me."

"I suppose I hit myself on the head, too, to make it look good."

"Why not? Makes your story look better. I figure you started the fire in a couple of spots to make sure they couldn't save it, then found yourself in a shit load of trouble and had to bail through the window."

Gray said nothing to counter the detective's theory. "So what do you want? You seem to have made up your mind already. Beats having to work any harder at it. You arresting me?"

"If it were up to me I would, but some aren't convinced. I don't think it will take much more to convince them though. One thing to think about. I talked to your neighbor across the street. She said she thinks you had the little girl over to stay one night. Is that a fact?"

Gray knew better than to bite. "You'll have to ask my neighbor. I'd get to her before noon though. Might be somewhat more lucid than in an afternoon. Now, if you're not here to arrest me, this interview is over."

Chavez pointed at Gray's hands. "I see you've managed to cover up those scrapes you had on your hands, the ones you claim came from a set-to at some food place? That was on some painting trip you said you were on." Chavez moved toward the door where the young cop stood waiting, then stopped. "Oh, for your information, I spoke with someone up there at that gas station place this morning. You know the one I'm talking about, on Highway 395. They said no one has robbed the place lately. In fact, the guy I spoke with says he's the owner, and he worked there the night you claim you had that scrap. So, unless there's another place up there I don't know what to tell you. Sounds like your story if full of holes, doesn't it? Sure makes me wonder."

The news stunned Gray. Chavez couldn't have talked to them. "I don't know what to tell you detective."

"Figured you wouldn't," Chavez said as Officer Gomez opened the door.

Out on the porch Chavez stopped. "I'm sure we'll have more questions later. I wouldn't want you to do anything like packing up your car. Might give us the idea you're going somewhere in a hurry."

Gray finished dressing and went into the kitchen to pour a cup of coffee and walked outside to sit on the patio. If Chavez had his way, they would arrest him and begin the process of tearing his story apart until they formed the picture they wanted. The case would be as good as solved. He had to admit the circumstantial facts had begun to mount against him, and if what Chavez said about the mini-mart was true, everything else made his story worthless. And his comment about running, was that to scare him? As far as the mini-mart was concerned, either Chavez was lying to gauge Gray's reaction, or someone was lying to the detective. Gray knew that's where he needed to start.

He picked up the phone and called Juarez's number, leaving a message on the tape. Paco Juarez's connections in the Vietnamese community in Westminster were as good as anyone not from that troubled country, and if anybody knew anything about the mysterious clerk at the food mart, it could be found in that suburb of Orange County.

23

Simone's session with Detective Mondavi left her with a major unanswered question. Senator Davis would want to know about the missing child. Was she the grandchild they never knew they had, the only grandchild of a couple who wanted one so desperately? Simone could visualize the pressure suddenly descending on Detective Mondavi and the Laguna Mesa Police Department once the senator was informed.

As soon as she returned to her room, Simone took a bottle of water from the small refrigerator and settled into the chair on her balcony overlooking the ocean. A half dozen sailboats gracefully maneuvered through the swell, some slipping north toward the gray-green bulk of Santa Catalina Island, while others ran with the wind, toward the harbors at Dana Point or farther south to San Diego.

Simone dialed the senator's cell phone, expecting to leave a message. To her surprise he answered on the second ring. She confirmed what they had expected. She said the police would wait until the corner verified the identification. Simone could tell by the senator's voice that his next step would be the most difficult, telling Susanna about their possible grandchild that couldn't be found.

With a deep sigh she hung up and ran her hands over her face, wiping away a tear that clung to the corner of her eyes. She tried to imagine what lay ahead for all of them.

For a moment her mind flashed back to the letter she had received from Paris. She knew the problem would need to be dealt with, but for now she would buy a little time. Perhaps, for the right price, it could be buried forever.

Another thought came to her. It was worth a call.

Detective Mondavi answered his page but hesitated at her request. When she explained why she wanted the boyfriend's phone number and address, he gave it to her with what seemed to be reluctance, advising her that the man was still considered someone of interest in the case.

Simone called the number. The message machine said to leave a number, nothing else.

With two options left, leave a number and wait to see if he called, or drive over to the man's house, Simone decided on the later, dropped her phone in her purse, and picked up the car keys.

She followed Pacific Coast Highway through its junction with Laguna Canyon Road, where the volleyball courts competed with sun worshipers for the limited amount of sand available. From there the highway continued south into the small town of Laguna Mesa.

As she turned onto the street Mondavi had named, she questioned her reason for going, wondering what it was she expected to obtain from this visit. Perhaps she would learn something about Bethany Davis and her daughter, something she could take back to Senator and Susanna Davis. Maybe nothing, other than being able to give them some peace of mind, that possibly Bethany had gained a degree of happiness before her death. Even some information about the man their daughter wanted in her life.

The house sat toward the back of a large lot. She figured it had to have been built at a time when California coastal property was reasonably affordable. The lawn looked freshly cut and the bordering flowerbeds showed recent care.

The man answering her knock wasn't what she expected. Not nearly as tall, or as bulky, as someone who might assault a police officer in his own office, but rather lean and slender. He stood at the open door waiting for her to speak, wearing an apron spattered with paint and holding a handful of brushes. Scrapes and burns marked his face. His hair, what there was of it, left him looking like someone auditioning for a punk rock band. She stifled a laugh, then noted similar burns and abrasions covering his arms.

But it was the eyes that held her in their grasp, gray-blue, like a frozen glacial lake, hard, unblinking, and penetrating. She shivered, thinking she would never want to be his enemy, and she doubted being a friend would be all that easy.

She glanced at the slip of paper in her hand, realizing an uncomfortable amount of time had passed. "I'm looking for a Conaire Gray."

He nodded.

"My name is Simone St. Pierre. Detective Mondavi gave me your name and address. I called earlier but then came by hoping you were in."

"And you want what?"

God he's cold, she thought, holding out a business card. "I work for Senator Jefferson Davis. He asked me to come out here to find out about the woman who was murdered. The detective said you were the one who told them she was the senator's daughter."

He stood holding the card and said nothing.

"I understand you and Ms. Davis were close. I don't know how much she might have told you about her relationship with her family, but anything you could tell me about her I'm sure would be greatly appreciated by the senator and his wife."

"I'm sure, but you haven't mentioned the girl. She seems to have been lost in the shuffle."

"The child, of course, I didn't mean to leave her out. Do you have a few moments to talk?" Simone said, not totally familiar with the uneasiness she felt in his presence. She stood waiting for an answer, feeling his eyes on her, not undressing her as most men did, but looking into her eyes to calculate the response.

Finally he stepped aside and allowed her to enter.

She glanced at the burns and abrasions again as she passed, thinking he must be in pain. "How long have you known about Ms. Davis and her father?"

"For a while."

"And you weren't curious. After all, not everyone is the daughter of a United States senator."

He shook his head slowly all the while staring into her eyes.

Simone walked into the room, picking up the faint odor of paint and turpentine. But what struck her was the neatness and sense of design in the furnishings. Not expensive, but warm and inviting and carefully chosen, unlike many of her friends whose homes were furnished by some of the top boutique stores in New York City. The purchases meant to impress ended up creating an environment she wanted to walk through but never remain in for any length of time. As she turned she noted the framed reproductions on the walls. She felt let down at the use of canvas transfers made to look like original oil paintings. It cheapened the original effect the room had on her.

"How did you and Ms. Davis meet?"

For a moment she thought he hadn't heard.

Then he said, "We met at a gallery up the coast, in Laguna Beach, about six months ago."

"And you started seeing each other?"

"Something like that."

"May I ask how serious it was?"

After a moment he said, "We talked about marriage."

"And the little girl, she was what, six? That didn't bother you, her having a child?"

He shook his head again then said, "Is, not was. She's still alive."

Simone waited, hoping he would tell her more. When he didn't she continued. "I know the senator will ask, or his wife will. You can imagine how they must feel after all this time. They believed she had died a number of years ago."

She felt his eyes on her. Again she waited for him to speak.

"Bethany and her father were never very close. She said she always felt they lost contact after her brother died," he said.

"That's what I understood. Did she ever say why? I mean, I've known the senator and Mrs. Davis for a couple of years, and worked very closely with them, yet I can't recall them ever saying exactly what brought about the separation."

"It was a personal issue. Look, if you want to know what she was like, I can tell you what I know. There are many periods in her life she wouldn't discuss, even with me."

"Yes, I'd like to hear what you can tell me. I know they'll appreciate it."

"All right. I have things to do, but I can spare some time," he said.

"Thank you."

"I haven't slept well and I could use a cup of coffee. Would you like one?"

"Yes, I would," she said.

She watched him pour the coffee into two mugs and gently nudged a black kitten away with his foot. "I haven't kitty-proofed the house yet. Somehow she got into some paint I had left out. This morning I found a couple of diminishing blue paw prints tracking across the top of a table. Luckily I spotted them before they dried."

She took the coffee from him and continued studying a painting of a Sierra Nevada mountain lake.

Some time passed, then, in a voice not above a whisper, she said, "You're an artist. Tell me these aren't yours."

"Why?"

Simone shook her head and moved across the room to another painting, a scene of towering elm trees in their brilliant autumn foliage against a backdrop of snowcapped Sierra peaks.

"This one's not signed either."

"Maybe it's not finished."

"My god, they are yours, aren't they?"

He handed her a mug. "It's what I do. I paint. Why, what's wrong with them?"

She shook her head. She didn't want to answer. She wanted to continue their discussion about Bethany Davis, but she had to ask. "Do you have others?"

"Some, why?"

"May I see them?"

He stood, holding his untasted coffee in his hand as if the decision was in doubt, then led her through the house to a room in the back.

Simone caught her breath at the array of canvases on the walls and floor. She moved from one canvas to another, sometimes picking one up and placing it in a better light, or viewing it from across the room. It seemed hours before she spoke. "Where did you study?"

"Some in Montana, mostly up the coast a ways."

"No, no, I mean your formal training. Who did you study under? Was it back east, New York maybe, or Europe? Did you go to Paris?"

Gray shook his head. "No, nothing like that. My mother loved to paint; she was very good. She took me out to places near where we lived and showed me how the mountains in the distance could be framed by the cottonwoods along the stream. Or we'd go down by the river where the spring floods had brought the trees down out of the mountains and piled them up on the banks, and in the bends. She used to show me how a scene is changed by where you stood."

Simone watched him lose himself in the painting. "And this is how you learned to paint like this?" she said.

"Some of it. She gave me old canvasses she had covered with gesso and I'd paint on them." She saw his eyes light up. "One year for my birthday she gave me a package of new canvas panels. The best birthday present I ever received."

She couldn't believe what she heard. "That's it? That was your training?"

"No. I spent a few years with a woman I met up the coast, near Big Sur. She taught me composition and color, and how to use a palette knife. She came from a family of artists. In her house she had a number of pieces by early California Impressionists. We would spend hours trying to capture what it was they saw when they painted them."

"I have a difficult time believing you."

"There's nothing else," Gray said.

She picked up a canvas and held it to the light. "This is Classic Impressionism, but here you have shades of French Barbizon, and maybe a slight lean toward Tonalism, wouldn't you agree?"

He laughed. "I have no idea. I couldn't define any of the schools that branched out from the Impressionistic period. I've read about them some, but that's as far as my education goes." He took the paining from her and placed it against the wall. "Maybe you should tell me how it is you know so much. I get the feeling you know a lot about art, and somehow I don't think it's from taking art appreciation classes."

Simone brushed past him, sending tiny shivers through her body. "I studied some," she said. She turned her back to him. It was better that way, listening to him without having to look at him. "None of your painting have people in them."

"I don't paint people. I only paint nature."

"Why, what do you mean?" she asked, still studying a mountain scene.

"Nature is true; nature is pure. It will never lie or deceive you. Now it's your turn, where did you study?" he asked.

"In New York some, then a period in Paris. I thought it was what I wanted to do. I studied at the shrine of Monet, in Giverny. I painted the lily ponds and the bridge, and sat with all the others and thought we were the elite of the intellectuals."

His face lit up. "You saw the master's work. I envy you. I've heard some still did that. Why did you give it up?"

"Long story and we'll leave it there." Anymore talk about Giverny would only bring back all the memories it had taken years to repress, though after that morning everything was out in the open again.

"So Impressionism was your love. American Impressionism also?"

She laughed. "Oh yes, my whole family felt I betrayed them when I gave it up. For my graduation from Bryn Mar, my grandfather presented me with a Childe Hassam."

Gray laughed. "Sure, a Childe Hassam. What's the going price on probably America's finest Impressionist?"

He was making fun of her, the idiot. What did he know about her or what her family could afford? "I don't discuss prices, and I have no need to convince you of its existence. In fact, you're one of the very few people who know about it, and I don't know what made me mention it." She made one last sweep of the room before walking out of the studio.

"Ms. St. Pierre, you haven't said anything about my work."

She turned to face him. "What about it?"

"You come into my home and pick up one of my pieces, and then ask to see others. You brag about places you studied, then try to impress me with your knowledge. So, with all of this knowledge, I'm simply asking, what do you think of the work?"

She stared at him in disbelief. He was laughing at her; she knew it. *You bastard.* "What do you think? They're magnificent, the best work I've seen in years and you know it, but you had to make me say it?"

She watched as he picked up the painting she had held in her hands. He placed it on an easel. "No, nothing like that. I wanted to know how you felt about them, truthfully. It wasn't meant for any other purpose."

"Well, now you have it, for what it's worth. Now it's your turn," she said. "Before, I felt I might be asking something you would rather keep to yourself, but you've already put away that point. I'm curious, what happened to you, your face and arms I mean?"

Gray told her about the fire and the questions Chavez had posed.

Simone asked, "Do they believe you about someone being in the house?"

"If they did, they're not admitting it. Listen, I don't want you leaving with nothing. You can tell Davis…Senator Davis…and his wife that Bethany wanted them to know about their granddaughter. She just wasn't sure about the reception she would receive."

Simone remembered the anguish Susanna Davis was suffering. "I think I can say they would have done anything to have been reunited. Any animosities they might have had were long forgotten."

She watched him process the information, then walk across the room and open a drawer in a small end stand. He took out a photo and handed it to her. "We were all on the beach when we had it taken. I know Bethany would have wanted them to have it."

Simone took the photo and slipped it into her handbag. "And you? What will you do now?"

He shook his head. "Nothing until I find out about the girl. If she's alive or not. Now that Davis knows that it was Bethany, he can help us find her."

"I'm sure he will. Thank you for your help. Simone walked back to her car. Before driving away she looked back at the house. He still stood at the door. Something told her there was more to the story than anyone had admitted.

24

The house had become a prison. Gray wanted Mondavi to call and say they had found Carlie and she was okay. He wanted Paco to call and tell him he had information about the food mart. But what he wanted above everything was the feeling that he was in control.

He headed for the kitchen to kill time and see what there might be to eat. Carlie Kate's old paint box lay on the floor beside a stool, its drawer sprung from the collision with the window. Gray picked it up to put it on the stool. The drawer fell out, scattering an assortment of old tubes of paint and a half dozen brushes he had given Carlie. A small black notebook lay among the tubes of paint. He tossed it on the table and walked back into his studio where the scent of the woman's perfume still lingered. Her presence had weakened him. He thought about his feelings for Bethany and wondered if their few months together awakened in him his ability to appreciate companionship and love. Even the thought of the young paramedic who had treated him the other night brought a warm glow.

The phone rang.

Paco Juarez suggested they meet soon, and Gray filled him in on Chavez's visit and Davis's aide.

"Where are you?" Gray asked.

"Seal Beach."

"How about grabbing dinner while we talk, someplace in Newport Beach maybe?"

"We can do that. Also, I made a few calls about that food mart. Interesting, but logical, if you know anything about these people."

"Hold that thought for dinner," Gray said. "I've got a couple of other things that came up. I don't know what's going on Paco, but it smells."

They agreed to meet, over Juarez's objections, at an Italian restaurant on the coast highway.

The kitten jumped up on the kitchen table and pawed the black notebook until she succeeded in pushing it off the table, then sat down to admire what she had done. Gray picked up the notebook, casually thumbing through it. Scrawled numbers and Hispanic names filled the pages. On one page a series of large dollar amounts appeared beside what looked like addresses. The numbers staggered

Gray. On one line someone had penciled in $413,000 beside an address on a street Gray knew was in nearby Azusa. He turned the page. Two words, *nespelam* and *colville,* were underlined.

Gray leaned back against the edge of the table and continued turning the pages. Nothing in the book gave him any information that might help him discover how the book ended up in the girl's seldom-used paint box, or who it belonged to. If Carlie wanted to paint, Bethany would bring her over to his place where he would set her up with a canvas tarp under her chair and a large box of wipes for her hands. He thumbed through the notebook again and noticed the strong smell of tobacco smoke. He flipped the book onto the table, then had another thought and dropped it in his pocket, wondering what Juarez had found out. Gray still couldn't believe the confrontation at the mini-mart, and the clerk's sudden flight, were denied, or why someone claiming to be the owner swore he worked the mini-mart that night.

When Gray reached Newport Beach, the street lights were beginning to soften some of the harsh corners of Orange County's premier city. Gray drove past the Balboa Bay Club, noting the forest of masts of the sailboats hugging the confines of their expensive slips.

He spotted Juarez leaning against the light post in front of the family-owned Italian restaurant, looking as out of place as a wedding dress at a funeral. Gray pulled the Jeep into a parking spot and eased his sore body out of the car.

Juarez dropped his cigarette on the sidewalk and ground it out with his heel. He tilted his head to the side studying Gray. "This is new; the haircut I mean. Looks like you had a problem in the kitchen."

"You might say it got a little too hot for my liking. You want to eat or stand out here and discuss my appearance?"

Juarez opened the door. "I hope they have tacos or burritos on the menu. Doesn't seem likely though."

After giving the hostess a name, they walked out into an open-air courtyard and bar to wait for their table. They pulled wrought-iron chairs out from a low table and sat beneath the branches of an olive tree. Gray ordered a glass of red wine, much to the disgust of Juarez, who ordered a Corona, grimacing when the waitress asked him if he wanted a glass.

Gray quickly filled him in on the attack and fire at Bethany's house.

"What did your detective say about who might have attacked you?"

The waitress brought the beer and wine and placed them on the table, taking Gray's twenty. The television beneath the canopy over the bar was tuned to a Lakers' game. Someone had turned the sound off.

"They said it was probably local kids looking for something to sell."

"You believe them?"

"No way. The guy who I saw was no kid."

Juarez squeezed the slice of lime into his beer and pushed it into the bottle. "Time was you could take care of yourself, situation like that."

"We going to discuss more of my shortcomings? Time was you didn't mix your beer with little pieces of fruit either."

Juarez grinned, then turned serious. "Okay. Now, why we need to talk. I spoke with some people I know in Little Saigon. That's Westminster to you. It seems a local entrepreneur, you might call him, has been branching out with his range of investments, and heard about this mini-mart gas station combo up there in red-head country, and thought it could be a money maker. Most liquor stores are sources of wealth in the Vietnamese communities. They don't pay their help much, stock anything and everything that'll sell, and don't worry too much about expiration dates on food items. Prices can be jacked up, 'cause from what you tell me there's not much in the way of competition."

Gray listened and remembered there was something else he hadn't mentioned about the attack at Bethany's house.

"So, it appears the same night you were up there and run into these red-heads—"

"That's red-necks, not red-heads," Gray corrected.

"Yeah, well, whatever you want to call them, they're *pendejos* to me. Anyway, let me finish before you say anything else. Seems a second or third nephew of this entrepreneur's wife comes into town late and in a big hurry. Next thing you know he's at LAX and doing a vacation jaunt to the old homeland. Story goes, the kid's here on an over-extended visa and working for rice money up at great-uncle's place of business, when these two *pendejos* get the crap beat out of them. Now, luckily for this Asian Donald Trump, he has decided to check on Momma's sweet little second or third cousin and gets there in time to clean up the mess you left behind. Follow me so far?"

"So far."

"So, these two *pendejos* say they're going to sue, at least the one that can still talk says that. So a little grease, or rice, changes hands and all is forgotten until your friend from the police department calls."

"Detective Chavez?"

"Right, and the word is, much to the delight of this owner, he appears to be pleased with the answers he received."

Gray mulled over the story while Juarez motioned to the waitress for another round. She said their table was ready and she would bring the drinks there.

Juarez studied the menu before laying it on the table and pointing. "What is this *parma* something, or *penne puttanesca?*"

"That's veal parmigiana. You'll love it, trust me."

"How do you know I'll love it? We could have gone to someplace that serves real food. I saw one down the street."

"Because the Italians taught the Mexicans how to cook, you can't miss," Gray said as he signaled for their waitress.

She came to the table and pulled her pad out of her apron pocket, then grimaced when she looked at Gray. "Ehh, does it hurt much? You know, like your face is…."

"Only if I have to repeat my order, so start writing."

"Well, okay, like, I was just wondering," she said, looking at Juarez for help. Juarez shrugged in reply.

Gray ordered for both of them and waited for her to leave before asking Juarez, "You think the guy can be convinced to tell the truth?"

"Wouldn't count on it. There are probably a few more things about the place he wouldn't want anyone looking into. Fact is, I'm surprised they haven't arrested you already. Your neighbor friend's not helping your cause from what I hear."

"Friend?"

"You know what I mean."

Their waitress placed a large cauldron on the table and ladled out two bowls of steaming vegetables soup. She mixed the salad and divided it between them before leaving.

Gray filled Juarez in on Simone's visit and the pressure he hoped Davis would bring in the search for the girl.

Juarez finished his soup while he listened, then said, "The Colonel's come a long way."

"Yeah, well, he's a senator now. Brings back the times we wished we could have settled with him, doesn't it?"

"Sometimes it's better to move on and leave things unsettled," Juarez said.

"I don't think I could ever do that."

"Put it away, Conaire. You had six months with her and that's more than either of you expected."

"It should have been longer."

"And we shouldn't have gone."

"I'll never forgive him, Paco. What he did to us."

"You more than me, but like they say, life goes on, and, don't forget, it wasn't only him."

"Wouldn't do our longevity good to forget them," Gray said.

Their meal arrived, accompanied by another glass of wine and a beer, compliments of their waitress, who said she felt bad about what she said. When she reached over to pick up the empty soup plates, Gray saw the tattoo on her forearm and remembered what it was he wanted to ask Juarez.

"The other night at Bethany's house, the one who jumped me. It was only for a second, but I saw this weird looking tattoo on his arm. Looked like a big X in a kind of script writing and the number 3."

Juarez frowned, then took a pen from his pocket and smoothed out his paper napkin. He wrote X3 in script and handed it to Gray. Something like this?"

Gray nodded. "Yeah, that's it. You know what it means?"

"I know what it means, although I can't understand what it would have to do with Bethany."

"What is it?"

"Stands for thirteen, the X for ten and then the three. Thirteenth letter of the alphabet is M, which represents *La Eme*. It's a jailhouse tattoo for the Mexican Mafia."

Gray puzzled his brow. "Mexican Mafia? Why would they be in Bethany's house?"

"No idea," Juarez said with a shake of his head. "Did you mention this to either of the detectives?"

"No. Didn't remember it until today. Who are they, anyway?"

"Remember our friend Pacheco, at the park?"

"The one with all the followers."

"Well, these guys would use guys like Pacheco to run errands for them. Very probably they're *sureños*."

"*Sureños?*"

"Basically southern gang members who band together in jail for protection. Their enemies are the *norteños* from up north, who are led by the *nuestra familia*. The ones from Northern California are usually a couple of generations deep in the old US of A, whereas the *sureños* are either the product of farm laborers or illegals. The northern group figures this is their territory. Consequently, if the two not kept apart in the prisons, they have a tendency to riot and kill each other. Some think that's not such a bad idea."

"Still doesn't make much sense," Gray said.

"Something I've learned to be true: bunch of things that don't seem to make sense end up making a lot when you put them all together. You just need to find the key."

Gray signaled to the waitress for the check. "Sounds like this whole situation."

"Exactly. My concern is that these guys in Laguna Mesa PD aren't looking at anyone else right now. From what I've learned from my sources, this Mondavi knows his stuff. I know you didn't do this, but my advice is start figuring out your fallback because you may need it."

"Chavez made a comment about that, about my not planning any vacation soon."

The waitress dropped off the check and smiled. Gray reached for his wallet and brought out the black notebook instead. He tossed it over to Juarez. "See if you can make anything out of this."

Juarez flipped through the pages, stopping occasionally to read something. He looked troubled. Gray waited while Juarez pulled out his cell phone and punched in a number, holding up his hand for quiet.

Gray couldn't follow the conversation in Spanish, but Juarez appeared agitated. He hung up and dialed another number from the book. This time the tone of his voice told Gray that Juarez was asking questions. He hung up and stared at the phone before turning over another couple of pages in the book.

Gray grew impatient. "Come on, Paco, who did you call?"

"The first one happened to be the chief of police in Mexicali, and he wanted to know how the hell I got his number, since it is a very, very, private number."

"And the other one?"

"Oh, that was only a federal judge in Tijuana. I could hear a couple of very young-sounding ladies in the background who wanted him to come back and play with them, so he was probably too occupied to worry about the call. The fact that he answered it at all could mean anyone having the number is real important to him. He may not be a problem, but this police chief may try having my phone number checked out."

Gray remembered the dollar figures listed beside the names. "You think the money amounts mean anything?"

Juarez nodded. "I don't know what you have here with this book, or how the hell it ended up where it did, but I have a feeling whoever it belongs to might want it back. There are a couple of other numbers I'd like to check on but not on my phone. By the way, how did you get your hands on this?"

Gray told him about the fire and the paint box. "You think it might be why they were in the house, looking for this?"

"I think that's a pretty good guess."

"Keeps getting stranger and stranger, and as to how it ended up where it did we may never know," Gray said.

"Remember what I said about the key. This may be it."

Gray paid the bill. Juarez said if they had gone to one of the food wagons he knew of they wouldn't have to leave a tip. Gray noted that Juarez hadn't left the tip, he had.

Traffic on Pacific Coast Highway had thinned considerably so they jogged across the highway and walked the two short blocks to the beach. They found an empty bench and brushed off the sand.

"How come you didn't give that book to the detectives?" Juarez wanted to know.

"I just discovered it today. The way they're looking at me, they may not want to look at something that doesn't fit their scenario."

They sat engrossed in their own thoughts. Gray absently watched half a dozen surfers bobbing on their boards, looking like some of the seals that make such pests of themselves in the harbor. With the light fading quickly, he watched as two rose up on their boards to try for one of the last decent waves of the evening.

"What do you think I should do with it?"

Juarez let his breath out slowly. "You can't be sure from a couple of phone calls, but you and I gave up believing in coincidence years ago. That thing you have there could be dynamite in the right hands. It could also be deadly for whoever has it."

"It could also be the key. You said so yourself."

25

The first call for boarding came as Simone wheeled her carry-on into John Wayne Airport. Quickly, she printed out her boarding pass and joined the line for the security check behind a woman with a young girl. The girl wrapped her arms around her mother's leg and gazed up at Simone, while her mother chatted on her cell phone.

Simone checked her arrival time and called Senator Davis. Mariano answered, sounding reluctant to summon the senator.

Simone insisted.

The senator cut her off before she had a chance to speak. He asked for her arrival time and said he wanted to see her as soon as she landed. He hung up before she could ask any questions.

The flight gave her the first opportunity to analyze her reaction to Gray. Simone's first impressions about people seldom changed. As far as she was concerned, Gray was an arrogant, self-centered, typical male with a self-inflated ego. She had to admit it wasn't him that made her angry; it was his damned paintings. It made her wish his work could be described as slightly above average. Something tourists visiting the West Coast art colony of Laguna Beach would buy to take home and hang over a couch, alongside a copy of their prized Thomas Kinkaid. Instead, she felt the angst of envy that such work would fall into the hands of people with little taste, but had the money to purchase them. Simone knew she would love to have bought one herself, but definitely not from him.

She dozed until feeling the plane begin its descent, her mind returning to the problem lying on her entry table, the one making reference to a time in Paris. She chuckled without humor. Possibly her past would make no difference to her future if the senator chose not to run for re-election. Still, a decision would have to be made.

An hour later Mariano led her into the senator's library. Susanna Davis sat on one end of a leather couch, clutching a photograph in her hands. Tears dampened her cheeks.

Simone sensed something besides Bethany's death was involved in their obvious distress.

"Thank you for coming," Senator Davis said. "I'm sorry I was so abrupt on the phone. I couldn't discuss what I'm about to reveal, as you'll understand when you hear it."

Simone placed her handbag on the floor beside her chair. "I hope it isn't more bad news, Senator."

He held up his hands. "Wait. Before we begin I need your absolute assurance that not a word of this conversation leaves this room. Your full guarantee, you understand?"

"Of course, you have my word, Senator," she said. She studied him as he turned to his wife, who nodded silently.

"Very well," he said, then continued. "An envelope arrived early this morning. I wasn't here at the time. One of the house maids signed for it and placed it on the stand by the front door. She went off duty without informing anyone of its existence. Mariano discovered it and brought it to me."

"Is it about the girl?"

"Yes, people have contacted us, but it's not money they're after. It's something else."

Simone stared at the senator, wondering what someone might want from him. It had to be something to do with his position. "Can you tell me what they want?"

Senator Jefferson Davis got up and crossed the room to sit beside his wife. "As of this moment we can't be certain they have the girl, or if the girl is who they say she is. They sent a photo, but it could be any young girl."

Simone remembered the photo in her handbag and pulled it out. "When I spoke with the person she was seeing, he gave me this to bring back for you. If there's any doubt about what the girl looked like, this should dispel it. The three of them were on the beach when this picture was taken."

Susanna Davis's trembling hand reached for the photo. She slipped on her glasses and stared at it for a moment before her jaw dropped. "Oh, no," she cried.

Senator Davis eased the photo out of her hand and looked at it. "Oh my god," he cried. "It's impossible."

Susanna Davis bit her lip, tears resuming their flow down her cheeks. "It's not only possible, Jefferson, it's true. Somehow she found Conaire again."

Simone waited for one of them to explain their bewilderment.

Finally the senator spoke, holding up the photo for Simone. "This is the man you spoke with, Conaire Gray?"

She didn't have to look at it again. "Yes, do you know him?" she asked. Gray had made no mention of knowing the senator.

Senator Davis passed the photo back to his wife and looked away. "Yes." He stood again and walked to the window, looking out onto Susanna's flower garden.

Simone waited, wondering if he would continue.

"Conaire Gray was a member of my command."

It took a moment for Simone to see the connection. "Did he know your daughter then?"

Susanna Davis spoke up. "Yes, they were very close."

"What happened?"

The senator chose to answer. "We didn't feel it was a good match for Bethany. Her mother and I felt there was someone out there who could give her a more socially acceptable future than Gray."

"Why, what was it about him you didn't care for?"

"You shouldn't have a problem understanding. Your background and family in New England have many of the same prejudices as the South. Mrs. Davis comes from an old Charleston family, considered one of the more prominent names in South Carolina politics and its social register. My own family, although not spoken of in the same circles as hers, was such that it allowed me to be acceptable to them. Having graduated at the top of my class at the Citadel also helped."

"I'm sorry, I don't understand, Senator. What was it that made him so unacceptable?"

"Conaire Gray's grandfather is a full-blooded Blackfoot Indian. Conaire himself spent a number of years living on a reservation in Montana. Hardly the suitor we wanted for our daughter."

Simone knew the reaction her own family would have to her bringing home someone like Gray. The image of the damaged hair held back with a beaded headband now made sense. Not meant as a fashion statement, rather a cultural tradition. "So, what happened?" she asked.

"I had Gray transferred and made her break off all communications with him."

"I don't see how this has anything to do with your daughter's death."

Senator Davis closed his eyes and lowered his head. "I can't tell you any more than what I have already told you. You'll have to trust me."

"Oh, for God's sake, Jefferson," Suzanna said. "You can't ask Simone to cover for you and help keep this whole affair out of the newspapers without telling her the whole story."

Senator Davis nodded and rang for Mariano, and asked that coffee be served immediately. Ten minutes later Mariano returned with a thermos and a serving tray, and left the room with instructions from the senator was not to be disturbed.

"You must understand, Simone. What I'm about to tell you could place you in grave danger if you were to acknowledge it to anyone. For your own protection, I cannot put names to any of the others involved. Suffice to say they are, for the most part, all highly recognizable names, and men in their positions would resort to measures guaranteeing their secrets remain that way. And they have the power to do so, believe me."

Simone couldn't deny her curiosity in what appeared to be something much greater than a robbery gone bad in Laguna Mesa. However, in the years she had known the senator, she could not recall an instance when he had exaggerated an issue. The information he intended to divulge would place her in danger. Did she want to know, she asked herself? She made her decision. "I understand, please go on," she found herself saying.

"Very well. At the time we're talking about I had under my command a First Marine Force Reconnaissance Company. I don't know how much you might know about such a group, but I can tell you they were some of the most highly trained fighting men we had. Highly skilled, highly motivated warriors, who would follow you into hell itself if the mission warranted it. I remember you once expressed your disdain for such men, calling them arrogant psychopathic warriors, but there are times when that's what's needed to complete a mission others might find contemptible but necessary. This was, as I said, about eight years ago. Susanna and I had lost our son a short time before."

"How did that happen, senator? You've never spoken about it," Simone said.

"It's not something we speak about. He was a couple of years older than Bethany, a brilliant mind, a big handsome young man who could have gone almost anywhere in life. Unfortunately, he met some people his own age who were experimenting with the drug of the day. Young Thomas found he couldn't resist their power. One night he and two others attended a party at someone's house. They found him in an alley the next morning. He had taken something that turned out to be tainted. He died in apparent agony."

Simone was beginning to understand what this new development with Bethany and her daughter meant to the senator and his wife. First a son, then a daughter, and now the possibility of having a grandchild in danger of losing her life. She waited for the senator to continue.

"You can imagine our anguish. I'm afraid I voiced my desire for revenge against those responsible for selling these drugs to our young people. Well, it wasn't long after that I was approached, very discreetly, by a handful of like-minded men who felt as I did. Some were military men, others were not though they did work for the government and that's all I'll say. We were not all from the same backgrounds or training, but many of us had lost loved ones to these drugs and shared the same anger and desire to work against this infestation threatening the future of our country."

Susanna Davis laid her hand on her husband's arm. "Jefferson, we know how you felt. I would have happily seen them in hell as well, but this is about what happened. Why not tell that story?"

"Of course, I was only trying to fill in some background. Anyway, a plan was put together to take the fight directly to those responsible."

"Senator, was this here, in the States?"

"No, the bulk of the drugs at this time were coming out of Mexico. You see, the crackdown in Columbia had destroyed the Cali and Medellin cartels. They had been using Mexico to handle the transportation of the drugs until some in Mexico decided to cut out the Columbians entirely. As I was saying, a plan was set in motion to take out the leaders of the cartels proliferating in Mexico. As it happened, one of the members of our group had direct knowledge of one such drug lord, a man by the name of Emiliano Montoya, who fancied being called Don Emiliano. At the time I would have gladly seen to the death of a hundred of them for what they had done to our son."

"You might wonder, Simone, whether I was aware of what was going on," Susanna Davis said. "I was not entirely unaware. However, Jefferson felt I would be better served to not know who was involved."

"Did you ever find out? Who was involved, I mean."

Susanna Davis said, "If you mean those who Jefferson was working with, yes. Go on Jefferson."

"In the plan, I was to furnish the ones we would send on the mission; others would provide intel and transportation, et cetera."

"Was there government authorization for this plan?"

Senator Davis paused as if wondering how much he could say. "Not by those who you might think would need to do so. Others agreed to do their part as long as nothing could be traced back to them."

He went on to explain that it was a "Black-Op" and that a great amount of effort went into it to ensure no one would ever discover its existence.

"My god, and in America," said Simone when the senator had finished. "Somehow we don't believe our own government would do something like this."

"Not our government, Simone," Susanna Davis interjected. "*People* in our government. And Jefferson was a part of it."

"Are Gray and Juarez still being watched?"

"Yes, but the surveillance level has decreased considerably," the senator replied. "Maybe once or twice a year they're monitored. To wrap this up, I'll simply say that Gray was never the same after what happened. We had to ask ourselves if we wanted to take the chance of putting him back into a dangerous situation where lives depended on his decision to shoot, so I had him transferred to a post where he could complete his enlistment without being sent into a war zone."

"And that transfer also broke up his relationship with Bethany," Susanna Davis said.

Senator Davis patted her hand. "Unfortunately we failed to realize the depth of her feelings toward him."

"And they never got together again, or communicated?" Simone asked.

"Oh, they tried, but we intercepted their attempts," Suzanna Davis replied. "We thought it best for her. But we were wrong. So wrong it cost us our daughter."

Senator Davis wrapped his arms around his wife and held her. "Bethany left one night. We thought she would come back after a few days, until we discovered she had cleared out a very substantial trust fund Susanna's father left her. We never heard from her again."

"Until now," Simone mused. "But somehow she and Conaire found each other."

"Yes."

"So this man, Montoya, is the one responsible for Bethany's death?"

"It would seem so," the senator said.

"And he has your granddaughter?"

"Yes. The picture they sent matches the little girl in the one you brought back from California. It's our granddaughter."

"Senator, you said it's not money they want. What is it?"

"He wants the name and whereabouts of the man who killed his daughter and grandson. In other words, he wants Conaire Gray in exchange for our granddaughter."

"My God, what will you do? Can't you contact anyone, the FBI, the CIA. There must be someone," Simone said.

Senator Davis gestured toward the folded letter on his desk. "It's all there. Wherever he got his information, it appears pretty close to the truth. He knows a great deal about what went on and who was involved in the operation, or most of those involved. In the letter, he said the girl will die at the first indication that I've contacted the police, or any other agency, and since he's responsible for the death of Brittany, I believe he will do whatever he says."

Simone closed her eyes and pressed her hands to her forehead. This could not be happening, she thought, not in this country. But it was. "So, Senator, what's your next step? What will you do?"

"Until you brought us this news about Conaire and Bethany, I wasn't sure what I could do. So what I'm faced with is this: Do I compound the mistake I made eight years ago and give this drug lord the name of someone I'm responsible for sending on this mission? Or do I lose the granddaughter we never knew we had? How can I live with either?"

The silence hung in the air, disturbed only by the gentle tapping of a tree branch against the library window. Finally Simone spoke. "I don't know how this will be taken, but I've just come from meeting this man, Conaire Gray. He loved your daughter. He loves your granddaughter. He hoped to marry Bethany. I think you have to tell him about this letter before you make your decision."

"She's right, Jefferson," Suzanna Davis said. "Maybe the two of you can find a solution. At least try."

"Maybe you're right. One way or the other, I would have informed him of my decision," Senator Davis said, looking at Simone. He appeared to think about what he wanted to say. "Will you go back and speak to him? I have a feeling he wouldn't accept my call."

She considered how to approach Gray, knowing how much of her earlier impressions were wrong. "Certainly. I'll catch the first flight out in the morning. But Senator, the police are still asking questions, and sooner or later something is going to leak. You know how that works."

"Yes, I have to address it immediately. What was your impression of the detectives involved? Can they be trusted if the situation is explained to them?"

She didn't need to think about her answer. "Talk to Detective Mondavi, no one else. I think you can trust him."

"Good, I'll call him. I'll use national security as an excuse to keep a lid on the information. It's obvious I can't tell him about the letter. There are a couple of other calls I must make in the morning that will need all my powers of persuasion."

"How long do you have?"

"The letter said I'm to call and leave a message by tomorrow evening. I'm going to ask for additional time and say that the information they want is being sought. By then you'll have talked with Conaire."

"Very well, Senator, I'll call you as soon as I've finished speaking to him." Her mind spun with the problems facing her and how she would approach him.

She left the house and went to her car, but before starting the engine she checked her phone for messages. She groaned when she saw Sergio had left another. He would be waiting at her condo if she didn't return his calls. She dialed Conaire Gray's number first.

When he finally picked up, she discovered she had been holding her breath. "This is Simone St. Pierre. I was there earlier today. Please don't ask any questions. I can't answer them. It's about the girl and I need to see you tomorrow morning."

"Is she alive?" he asked, his voice close to breaking.

Simone hesitated before finding her own voice. "Yes."

On the way to her condo Simone pulled up to a mailbox and dropped an envelope through the slot. She knew the money would only buy a limited amount of time.

26

Conaire Gray placed the bowl of food on the floor and scratched the ear of the kitten, who arched her back before rubbing up against his leg. "Can't remember what she called you little one. I suppose I'll have to come up with something."

Simone had called a little after seven with her flight number and arrival time. She wouldn't say anything other than Carlie Kate was alive and could Gray meet her at the airport, since she had managed to get a return flight later that afternoon.

With the flight due in an hour, he figured he would rather wait at the airport than wander around the house watching the clock. He rinsed his coffee cup in the sink and scratched the kitten's ear again before picking up his car keys.

Half a block from the house he passed a patrol car parked in front of a fire hydrant, the driver pretending not to be paying attention to him as he passed. Gray wondered how long they expected to put someone on him twenty-four hours a day, unless they expected to make an arrest soon.

Airport traffic was light and he found a spot on the ground floor of the underground parking structure. Inside the terminal he checked the flight status board and saw her flight would be on the ground in fifteen minutes. He called Paco and left a message.

Twenty-five minutes later she entered the concourse. He watched the self-assured stride of someone who knew where she was going and didn't care how many watched her along the way.

Gray moved away from the wall and worked his way through a crowd of Japanese golfers, presumably on a two-day excursion to Pelican Hill Resort and golf course.

When she saw him, she held up her hand and shook her head. "Not here, please. Is there somewhere we can go? I haven't had much sleep."

To Gray she didn't look as if she hadn't slept. In fact she looked as if she had just walked out of a fashion magazine, wearing simple washed jeans with a loose-fitting cotton blouse and sandals, her long blonde pony tail held in place with a marine blue Gucci scarf.

Neither spoke as he pulled the Jeep out onto MacArthur Boulevard and drove toward Jamboree Road. A Starbucks catering to students from the university usually had open tables at this time of day. He felt her studying him.

"You got a haircut since yesterday," she said.

"Headband won't fit now."

"What a shame. It was rather novel."

"Listen, I need to know."

"I'll tell you everything we know as soon as we talk. Right now all I'll say is the same as what I told you last night. We've heard that she's alive."

The coffee shop parking lot was half empty. He pulled the Jeep in between a gleaming Mercedes and a Lexus with dealer plates.

A few tables were occupied by students with their laptops open and school books piled alongside. Two businessmen worked their cell phones beside a table with four middle-aged women wearing designer workout clothes. Pastries and lattes seemed to be their preference.

Gray ordered her a non-fat vanilla latte with an extra squirt and plain coffee for himself. He watched her fidget while he waited for their order. If Carlie Kate was alive, why was this woman so disturbed, and why did Davis think it necessary to send her back to see him? It made no sense, but then nothing had lately.

"All right, this has gone far enough," he said, placing her latte on the table and pulling out a chair. "Where is she and who has her, and how much do they want? Shouldn't be a problem. The senator and Mrs. have money."

Simone sighed and wrapped her hands around her cup. "We need to talk first, about you and some things about your past."

"What things? My question is pretty simple. Where is she?"

"Do you know a man by the name of Emiliano Montoya?"

Gray frowned, "No, who is he?"

"Okay, you need to think back. Last night Senator Davis told me the story about what happened eight years ago, when you were sent somewhere by him and others."

Gray froze, his coffee cup suspended in mid-air. It never happened, according to all records. No one was permitted to discuss it. What right did he have telling her about that mission? He took a slow breath, concentrating on maintaining his emotions. "I don't know what you're talking about."

"Yes, you do, and I've also been told you would deny it, and why. But we have to talk about it, because what's happening now is the result of what happened then."

"What did he tell you?"

"He said that you and another man were sent somewhere to kill someone," Simone said, her voice dropping to a whisper.

Gray stared at her, his face still expressionless. Minutes passed as he waited for her to continue, knowing that all the demons inside his head were gathering to relive their birth.

"Emiliano Montoya is the man you were sent to assassinate. He has the girl."

The horror fought to overpower his resolve. He closed his eyes, knowing the penalty for what he had done was now being assessed. Neither spoke while a new group of morning-meet-up women took the table next to them, all talking at once.

Gray buried his head in his hands, then took a deep breath. "Not here," he said, rising from the table.

They walked down the tree-lined street to a small park and found a shaded bench. The ocean breeze stirred the leaves overhead.

"I love the smell of eucalyptus in the warmth of summer," he said. "Do you know they're not indigenous to California? Some people thought they could make a fortune by growing them and making lumber out of them. I heard Jack London was one. Found out about the only thing they're good for is creating a wind break."

Simone laid her hand on his arm. "Conaire, we need to talk about it."

"I know, but where to start is the question. If what you're saying is true, do you have any idea what it means, to me?"

She shook her head. "What do you mean?"

"Bethany's death, Carlie Kate being taken, and only God knows what will happen to her. Why, because of me, because of what I did."

"Conaire, the senator told me what happened. There are others who are just as responsible. It wasn't only you."

"It might as well be. What do you know about the others involved?"

"Only that they exist," Simone said. "The senator wouldn't tell me who they were. Do you know?"

Gray waited while two young girls on skates passed, their arms swinging wildly to maintain their momentum. "Some I know about," he said with a nod.

"Would they help if asked?"

He laughed bitterly, then turned sober. "Forget that you ever heard there were others, if you value anything, and even standing here speaking about it is a threat to your life. They would probably help this Montoya if they could. One less loose end for them."

"I've been told that already, by Mrs. Davis."

"What is it this Montoya wants for Carlie? How much is he asking for?"

Simone touched his arm again and shook her head. "He doesn't want money."

"No? What then?"

"He wants the name of the person who killed his daughter and his grandson. He wants you."

27

Caesar Castillo lit a cigarette and opened his portfolio. "We have been very fortunate in finding someone in this Laguna Mesa place."

Emiliano Montoya sat back in his chair, his eyes gauging the reaction in his son's eyes to this information. Edwardo Fuentes, who had just returned from mailing the letter to Senator Davis, sat beside Miguel.

Montoya spoke to Castillo. "This man, why has he agreed to help us?"

"The man has very expensive tastes, as does his girlfriend. She is the wife of a politician who could do much damage to him if he did not offer her those things she craved."

Montoya grunted. "And you are sure he can help?"

"Actually, he has already earned his reward," Castillo said. "It appears the vehicle transporting Miguel's DNA had the misfortune to be run off the road. No one was seriously injured, but someone who stopped to assist opened the container containing the samples. It now appears they have been rendered useless by becoming contaminated."

"That is unfortunate. Miguel should count his blessing, as they say. And what did this man say about this thing that Miguel has lost?"

"Nothing was found in the house."

Montoya tapped the top of his desk with his fingertips. "And those you sent to look?"

Castillo shook his head. "They found nothing either. But while they were there someone showed up. They overpowered him and set the house on fire. If the book was there, it is gone now."

"Then perhaps we are in the clear. Now," Montoya said, turning to Fuentes. "This child, will she be a problem?"

Fuentes sat back in his chair and laughed. "She is good, but she is like a woman deceived. I have never seen a child with such a temper. I asked her if she needed anything before I left, and she wiped away her tears and stood with her little arms crossed and said we would be punished for what we did to her mother."

Castillo looked up from his papers and said, "We are to be punished?"

"She said someone named Conaire would come for her, and when he did we would regret it. It would be better for us if we let her go now, before it is too late."

Montoya held his hands apart. "Who is this person she speaks of? Is he a policeman?"

Fuentes shrugged. "I believe he was the woman's boyfriend. The girl said he is an Indian."

Montoya looked confused. "Does he come from India?"

"I don't believe that is what she meant. I think she believes he is an American Indian."

"Ah, yes, one of those Indians up there who drive old trucks and beg for our drugs," Montoya said. "I do not think I will lose sleep over this. But I must warn you. Do not accept this child into your heart. I can see it on your face. She will know too much to be allowed to return when this is over."

"*Si*, Don Emiliano, but it will be hard no less. I beg of you that you do not ask me to do it."

"I understand. Now go. You have done well." Montoya turned back to Miguel Zapata and Castillo. "We have not spoken of it, Miguel, but your trip to the north also included a visit to the people in this city. Did it go well?"

"Shit, all they were concerned with was how much money they were to get. If we do not keep an eye on them, much of this money will go into their pockets."

"As long as it gets them elected to their city council. Once they are in place we will control them, and we can begin acquiring the small businesses that Castillo here will use to clean up this money of ours. This business of ours, Miguel, cannot go on forever. We must consider the future."

Miguel Zapata gazed up at the ceiling, his face etched with anger. "How much money do you think you will make from these little businesses you want to buy? I can make more money in a week than you can in a year. They say you are becoming too soft to hold our territory and drug routes."

Emiliano Montoya knew the day was fast approaching when he would be faced with making a decision about his bastard son. He needed this thing he was involved in to be over quickly.

Castillo's phone began to vibrate as Montoya opened the handcrafted wooden humidor and extracted a cigar.

Castillo placed the phone to his ear as he walked off some distance. A moment later he pocketed the phone and returned to his chair.

Montoya sensed something was wrong. "What disturbs you?"

"It is from the senator. He says the information you seek is not readily available and he wishes for more time."

The unwrapped cigar crumbled and fell to the floor at Montoya's feet.

28

It took a moment for the implication to sink in. "He wants my name, not money?" Gray said in disbelief. "That's all he wants? You mean if Davis gives this guy my name he'll let her go? Will they do it as soon as they hear from him?"

"They didn't say, or at least the senator wasn't told."

"Then why are you here? Hasn't he told them what they want to know?"

"No," she said. "Senator Davis said he was responsible for sending you. He said he wouldn't give them your name without your consent. He said he owed it to you."

"That's most considerate of him," Gray said. "If he hadn't got himself lost in his quest for revenge, none of this would have happened. But it's done and I'm living with the consequences. Why? Because eight years ago I was sent by people I trusted to do something that was very wrong. I was sent to kill a man, but the wrong people died. I guess you can say I murdered them."

"But others sent you, yet you're saying that after eight years it still bothers you?"

"I live with it every day of my life."

"God, how terrible."

"Not consciously. It's a scene that plays itself out in my head. Sometimes I hear a backfire that sounds like a gunshot and it starts. Sometimes it's a group of people gathered together, like at a party, but more often it's seeing a woman with a child in her arms."

"Would you tell me how it happened?" she said.

"Why?"

"I don't know, really, but maybe it will help me understand this whole affair. You wouldn't know, but it's having a profound impact on my life also."

He didn't know whether to believe her or not. If Davis had told her everything, including the existence of the others involved in the planning and logistics, it put her in danger as well.

Gray leaned back against the tree and folded his arms across his chest, wondering where to begin. He had told no one the story since their debriefing. "I don't need to go into how we got there, maybe they told you already, but we were in place for three days. We lived in a shallow hole in the ground waiting for our opportunity. Our target never gave us a clear shot until the third afternoon. Cars began arriving in the morning with a bunch of people for a party of some sort. This place had a large outdoor patio. We watched our target move around among his guests until he moved off by himself to talk on his phone. We figured we were about eight hundred and forty yards away, not a difficult shot for me."

Simone sat back down on the bench and leaned forward to listen. Sunlight filtering through the trees danced across her cheeks. "The senator told me you were the best he'd ever seen."

Gray laughed bitterly. "Yes, so they said."

"Please go on. What happened?"

"This guy you say is Montoya walked over beside a very large potted plant, more like a tree. What we couldn't see was a door to the house that was hidden from us by the plant. It hadn't turned up in any of the high-altitude surveillance photos. Everything was perfect. This was the moment we had waited for. The man in my sights was attempting to overthrow the government of a friendly country, or so we were told. God, how naive we were then."

"But you believed that."

"Yes. The ones who told us this were very good. Real government officials. Although it could never be made public, the people in power would be proud of us, they said. So there we were, waiting for the chance to make them proud."

"You did what you had been ordered to do," she said.

"Ordered, no. The way they phrased it, we volunteered. Anyway, everything flowed toward the moment we had prepared for. I had him centered in my scope. I took the shot."

Gray stopped speaking. His eyes stared off into the distance, to that spot high on a mountainside in Mexico. Then in a whisper he said, "At the instant my mind gave the order to shoot, the man turned. Behind him stood a woman with a child in her arms. I can see every frame like it was an old movie. I can hear the bullet strike. I hear her gasp. I see the blood explode from her body. She and the child fall to the ground. I can't take my eye from the scope of my rifle. I can't understand how I missed, but there he is, my target, only now he's cradling two bodies to his chest. My partner knocks the rifle from out of my hands and pulls me to my feet, and we run."

Simone stared at him as in disbelief. "And now it's come down to this."

"Yes, and now this. For what I did, Bethany's dead, and he has a little girl who he threatens to kill unless he can kill me," Gray said, looking into her eyes. "He wants his revenge."

Simone nodded.

Gray shrugged. "Who can blame him."

He waited for her to speak. He could see the horror in her eyes, but he needed her to see that the responsibility for all that had happened belonged to him.

She clutched her empty cup in her hands and followed his gaze out over the playground full of children and their protectors. Finally, she asked. "What happened to the one that was with you? Does he feel the way you do?"

"I've known him since our first days together in the Corps. We knew each other's every move; we trusted each other as much as any two people can. Once they convinced us that what they asked of us was of national importance our lives were as one."

"When did you find out it wasn't? True, I mean."

More time passed. More children screamed in mock terror. More mothers picked their offspring up out of the dirt and scolded them. When exactly did he realize it was not what they claimed? Was there a time when he questioned the mission before they went?

She moved to his side, but her presence, so close, unnerved him. He took a step away. He needed space to finish the story. "It took a while before we were sure. We talked about it. It didn't add up when we had time to put it all together, later, when it was over. That's when we decided we'd been pawns. They used us."

"Couldn't you talk to someone about what they had done?"

"No. After we got back, they buried us in a small base somewhere in North Dakota. We were told by very persuasive people that if we decided to take our story anywhere, we would simply vanish. There was no doubt in our minds. We believed that part was true. Probably still do. They're still out there. They haven't gone away. They still watch, and they're more powerful today than they were then." Gray watched the children frolicking on the swing sets. He felt at a loss as to where to go next. "Did Davis give you any hint about who this Montoya guy is?"

Simone brushed a loose strand of blonde hair away from her mouth. "Something was said, briefly, in passing, about an involvement in drugs."

"Drugs, in Mexico. Makes sense. I know someone who might know." He pulled his phone out and tried Juarez's number again. He got lucky and quickly filled him in on Simone's information. He listened a moment, then gave directions to the park.

"What did this person say to you? It must have been serious by the look on your face."

"He said to wait for him, about fifteen minutes, twenty at the most, and not to move."

"You look concerned."

"This person doesn't scare easily, but I could tell the news shook him."

Thirty minutes later he saw Juarez coming across the park. Gray pointed him out to Simone. "The other guy that went with me was Francisco Juarez. I call him Paco. That's him."

"He looks like a younger version of that actor, James Olmos."

"Don't tell him that. He thinks he's better looking."

Gray nodded to Juarez. "This is Simone St. Pierre. She works for the Colonel, I mean Senator Davis. She's touchy about proper titles."

Juarez shook her hand and studied her a moment. "*Mi amigo* says you brought news about the girl."

"Yes, there wasn't much information in the message the senator received. I'm sure Conaire filled you in on what we know."

"Yeah, well, this gives the whole thing a different perspective, doesn't it?"

"Conaire said you know something about drugs and the drug trade. Have you ever heard of this person, Emiliano Montoya?"

"Ma'am, I live and work in a town called Santa Ana. It's up the road a few miles, but it's in a different world. Drugs are around me every day."

Gray had remained silent but couldn't wait any longer. "Do you know about this guy she's talking about?"

Juarez slipped his arm under Simone's and smiled. "Let's take a little walk like we were all a big happy family." He led them to a secluded picnic table, away from the playground and the street.

"Paco, let's have it," Gray said.

"Jorge Emiliano Montoya, or as he likes to be called, Don Emiliano. I know of him. It's impossible to be around drugs without knowing who he is."

"Did you know he was the one we went after?

Juarez shook his head. "Not then, but a few years later I started to make some innocent inquiries, the kind that wouldn't get back to the wrong people. With the answers I got, it wasn't hard to figure out."

Gray couldn't believe what he was hearing. "And you never told me?"

"Why? You had enough to worry about, and there wasn't anything you could do about it, except worry more."

Simone held her hand up. "Okay, you two, let's get back to this guy. Who exactly is he?"

"I'm surprised your senator sent you back here and never filled you in. He sure as hell knows. Emiliano Montoya is what you call a drug lord, or drug baron. He is the head of the Hidalgo drug cartel operating out of the Mexican state of Michoacán. It's not like the

Cali, or the Gulf Cartel, or any of the others that make headlines in Mexico. Montoya keeps a low profile and pays his politicians and federal officials well, and their job is to keep him out of the media's sights. Doesn't mean he's any less deadly. Far from it. Montoya's had many bodies buried, and many left on public display as a warning. His drugs are top of the line and he's not greedy. If you're dealing drugs for Montoya, you're the New York Yankees of the trade."

"And now he wants my name in exchange for Carlie Kate," Gray said.

Simone asked, "How was he able to manage it, finding the woman? The senator's had people looking for her for years. And then to send people up here and do what they did."

Juarez said, "Maybe he just got lucky, but you can bet he's had a hell of a lot more people looking for her than the senator has."

A cell phone buzzed softly. Simone reached into her handbag and glanced at the screen. "The senator's calling." She moved off a few feet to take the call.

Gray rubbed at a raw spot on his cheek. "What do you think, Paco, since you're a detective, sort of?"

"About?"

"The whole thing. I can understand them coming up for Bethany and using her. But why kill her, and then take Carlie Kate? And what about the fire? Do you think they're connected?"

"I've been wondering about that myself. A couple of things seem out of place. Maybe Bethany's death was an accident, and their only option was to take the girl instead. But jumping you in the house and then setting it on fire was for some other reason, although the tattoos you saw tie the two together."

"How? Why?"

Juarez pulled the black notebook out of his pocket and handed it back to Gray. "We talked about it. Now I'm convinced. This has to be the reason. They came back to find this and that makes it very important to someone."

"You might be right," Gray said, leafing through it before putting it in his pocket. "Did you learn anything else from it?"

"Not much, but some things definitely need checking out."

Gray heard Simone's quick intake of breath. Her conversation ended and she walked off by herself. "You know, Paco, you don't need to get involved in this. It's not your war, and this guy doesn't seem to know about you. It's all about me."

"Things change. Sooner or later he'll find out about me if he asks enough questions."

Simone walked back, her face a mask of concern. "The senator had asked for more time on the pretense the information on your whereabouts wasn't readily available. He thought he might be able to negotiate."

"What happened?" Gray asked.

"He received a new message less than an hour ago. Somehow this Montoya believes the senator knows where you can be found and is stalling."

Gray thought about it. "Odd he didn't know until you went back and told him. I wonder what else he knows."

"You're right. Nevertheless, the message said twenty-four hours maximum or…." She looked across the grass toward the playground.

"Or what?"

"Or they'll start sending her back in pieces. Small pieces."

"God, no," Gray gasped.

"She means nothing to them," Juarez said. "People's lives are cheap to him."

"All this because I missed him," Gray said. "How things would have been different if I had killed him."

"But it is as it is, and you have to decide what you're going to do," Simone said. "The senator has only until this time tomorrow to give them the information they want."

Juarez nodded in agreement. "She's right."

Gray crossed his arms. "How much time do you think I have?" he asked Juarez.

"Hard to say. Depends on whether he wants to kill you or grab you like they did with the girl. My guess is he'll send someone to get rid of you quickly and not take any more chances. He's too exposed if he tries launching another kidnapping. I'd say thirty to forty-eight hours at best, but it could come even sooner."

"That long, huh? I'd be pushing it if I were easy to find in three or four days."

Juarez nodded his head slowly. "With the people he has at his calling you'd probably be dead in that time, unless you decide to fight back."

Gray shook his head. "No way to fight them without doing exactly what they want to do to me, except I've got nowhere to run afterward."

"What will you do?" Simone asked.

"Not much choice since I can't sit in the house and wait, and I can't go to the police. The only thing left is to leave."

"Where will you go?"

Gray wasn't sure about that himself, but there was one place he would have a better chance of keeping out of sight. "Montana maybe. It's a big reservation and I know everything there is about it, but don't tell Davis. I wouldn't want him passing it along."

Juarez blew out his breath. "Poses a problem, doesn't it?"

They had discovered over the years their thoughts often ran along similar lines. "Yeah, I've thought about that, too, but what choice do I have?"

Simone looked confused. "What are you two talking about?"

"The whole situation," Gray said. "As long as they chase after me, the longer they'll keep Carlie Kate alive. But how long do you think it will take before someone figures out he has her? He can't take that chance."

Gray knew Juarez had something he wanted to say. "What is it?"

"First, get a new phone right away and call me with the number so we can stay in touch. I'll check my sources and see what I can find out."

Gray nodded. "First thing on my list, but that's not what's bothering you is it?"

"If they get you, what makes you think they'll let her go? She knows too much. If she disappears, who's to say they had anything to do with it."

Simone interrupted. "Oh no, they wouldn't, would they?"

Gray looked at Juarez a moment. "You're right. I guess I might have to consider another option."

"What's that?" Simone asked.

Grays thought about her question a moment before answering. "I have no idea."

29

Gray watched her give the boarding pass to the airline representative and walk toward the entrance of the ramp. At the last moment she turned and looked back, the faintest hint of a sad smile on her face, and mouthed the words, "Take care," then she disappeared into the tunnel. He wondered if he would ever see her again.

As he drove down Jamboree Boulevard, his thoughts raced over the multitude of things that he needed to do. First, a new phone at a T-Mobile outlet off Newport Center Drive.

It took thirty minutes to fill out the paperwork, pick up the phone and car charger, and buy the minutes for the phone. Before leaving the parking lot, Gray left the new number on Juarez's message machine and, as an afterthought, did the same on Simone's.

He went over his options. Best he could come up with was run or stay. Pretty simple.

If he stayed, and Juarez's warnings proved right, he would have to protect himself using as much force as his pursuers. And what would be the consequences of taking more lives without the protection of a license, be it military or civilian law enforcement. Would they agree it was self-defense? Possibly. But Gray also knew the law in such cases moved with the speed of approaching winter, and in the meantime others would follow as avenging angels bent on killing him for their reward of a guaranteed supply of premium mind-altering drugs. And could he live with the knowledge of the lives he would have to take, even if they were thugs for the cartel?

Gray knew the only path he had held a catastrophic unknown. How long would Montoya keep Carlie Kate alive if the cartel couldn't find him, and what would his life be like if they killed her to cover their tracks?

By the time he turned onto his street he had a mental list of the preparations he needed to make. The patrol car at the end of the street had moved into the shade, its occupant dozing as Gray pulled alongside and slowed. He tapped the horn, rousing the young cop, the same one who took his report the night of the fire.

He placed a call to the bank and told his account manager he would like to pick up a considerable amount of cash in the morning. She said she would have it available that afternoon.

Next he called Dorothy and arranged to drop the kitten off later in the day, reluctantly denying there was any new information. He then wrote a note for Richard at the gallery, explaining the situation as vaguely as he could, and dropped a house key in the envelope. Gray asked him to pick up his mail and take care of any bills and, as an afterthought, to take back to the gallery and store two paintings by Granville Redmond and Edgar Payne that had too much value to be left in the house in his present situation.

Gray glanced at the clock for the fourth or fifth time, calculating the margin of error at an hour or two. He figured he had until the following night. The next day he planned on making a show of living normally, maybe even shopping for groceries to keep Detectives Mondavi and Chavez as relaxed as possible.

Juarez sent him a text message saying he received the new phone number, which reminded Gray that Juarez had returned the notebook. He found it on the table, beside his keys and wallet.

With nothing left to do but wait, Gray checked on an address that was only an hour away.

It appeared the patrol car had found something better to do, the spot in the shade beneath the big tree being occupied by a Pizza Hut delivery car.

The place he was looking for was a couple of blocks off the 605 Freeway in the town of Azusa. Gray remembered hearing the town name was thought up by progressive-minded city council members who claimed their fair city had everything in it from A-Z in the USA. Somewhere along the line it appeared the town had fallen on hard times. Wedged between the San Gabriel Mountains and a flood-control basin, it had become an enclave for minority groups, legal and illegal.

The address belonged to the Fourth Street Self Storage yard. The buildings were surrounded by a chain-link fence topped with razor wire and heavily impregnated with tumbleweed. He pulled into a parking spot in front of the office and looked the entrance over carefully. The only gate could be seen from the office window.

Inside, a heavy-set Hispanic with gang tattoos informed him there were no empty units. He shook his head when Gray asked to be put on the waiting list. A bank of closed-circuit TV monitors filled one wall of the small office. Gray studied the chart of the storage spaces while the man behind the desk answered the phone. A unit number, matching a number listed beside the address in the notebook, was taped to one of the monitors on the wall. All the other cameras directed their attention to the alleyways inside of the facility. Whatever was in the unit was worth more attention than the rest.

Gray left the office, and as he backed the Jeep out its parking slot, a golf cart with an armed guard pulled up to the other side of the gate and stopped. Gray figured that whatever was in that locked and guarded unit would not be forgotten.

The woman at the bank called to say the cash withdrawal he had requested was ready. He thanked her and told her he would stop by later in the day. With this in mind, he pulled off the freeway, found an REI store, and purchased a small duffel bag.

She was waiting when he entered the bank and led him to the safe deposit box area. She closed the door while he counted out the cash he had requested.

"You realize I have to report this transaction to the IRS?" she said.

"I take my money out of the bank and you have to report it? Why?"

"Anything over ten thousand dollars in withdrawals has to be reported."

Gray stuffed the banded bills into the duffel. "But it's my money."

"Doesn't matter. And if you were to make a couple more large withdrawals, even if they were less than ten thousand, I'd be required to report them also."

Gray shook his head. "Need to have something for our government employees to do I suppose, but I hope this is the only withdrawal for a while."

Fifty minutes later he pulled into his driveway and put the Jeep in the garage. He tossed the duffel on the kitchen table then took the envelope addressed to the gallery owner and walked out to his mailbox by the street.

A late model, fire engine-red Chevy came down the street and slowed, its occupants stealing glances at him as they passed.

Gray watched the car turn the corner at the end of the block, thinking it was out of place in this area. The neighbor across the street came out of her house wearing little more than what would get her arrested for indecent exposure.

He heard the high-pitched sound of a car engine rapidly accelerating and watched as the Chevy raced toward him, the windows down and two of the passengers leaning out. Gray saw the shotgun pointing out of the back window and reacted, diving toward the grassy swale separating the street and the sidewalk. It offered little protection, but he had no other option. He heard the blast and felt the burning impact from the small pellets. A rapid burst of shots from a handgun splintered the wooden post of the mailbox. He rolled away from the retreating car as several more shotgun blasts sent pellets slicing through the air above his head to ricochet off the pavement and nearby cars. He heard the tires scream as the driver slammed on the brakes.

Desperate for shelter, Gray rose to his feet as the engine revved up and the Chevy raced backward. Gray crouched, waiting until the last moment before sprinting across the street.

The Chevy shot past, heads pivoting in confusion as they tried to spot him. Gray spun around and raced back across the street, hoping to confuse the shooters and give himself time to reach his open garage. But the Chevy driver quickly swung the car over onto the sidewalk and gunned the engine. Gray took a hurried look over his shoulder and saw the car hurtling toward him. Up ahead, his neighbor's thick hedge offered some protection. It wouldn't stop the car altogether, but it might distract them long enough for him to make it to his house. But even if he made it, he had nothing to defend himself with. He had sworn never to use a gun again.

The car closed rapidly. He couldn't take a chance of losing precious seconds by looking back, and if he tripped, the car would smash him to the ground. The stump of a thick tree branch in the corner of the yard hung out over the hedge and sidewalk. Gray raced past the tree and launched himself into the air, hearing another series of pistol shots, punctuated by a blood-curdling scream, as the car hurtled past. He felt a spray of wetness splash his face. He hit the ground hard, then rolled over onto his knees and saw a handgun lying in the grass. Some distance off tires screamed on pavement, followed by the sound of a siren.

Gray remained on his knees while he took a quick inventory of his body. Blood trickled down his arm and onto the grass. He ran a hand over his face and glanced at it. There wasn't as much blood on his face as indicated by the wetness of his shirt and arms, making him wonder where else he was hurt.

Then he saw an arm lying in the grass, or the torn remains of an arm. Gray did a panicky double check to assure himself it was someone else's and, satisfied, he pushed himself to his feet as the sound of multiple sirens rent the air. Two patrol cars came to a screeching halt, effectively blocking the street to all traffic. He wondered if the patrol car assigned to keep an eye on him had managed to initiate a pursuit of the Chevy.

Gray called out to one of the approaching patrolmen and identified himself. The first cop yelled at Gray to lie down and put his hands over his head. Gray felt the tension in the air and did as he was told, then said, "There's a gun lying over here on the grass."

"You stay where you are and we'll get to it," the first cop answered.

"Okay with me, but when you do you'll find someone's arm lying over there, too, and my guess is it belonged to the guy who lost the gun."

"Shit," the young cop said, staring down at the severed arm.

Gray guessed the small town didn't produce too many mangled limbs lying on lawns.

A dark-blue sedan pulled to the curb beneath the streetlight. The driver stepped out and reached back for his jacket. Gray recognized Detective Mondavi, who took in the scene and whistled softly. He walked over to where Gray lay with his face in the grass.

The detective stood above Gray and directed his people to search for any other interesting things in the grass, then knelt down. "You've been living here in my town all these years and never caused a peep and now this. I have a murder, a missing child, a home burglary and fire in conjunction with an attack, and now this, our quiet little town's first drive-by shooting attempt. And you're involved in all of them," Mondavi said.

"You mind if I get up?" Gray asked.

"Sure, why not? And then just maybe you can tell me what the hell is going on."

Gray pushed himself to his feet and looked around. The cop who discovered the arm was following a trail of blood. Another stood beside the gun lying in the grass.

Gray looked back at Mondavi and shrugged. "You're the detective. You tell me."

Mondavi stepped in close to Gray, making him back up half a step. "Yes, I am, and I can tell you this with certainty. You know more than you're telling me and that really upsets me."

While Mondavi vented his anger, Gray took a moment to think about what had happened and the first thing he came up with led to the Colonel—Senator Davis. Simone must have called the son of a bitch, and he had immediately passed on the information to Montoya. How long had it been, six hours? It proved one thing though. Two, actually. Montoya's reach was long, and he was in a hurry. Gray shuddered. What would this mean for the girl?

Another cop came over and pulled Mondavi to the side.

A paramedic van had pulled up and the flashing red light shut off. Two occupants jumped out and began assembling their gear. Gray caught a glimpse of short blonde hair on one of them and winced. He knew a lecture was in his near future.

Detective Mondavi came back. "They found the car and the guy who left the arm behind. The guy bled to death and the others scattered, but San Diego PD picked up one of them. The guy didn't want to talk, but we did learn they're from Logan Barrio in San Diego. Bad bunch to be on the wrong side of."

Gray listened while Mondavi filled him in on what they had learned. "Looks like whoever was driving got too close to that sawn-off tree branch. Man, I'll bet that smarted. Makes you wonder if there is a God, doesn't it?"

The blonde paramedic who treated him at the fire stepped past Mondavi. "Excuse me, Detective. I'll need to look at our victim. How about that? My first today."

Mondavi moved aside. "I don't think he needs much attention, but you can have him for a few minutes while I check on the rest of the situation. All that shooting and nobody else hurt is a minor miracle. Must be my lucky day."

"Sarcasm doesn't become you, Detective," she said with a grin.

Gray shook his head. "You again, how lucky can I get. Wilson, right?"

She wiped off his face and helped him remove his shirt. "Yep, that's me. Says so right there on my badge. Seems every time we run into each other I'm helping undress you. People might start to talk. Anyway, it looks like three of whatever it was they were using got you. I'd say bird shot. If it had been double-ought things might be different."

"You know the difference. I'm impressed," Gray said.

"My dad used to take me duck hunting every season. Bought me a yellow lab pup in an auction at a Ducks Unlimited dinner one year. My mom had a fit when she found out how much he bid on that dog. He tried to convince her it was in a raffle, but she never bought it. You still have that little kitten you rescued?"

"Yes, and it didn't cost me a cent, although I doubt it would be any good duck hunting. I have a lady looking after it for me."

Mondavi left the patrol car and headed back.

"You know there are easier ways for us to meet. Doing it this way is awfully hard on your body," she said with a giggle.

"You think I'm not doing all this to impress you?"

"Okay, I'm impressed, whatever that means, and you know where you can find me, so let's not meet professionally anymore."

Mondavi waited until she acknowledged his presence. "You about done with him?"

"He's all yours, Detective," she said, packing everything into an oversize tackle box.

Gray watched her, comparing the difference in the two women who had suddenly pushed themselves into his life. Both had the kind of natural beauty any woman would die for. He felt uneasy with Simone. With this one it was different, easy, with no hesitation in the casual banter, as if there was nothing to lose.

"You might stop in at the clinic in a day or two and have those holes checked." She stepped in front of Mondavi, blocked his view, and used a piece of gauze to do one last wipe on his face before helping him on with his shirt. "My phone number is in your shirt pocket in case you ever need it, professionally or otherwise," she whispered. "And since you never asked, my name is Claire."

"I thought it was just Wilson. But that might not be a good idea. I seem to be a magnet for trouble."

She winked. "Let me worry about that. Oh, by the way, nice haircut."

Gray blushed.

Mondavi waited until she was some distance off. He ran his hand over his shaved head. "You know this whole case gets stranger and stranger. First the chief wants us to put all our efforts into checking you out, and you know what, you were looking better and better for this every day. I was this close to having Detective Chavez you pick you up tomorrow, and now this."

"Does that mean I'll lose my watcher at the end of the street?"

"Yeah, the powers that be have sent out the word to drop everything and set you free, so to speak."

Gray smiled. "I guess a drive-by does change the focus."

Mondavi moved in closer. "It might, but I got the word, unofficially you understand, before this happened."

Gray studied the detective's face. "Before?"

"Before."

"I see your point."

"I don't know what you've gotten yourself into, but if it was me I wouldn't wait around to find out."

"You saying I should leave town?"

Mondavi nodded. "The sooner the better. I've read your military record. I'm surprised there aren't more bodies lying around."

Gray looked away. "I'm not that person anymore, Detective. I've changed."

Mondavi leaned forward. "You think so? My advice is, if you want to stay alive, find that person again before it's too late."

30

Simone St. Pierre settled into her first-class seat as the intermediate jet began to push back from the gate. She struggled to put her thoughts in focus, but the last couple of days had been so out of the ordinary nothing she did seemed to help.

She closed her eyes as the plane came to a full stop and the engines throbbed with power waiting to be unleashed. God, she felt tired. She wondered if she could afford the luxury of sleeping during the short flight back to Phoenix. A humorless chuckle caused the businessman in the adjacent seat to glance her way. No, sleep was not a viable option. That would have to come later, after she reported back to Senator Davis.

What had Conaire Gray and Francisco Juarez told her that the senator hadn't? Didn't the senator know that Emiliano Montoya was the head of a very successful drug cartel in Mexico? He had to know this, but then why not tell her. Was this his way of protecting her by not giving her too much knowledge? This was America. The whole damned situation should be turned over to the proper authorities. With the senator's position, the FBI and the CIA could be brought in very easily. Pressure could be applied on Mexico regardless of what some Mexican distributor of slow death warned. Or was the decision not his to make? She suddenly felt the unseen weight of the so-called *others* telling her there was more involved than she could see. Had Montoya warned the senator that involving the proper authorities could unmask everyone?

Simone flinched when she realized her fingernails were embedded in the palms of her hands. Juarez was right and she knew it, and she knew that Gray knew it, too. Why would Montoya risk letting the girl live? After all, there was no proof he had anything to do with it. Would she relate this to the senator?

The thought of Gray's predicament troubled her more than she wanted to admit. The first time they met she had left his house feeling stripped of her own sense of pride and achievement because of what she saw in his work. It had forced her to question the career path she had chosen. This feeling of apprehension had nothing to do with art. She put it aside, not wanting to explore it further.

She felt the plane begin its descent into Sky Harbor International Airport. In forty minutes she would be on her way to report to the senator, then he would start the clock on Gray's dwindling hours. Again, she posed the question, why did she care?

"Oh, Simone, don't do it," she mumbled loud enough for her seating companion to look her way again. *Don't let yourself develop feelings for him, please. He is absolutely everything you despise in men.* The last man she had felt this way about now threatened to reveal a past she had hoped was buried forever.

Which then made her wonder what it was she saw in him in the first place. What was he like beneath the pain that seemed his constant companion? Once, for the briefest moment, she witnessed the shadow of a smile in those blue eyes above those high cheekbones and bronzed skin. It appeared when he spoke about the girl and what her innocent love had done to transform him from the brooding introvert to someone who thought there might be a life in his future.

Simone sighed deeply, knowing her only hope was in distancing herself from him immediately and looking into her own future.

The plane touched down with a jolt, the engines screaming, and began its trip to the gate. She looked out the window, knowing that the inevitable message would be on her cell phone as soon as she turned it back on. She had to admit Sergio seemed to care, sometimes overly so, to the point of suffocation. But what about her Latin lover with the looks of a Brooks Brothers model? Could he be her future if everything else blew up? Maybe she had been too hard on him. Their last conversation revolved around her attempting to explain why this trip back to California was so important. She tried to remember how she answered his flood of questions, then shook her head in frustration.

Before she rose from her seat and picked up her briefcase a troubling thought began floating in the back of her mind.

31

Miguel Zapata heard the pounding on his door and rubbed the sleep from his eyes, cursing as when he tore off a scab from one of the deep gouges on his cheek.

Someone opened the front door and shouted, "Miguel, your father wants you."

He rolled off the bed and pushed himself to his feet, the hammering in his head unrelenting. "Shit, what is it he wants now?"

The guard laughed. "Did not tell me, but I am glad it is you he wants and not me."

Fifteen minutes later Miguel Zapata sprawled in the leather chair opposite his father's desk. Castillo sat next to him, his slim legs crossed and his ever-present portfolio on his lap.

Jorge Emiliano Montoya tossed a newspaper on the coffee table and settled back in his chair. A lazy spiral of steam rose out of the cup of Columbian coffee sitting beside the cut-glass ashtray holding the ever present cigar. The inch-long ash indicated he had been deeply involved in whatever was on his mind.

"So, why not tell me again what we have learned," Montoya said.

Castillo cleared his throat and glanced at Miguel before opening the folder tucked inside the portfolio. Miguel knew the look was a warning to him to keep his knowledge to himself.

Emiliano, we have learned the man's name is Gray, a Conaire Gray."

"Gray," Montoya repeated. He indicated to Castillo to continue.

"It appears the man lives in the same town as the woman."

Montoya frowned. "And why did we not know this from our source?"

"Perhaps he was not able to obtain it," Castillo said.

Miguel knew all of this information already. In fact, he had already acted on it. He hoped that once this object of his father's hate was taken care of his father would have more time to listen to some of the ideas Miguel had, ideas Miguel had already put into work.

Montoya flicked the ash off his cigar and leaned back in his chair. "By chance did this Gray know the woman?"

"He did," Castillo said. "This man was a current boyfriend."

"Then it is obvious he knew the woman before this. I find it odd the senator did not know."

"Our information indicates a wide separation between father and daughter. It is possible, but immaterial."

"If this man, Gray, was the woman's boyfriend at the time," Montoya said, "then is he not the one we had pushed the investigation toward. It would seem if we were successful and the police in this town arrested him, it might prove difficult to eliminate him."

Miguel let the conversation pass between his father and Castillo. He figured the man would be dead long before the police decided to arrest him. In fact, he might be dead already, if those he spoke to had acted immediately.

Castillo tucked the folder back inside his portfolio. "I felt it was important he not be arrested. I have already seen to it."

"I do not like these coincidences. I have spent eight years looking for this man. We find the woman and I put a plan together to use her to force this senator to tell us who the man is that murdered my only grandchild and my daughter. And now this." Montoya crushed out the cigar in the ashtray and stood. "He has been fucking her all along. Why did we not know this?" Montoya said, slamming his hand down on the desk.

Castillo shrugged.

"Very well," Montoya said. "Now that we know where to find him, have him taken care of."

"I will see to it," Castillo said. "I believe those we sent to search the home will see that it is taken care of immediately."

Montoya sat back down. "You will inform me as soon as it happens."

Castillo turned to Montoya. "Will this be the end of it, the death of this man?"

"In time the American senator will be told to forget what happened. I retain the information that could destroy his career and of those that assisted him. Who knows? I may need another favor at some time."

Miguel and Castillo pushed through the double doors, but Montoya had one last order before they were out of the office. "And see that the girl and the old man watching her are taken care of."

32

The last emergency vehicle pulled away from the curb, leaving only the neighbors standing around repeating to each other what they had seen and how close they were to the attack. Those in the two houses next to Gray's pointed out the gouges made by the wayward slugs from the handgun, all agreeing that it had to have been a .45 automatic by the noise it made. The pellets from the shotgun left little evidence of the attack, much to the chagrin of those who lined up to be interviewed by the news networks.

Gray, having shunned the microphones, closed his door and leaned back against it while attempting to release some of the tension brought on by his near death. He kept hearing Mondavi's words about being told to back off the investigation. Did that mean he knew about Emiliano Montoya? Gray didn't think so. Someone else was behind it. Could that someone be the Colonel—Senator Davis? Possibly. Like Mondavi had said, they were about to arrest him. In custody there was no way Davis and the others could get to him as easily, but left alone he became an open target.

Gray pulled off his shirt and carried it into the bathroom, dropping it on the floor beside the clothes hamper. The face reflected in the mirror little resembled the person from a few days earlier. The short hair, the raw patches of burnt skin peeking through the unshaven face, and the circles under the eyes brought about by Bethany's death and the worry over Carlie Kate. He turned slightly to view the patches Claire Wilson had applied to the pellet wounds. On one she had drawn a happy face.

Gray splashed cold water on his face, his thoughts returning to Carlie. Where was she? Had they taken her across the border? Or where they hiding her somewhere in the American Southwest? If she was still alive, he knew he was responsible for any chance she had. Gray dabbed his face with a towel, wondering how long it would take for the scabs to heal sufficiently to allow him to shave.

He realized he had not eaten since a light breakfast and rummaged through the freezer until he found a package of frozen chicken cutlets. He tossed them in the microwave to defrost and discovered a container of homemade marinara sauce Bethany had made. He put on a pot of water and grabbed a bag of organic wheat pasta while reviewing everything that had happened to date, beginning with Bethany's death. If the information in the black book was as important as it appeared to be, he at least had somewhere to start.

He stood at the counter and ate the hurried meal, rinsing off the dishes in the sink while coming to a decision.

In the garage, Gray piled gear beside the Jeep, one part of his mind thinking about what he should take while another churned through the choices Montoya had. Carlie was Montoya's leverage with Davis, so killing her would leave him with nothing to bargain with. That was a positive. Gray hoped that by staying alive he might keep her alive.

The clock read 3:00 A.M. If Montoya's arm reached out as far as Paco claimed, then Gray might expect new visitors at any time. He tossed the gear in the back of the Jeep and the duffel with the money on the passenger seat. With no idea in which direction to run, he decided to get on the freeway and let it take him wherever it led.

33

At 3:30 in the morning, Laguna Mesa slept to the gentle rhythm of the automatic sprinklers systems soaking the lawns and streets, regardless of the dire predictions of a possible water shortage.

Gray coasted down the street to Pacific Coast Highway. Two Laguna Mesa patrol cars sat side by side in the parking lot of the 24-hour café across the highway. He sat at the intersection for a moment, trying to decide which way to go.

With his windows down, only the hiss of his tires on cool pavement competed with nature's version of perpetual motion as wave after wave of the Pacific Ocean spent itself on the rocks and imported sand along the shore.

In his rear-view mirror he noticed a pair of headlights pull out of the café parking lot and follow. He turned up Laguna Canyon Road, the headlights keeping pace a block behind before they turned into the parking area for the Sawdust Festival, one of Laguna Beach's summer art exhibits. Mondavi had told him the surveillance had been pulled, so why was this car following him? Was it only a coincidence that the patrol car happened to be parked across the highway from his street? Gray pushed it out of his mind and worked his way up the winding canyon road.

A series of red cones and blinking yellow lights closed off both ramps onto Interstate 405, an arrow directing traffic up the road toward the on-ramps to Interstate 5, the main north-south artery from Mexico to Canada.

A Santa Ana Police Department car, its engine running, sat by the on-ramp. Gray accelerated onto the northbound lane, joining the only other occupants at this time of the morning, the big rigs thundering through the city, hoping to make it to the bottom of the twisting climb out of the LA Basin before commuter traffic brought travel to a standstill and turned the four- and five-lane artery into the world's largest parking lot.

Passing through Norwalk, Gray reached over to change radio stations and noticed a car on his left hanging back but still keeping pace with him. He hadn't noticed its approach. Another car held a position on his right, but a half dozen car lengths behind.

At what was once the famous cloverleaf interchange, Gray swung off onto the 110 Harbor Freeway, rather than head over the pass into North Hollywood. A glance in his rear-view mirror revealed both cars still holding their positions.

He tapped his fingertips on the steering wheel, glancing in the mirror again, then reached over to shut off the radio. A feeling of uneasiness crept into his stomach. Something told him he wasn't being paranoid. He knew nobody followed him out of Laguna Mesa, yet why were these two cars still hanging on.

Gray eased up on the gas and drained off some speed. Both cars quickly slowed to maintain their positions. He increased his speed slowly, noting they did the same. Okay, he muttered, what exactly is it you intend to do, and what are you waiting for? As if to answer the second question, the car following some distance back began to narrow the gap.

Gray took the long ramp onto the 210 Freeway in Pasadena, with both cars still on his tail. Traffic was building in the opposite direction as more cars joined the morning rush. He wondered what his tailers intended to do if they got close enough. LA was noted for its random acts of gun violence on its freeways and at this time in the morning no one would notice. Still, why hadn't they acted sooner, unless they were having someone run his plates to see if the Jeep was his?

Again, as if answering his question, the trailing car on his right moved up, blocking him from taking an off-ramp. Unless he acted fast, they would have him sandwiched between them. The Jeep could not match their speed, so he needed another option.

A quarter-mile ahead, two eighteen-wheelers lumbered along in the slow lane. Gray edged his speed up slowly, not wanting to alert his followers. He figured they would wait until all three cars had passed the trucks before making a move.

He saw the sign for the next off-ramp and knew this would be his only chance. He knew the road and doubted those following would be familiar with it, but it was going to be tight. If he could pull it off, it might gain him some distance and that was all he could hope for.

Gray slammed the gas pedal to the floor and shot for the gap between the two semis. Caught by surprise, both cars fell behind as he flung the Jeep into the space not more than two or three car lengths in width, earning him an earsplitting blast from an air horn of the trailing truck.

He swung the Jeep onto the off-ramp leading up to Angeles Crest Highway. Without braking, he ran the stop sign and made a squealing turn, punching the accelerator to the floor in hopes of gaining even more time, figuring he might have a chance if he could make it to where the road reduced to two lanes leading into the mountains. He stole a quick glance in the mirror. The lead car took the turn too wide and fishtailed across all four lanes before straightening out, the trailing car moving into the lead position.

The three cars shot out of the upscale residential area and onto the climbing, twisting road, where passing was almost impossible.

A hard curve to his left gave him a chance to see both cars squirreling through the turns about a quarter-mile behind. He didn't like how much they had gained in such a short time.

For the next couple of miles Gray saw them briefly as he used both sides of the road through the curves, hoping there was no oncoming traffic. He tried to remember the road ahead, especially where other roads led off the highway to run deeper into the Angeles National Forest. If he remained on this road, it would eventually take him to the little town of Big Pine, then Wrightwood. That possibility was out. They would catch him long before that. He needed another route, one harder for them to follow. Hell, he needed Jeep terrain. But where would he find that? A road came to mind, one he had seen the previous fall when he came up for a weekend hike. He tried to remember where it was.

Not willing to take a chance, he raced through the stop sign at the intersection of Angeles Forest Road. Ahead was a landmark that had been called Red Box for so long it had made it onto the maps and signaled the road leading up to the Mount Wilson Observatory. After that he would have a long stretch until Big Tujunga Canyon. If he could make it that far, he figured he could make the jeep road.

Through another sweeping curve and the road straightened out for a quarter of a mile. Gray stole a quick glance in the rear-view mirror. The lead car had moved up quicker than he expected. Less than fifty yards separated them. In half an hour, traffic would build on this road leading into LA. *I hope nobody chose to go to work early today.*

He tore through another curve, then another stretch of straightaway, and he knew they wouldn't pass this one up. The chase car pulled out into the oncoming lane and disappeared into his blind spot. He tensed, wondering what they had in mind.

The Jeep lurched to the right as the following car attempted to run him off the road. He pulled away from the edge and felt the second crash that sent him back again toward the low wooden railing, the only thing between him and a two-hundred-foot drop to the canyon floor below.

Gray jerked the Jeep hard to the left, using the weight and bulk of his heavier vehicle to push the other car across the highway to the dirt embankment. He pulled back into his lane, watching the wild dance the other car did trying to regain forward momentum. Gray figured he had gained time until he saw the trailing car pull around the first and take up the chase.

Ahead, a pickup came into view around a curve, forcing all three cars back into the right lane. Through the curve the three cars roared bumper to bumper. Gray knew he was running out of time.

The sign for Big Tujunga Canyon Road flashed past. Another mile ahead, but at this speed could he make the sharp turn without slowing down?

He heard the gunshots as his side mirror exploded. He jerked the wheel to the right as three star-shaped holes appeared in his rear window. Six inches closer and all his troubles would have been over.

With the side mirror gone, he stole a quick glance over his shoulder. The late model four-door that took over the chase hung back a few feet from his rear bumper. Gray whipped the Jeep over and hit the brakes, feeling the jolt of the collision and having the satisfaction of seeing the passenger in the front seat slam into the windshield. Gray jammed the accelerator down, feeling the surge of power from the big engine. He quickly gained distance on both cars, knowing he needed it in order to slow for the curve. A quarter-mile ahead he saw the sign pointing to the road entrance on his left. With any luck he could make the turn and gain valuable time on his pursuers.

He rolled the window down and recognized the unmistakable tinny chatter of an AK-47, the third-world's answer to open rebellion, feeling the thud of the heavy slugs slamming into the back of the Jeep. He gritted his teeth and tightened his grip on the steering wheel, waiting until the last minute to slow suddenly and throw the Jeep over onto the narrow two-lane road leading deeper into the mountains.

Still a chance to make it, he figured, as long as he could keep them behind and off balance. That Ak-47 made things a whole lot harder. But before he could start thinking he had a chance of escape he needed to remember how far that jeep road was and how it looked when he saw it. If he missed the road, it was all over. The Jeep couldn't take much more incoming fire. Many jeep roads leading off into the dense interior never advertised themselves, but this one had something that made him remember it, as if someone left a sign for others to follow. A rock on the side of the road, that was it, with a red arrow pointing to the left painted on it. But how far ahead, and how much speed would he have to bleed off to make the turn?

He floored the gas pedal in an attempt to gain distance, while using both lanes to keep them from coming up alongside and still watching for the rock with the red arrow. They closed to three car lengths. He knew if the road straightened out they would make another attempt to come alongside, and he would be at the mercy of an AK-47. The potholes and cracks in the road made it difficult for the one trying to lean out the window with the automatic. Instead he held the rifle at arm's length and ran through a clip. Gray saw the puffs of dirt and bursts of rock chips from the slugs.

Then abruptly the road widened into a third lane for passing. He hadn't remembered it. The lead car swung into the additional lane and crept up, with the trailing car closing quickly. They would have him trapped between them.

The round boulder with the red arrow flashed past. Gray hammered the brake pedal and threw the Jeep into a partial spin at the narrow opening leading into the heavy growth of fir trees. He slowed the forward momentum enough to throw the car into four-wheel drive, murmuring a silent thanks to Jeep for being one of the few four-wheel cars he could do that in. The Jeep bit into the rock and gravel, with the heavy Goodrich all-terrain tires sending up a spray of debris as he fishtailed up the incline.

Through the rising cloud of dust, Gray saw the second car spinning in the gravel, the first having missed the road. The Jeeps tires ripped at the gravel and rock, pushing the off-road vehicle up and over the high rocky crown of the road. He fought the wheel, waiting for the sound of the rifle to split the air again.

For a second he took his eyes off the gradient ahead and looked into the mirror in time to see the car following leap into the air, its hood flying open and coming down on whatever it had hit. Steam poured out of the broken radiator as the car tilted far over on its side before settling back on the rock that had ripped out its undercarriage.

Gray bounced around a sharp curve and stopped out of sight of those behind him. He heard the curses, followed by threatening screams. The AK-47 opened up again, clipping branches and leaves overhead. He drove a quarter-mile farther up the track and parked.

Slipping back through the trees, Gray crept to a spot beneath a canopy of overhanging branches and squatted down on his heels. Thirty feet below, four men argued vehemently while pointing up the trail and cursing the driver of the leading car which was hopelessly hung up on a rock embedded in the crown of the road. A trail of oil slowly worked its way down the road. In a fit of rage, one of the others pulled a pistol from his belt and emptied it into the engine compartment of the disabled car.

The flickering shadows filtered over Gray, his face blending in with the streaks of sunlight and shade. As if he were a part of the land and shrubs, he watched, motionless, his eyes memorizing their faces.

A thick-necked Hispanic, with shaved head and neck spattered with tattoos, pulled out his cell phone and studied its face. Gray wondered if any of them had ever been out of cell phone coverage before. The man punched in a number and waited. Two others began transferring their gear to the other car, while the driver of the disabled car pulled a handgun from the glove compartment. He started working his way up the steeply inclined road, his smooth leather soled shoes slipping on the loose rocks and gravel.

Gray eased into complete shade, then moved through the trees paralleling the road until he was ahead of the one coming up from below. He slid in behind a jagged wall of rock bordering the road and waited. He heard a muffled curse and eased around the edge of the wall. The man had slipped to one knee, his pants bloodied and shredded on the rocks. Gray stepped out behind the man and wrapped his arms around the man's neck in a figure-four chokehold. In a matter of seconds the man quit struggling and went limp. Gray dropped him on the ground, picked up the gun and walked back to the Jeep. He tossed the gun on the passenger seat and inspected the damage to the body and windows of the car. As an afterthought, he walked back to the unconscious man and striped off his shoes, tossing them into the bushes. He smiled, imagining what the man's feet would look like by the time he made it back to the others. As he drove up, the road he wondered what story he could concoct to tell the dealer when he took it in for a new rear window and mirror.

34

Gray located a dealership in Bakersfield that said it could have the Jeep ready in about five days. The service manager tossed the keys to the nearest mechanic and nodded her head at the car.

"Just out of curiosity, what happened?" she said. "Looks like somebody used it for a shooting gallery."

"I think it's an example of what happens when you put guns into the hands of adolescent males," Gray said.

She shook her head in sympathy. "I know a couple just like that. Could even have been one of my exes. Where did you leave it?"

"At a trailhead up in the San Bernardino Mountains, kind of remote place but I thought it would be safe. I was gone for three days and this is what I came back to. Lucky I could still drive it."

"Tough, but we can take care of most of it," she said. "You're going to need a body and paint shop to do the rest."

The temperature in Bakersfield hovered near the century mark. The hot air, pregnant with dust from the surrounding cattle ranches, blanketed the oil town. As one old timer related to him in Bakersfield drawl, "There's over fifty thousand steers out there and every damn one of them has four hooves, and it ain't rained in three months. Those steers are the greatest dust making machine God ever devised."

Across the street Gray spotted an In-N-Out Burger, a west coast hamburger chain that served some of the best burgers he could ask for. He picked up his order from the smiling worker and found an empty table under an umbrella on the outside patio. He pulled out his phone and punched in the number. Paco answered immediately.

Gray quickly related the two attempts in the last twenty-four hours. "Any thoughts?"

"Seems Montoya knew about you much sooner than we expected," Juarez replied. "How else could he send his *chollos* so quickly unless the Colonel didn't wait to pass on the information?"

"You're thinking the same as me. Why bother asking for more time and sending this woman out here to tell me about it?"

Juarez chuckled. "Every time we think we know what's going on something, or somebody, craps on our ideas. And in case you were too busy to notice, that wasn't just any woman came to see you, that was a whole lot of woman."

"Paco, buddy, I got a hell of a lot more things on my mind than noticing women right now. People keep trying to kill me. And what about those cops that followed me? They were the only ones who saw me leave this morning."

"You call that detective yet?"

"Not yet. He's on the list, along with that woman you were referring to. You hear anything else on your end?" Gray asked.

"You can't believe the shit I'm hearing," Juarez answered. "Be glad you made it out of town because they say he's offering a bounty in the high six figures for your Indian scalp. Makes me wonder why I saved your sorry ass all those times."

"Because you were a dumb Mexican and didn't know any better. Which brings to mind another possibility, if you think you can follow along. Could our senator have sent her down here to keep me in place for a while?"

"Man, that would be cold blooded," Juarez said. "But why, after all these years? And you know what I think of our Colonel. Still, I don't see him doing that, not on his own. He might though, under enough pressure."

A horn blared at the stoplight and someone voiced their displeasure for a moment. Gray could hear Juarez talking to someone.

"Listen, Paco," Gray said. "What about you? At least I know they're after me. You might not know until it's too late. Think about it, friend."

The service manager jogged across the street to tell him the car was ready. Gray told Juarez he'd call back if he heard anything new.

Gray called Mondavi, but the voice at the Laguna Mesa station said the detective wouldn't be in the office for the rest of the day. Was this an emergency, and if not, would he like Mondavi's voice mail? Gray hung up instead.

Gray returned to Jeep repair shop. The mechanics hadn't bothered taking off the stickers on the new windows. He didn't care—the bullet holes would draw all the attention.

Still not certain were he would go, he drove through fields of newly planted grapevines, amazed that there was still a need for more vineyards in California. He wondered if someday someone would realize that the Central Valley, one of the greatest food producing valleys in the U.S., if not the world, had been replanted with grapevines, and most of the country's vegetables were being imported from Central and South America.

Buttonwillow sat at the end of an Interstate 5 off-ramp. A place where a traveler could fill the gas tank before tackling the congestion of the city, or a place for truckers to spend the night and eat fast=food. Two or three motels served those in need of a few hours sleep and a shower, if they weren't too particular about the services offered.

Gray pulled into the parking lot of a shuttered convenience store, knowing he had put the call off long enough. He dreaded some of what she might say, but it had to be done before he got on the highway. The last thing he needed was having the California Highway Patrol pull him over for the flagrant violation of talking on his cell phone while driving. And what would they say about the obvious bullet holes in the body of the Jeep? Of course, if they could somehow concoct a reason to search the car without his permission, there was the problem of the duffel bag with ten thousand dollars and a loaded 9mm. With California gun laws, he could almost be charged with a capital offense.

"Is there any news?" he asked as soon as she answered.

"News? Conaire, is that you?"

"Yeah, it's me. Have you heard anything?"

"Maybe the next time you can say hello before grilling me," Simone St. Pierre replied. "No, we haven't heard anything. I would have called."

"I wonder," he said, then felt guilt for the sarcasm.

"Conaire, is there anything else? Where are you anyway? I can hear a lot of traffic."

"Doesn't matter. Listen, I don't know what you know, or how much your senator tells you, but you can tell him for me I think he's a lying, cold-hearted prick.

He heard the sharp intake of breath before she shot back, "Just what the hell do you mean by that?"

He felt his own temper rising. "I don't know what game he's playing by sending you out here to tell me this Montoya character wants to kill me, and hell, I would too if I were him, but then saying he had asked for another forty-eight hours. And he did all of this because he owed it to me? He sent me on that mission in the first place. He owes me a lot more than that."

"You finished?" she asked.

"Until I hear what you have to say."

"Then listen, if you want to continue this conversation. You can begin by explaining yourself if you know what I mean."

"All right, Ms. St. Pierre, but first I need an answer. And I'm not sure I'll believe you, but we can try."

Simone's voice crackled with anger. "Ask your question or I'm hanging up."

"Tell me something. When did Davis call the drug lord with my name and where they could find me, and do you know for sure?"

"Yes, I called him as soon as I got back. He wasn't there, but I left a message. He called me back to say he got the message and would wait until the last minute to call."

"And you believed that was the first time he called them?"

"Conaire, are you implying he called them sooner? Forget it."

"Really? Then explain this. Six hours after you left they came for me. This was no random drive-by shooting. They were after me."

He felt himself tense, holding the phone tight against his ear, waiting for an answer, wondering if he could tell if she was lying.

"Impossible," she said but he noticed confusion in her voice. "No, it couldn't have been like that. There's another reason. There has to be. You're obviously mistaken. I mean, what is it you're saying by they came for you."

"Hard to be mistaken about what happened. Four guys driving down the street, blasting away with shotguns and automatics. You know my street. They were waiting for me. You still think it was a mistake?"

"Are you all right?" she whispered.

"Nothing that won't heal. What about it?"

"Conaire," she said hesitantly, "I can't explain. I need time to think."

He waited for her to continue.

"I know him," she said. "The decision to give them your name nearly destroyed him. He is one of the most trustworthy and honorable men I know. There simply has to be another answer.

Gray believed she was telling the truth, as she knew it. He felt a sense of relief. "Simone, they knew who I was, and where to find me, long before the deadline was up."

"Look, I don't have an answer for you. Sometimes it's something so simple we overlook it. Give me time to think about it."

Gray wondered if he should tell her about the second attempt. He decided not to. "I can't afford to overlook anything. If you're being truthful, it would help for me to know what I'm missing."

"I wouldn't lie to you; that's not me. What will you do now?"

"I can't go home, at least not until this is over."

"So where will you go?" she asked, her voice coming across strained. "Can you go to that place where you said you grew up? You know, where your grandfather lives?"

"I'm not sure my presence would be welcome."

"Why?"

He had wrestled with the question for days. "My grandfather and I have our differences. Different life styles, different opinions. He wanted me to embrace my blood, be proud of my heritage. I thought they were all still living on past reputation and not doing anything to improve themselves. He never could understand why I walked away from living, and I couldn't tell him why so he felt I didn't trust him. We haven't kept in touch other than an occasional card."

"Can't you call him?"

"No phone. Doesn't believe in them."

He sat in the Jeep, his eyes following a tiny biplane as it swooped across the highway and dropped back down over a field, a light mist of liquid trailing into the air and settling on the crop. The plane's nose rose before the pilot banked hard and dropped back for another pass. "I've got to go," he said, hanging up before she could reply.

He started the Jeep and pulled onto the northbound ramp, going over their conversation again. A thought suddenly flashed before him. Paco had not asked where he was going. Maybe Paco didn't want to know. Why had she?"

35

We've had our differences. Wasn't that what he said to her? When was the last time he saw the old warrior? Six years ago, maybe, and then his grandfather had told him to start living again or go ahead and start to die. And Gray recalled storming out of the cabin in anger and driving away from the reservation, desperate to tell someone what had happened to him and what he had done. But it wasn't as easy as that. He remembered the warnings he and Juarez received from some very dangerous men. They had put the fear into him. He believed them. He swore he would keep their secret. But the secret had slipped out of the box and only time would tell if the warnings of the consequences would come true.

The interstate pointed north, almost a straight line through California and on to Canada. It knew its destination; he wished he knew his. A thought struck him. If he didn't know where he was going, they wouldn't know either. A picture of Carlie Kate, her long, sun-bleached hair tousled from the wind as she used both hands to hold it away from her face while she questioned him about one thing or another.

And what about Simone's last question? Would he call her? No, she had his number. If she heard anything new, she would call. Which made him afraid for her to call, since they had made it plain drug kingpin Montoya wouldn't let the girl go until the cartel thugs found him.

He turned on the radio. Dwight Yoakam was singing the praises of Bakersfield as a big rig swung out to pass another. The two behemoths lumbered along for a mile without any distance developing between them. Gray saw an off ramp and took it.

At the end of the ramp he faced another decision. He sat there until an antique Volkswagen bus, with two surfboards strapped to the top, pulled up behind him and he was startled by its horn. Gray turned west, the guys with the surfboards turned east, making him question their sense of direction, since the one basic need of a surfboard happened to be in the direction Gray had chosen. But this was California, so who knew what they were thinking.

The two-lane road led past a field of horsehead oilrigs patiently sucking the thick goo out of the ground and into a maze of rusting pipes. Then back again into an arid land of sage and mesquite, a land untouched except for the trash tossed out of car windows, a land needing only access to California's most valuable commodity, water, to turn it into more acres of grapevines.

A sign indicated the convergence of Highway 41. A car had pulled to the side of the road and an elderly couple stood and pointed their cameras at what appeared to be nothing more than a fence and more sage. Gray groaned, remembering a recent documentary he and Bethany had watched about the tragic death of James Dean, who was killed at this intersection years before. He wondered what the old couple hoped to see.

Ninety minutes later the twisting road emerged from a canyon and entered the outskirts of a town. A town built on the flats below the western slopes of the hills, facing a relentless ocean, and the nearly six hundred-foot plug of a long-extinct volcano. Morro Bay, once a quiet but thriving commercial fishing town, had in recent years built up its image as a tourist destination for those wishing an option to the more yuppie-oriented Cambria, twenty-some miles farther up the coast.

Gray turned off the air conditioner and rolled down his windows, luxuriating in the thirty-degree difference in temperature from the Central Valley. A heavy layer of clouds obscured the top of the rock, the protected home of Peregrine Falcon families. He found an outdated ten-room motel on a side street and checked in, the Pakistani proprietor explaining the availability of the continental breakfast served each morning, beginning at seven.

After examining the room, and the door locks, he grabbed the duffel and headed the few blocks to Main Street. What he needed was a cheap backpack to put the money and gun in. Everyone, at least those that looked like he did—partially shaved head, unshaven, bordering on the shabby—carried backpacks, not duffel bags. A small second-hand store had what he was looking for, something matching his appearance and not worth stealing.

Back in his room he transferred everything into the pack and added a mid-weight fleece top to cover the bundles of cash. On the bottom of the duffel he found the black notebook. He slipped it into a side pocket, along with the 9mm.

It dawned on him that he hadn't slept since the night before, and maybe it would explain his problem with trying to sort out the scenarios tumbling around inside his head like one of those winter scenes inside a glass ball filled with imitation snow. But first he needed to eat. He slung the backpack over his shoulder and walked to the line of waterfront shops and restaurants breathing in the distinct combination of salt air and fish.

Seagulls perched on pilings and railings along the walkway announced their presence, as if their characteristic yellow and white droppings hadn't. Out in the bay, seals barked their own attendance while heaving themselves up onto buoys or the decks of rarely used sailboats. Gray passed the wooden piers lined with functioning commercial fishing boats. At the far end of the pier a spanking clean Coast Guard cutter was tied to the dock, its flag flying high above the deck.

The restaurant offered a variety of local fish as well as the always available line of hamburgers and salads. A young girl wearing a shirt advertising the restaurant seated him by the window overlooking the harbor. After learning halibut was in season, Gray ordered a bowl of clam chowder and fish-and-chips.

He sat watching the sailboats anchored in the bay begin to swing around with the changing tide. An otter rose from the depths and rolled onto its back, clutching a shell to its middle. Gray's phone rang.

Only two people had the new number. It might mean Paco had information on the storage facility, or Simone had news.

"How did you get this number?" Gray wanted to know.

"I'm a cop, remember?" Detective Mondavi said. "Besides, I called your friend, Juarez, and convinced him to let me have it. I understand you called and, guess what, I drove past your place this morning. Somebody's been in already, unless you left the door open when you left."

Gray mentally thanked himself for dropping off the paintings at the gallery and brought up the reason for his call, the cops that followed him into the Canyon Road at three in the morning.

Mondavi swore he cancelled the surveillance but would look into it. His answer didn't satisfy Gray. Not everything was as it appeared to either of them.

Mondavi didn't ask where he was, or where he might go. Gray hung up after soliciting a promise from the detective that he would call if anything turned up about the girl. The waitress dropped off the platter of fish-and-chips and asked if there was anything wrong with the untouched chowder. Gray shook his head. He hadn't mentioned to Mondavi the Santa Ana PD car parked at the on-ramp of the interstate and being followed shortly thereafter. Was that a coincidence too?

36

Simone St. Pierre propped herself up in the bed and pulled the sheet up to cover her breasts. Sergio de Mello snored softly beside her.

In the soft gray light filtering through the curtains of the hotel suite, she focused on the dancing shadows on the wall and questioned the reason for her being there. After Gray's phone call, she had burst into the senator's home office, much to the affront she caused Mariano, who stood holding the door while she questioned the senator's word. She accused him of sending her on a mission for no other reason than to give Gray a sense of temporary safety while those who wanted him got organized.

Senator Jefferson Davis had reacted with total bewilderment and denial. She saw no indication he was telling her anything but the truth. Had Gray been mistaken in his assumption that the senator had sold him out?

But here I sit in Sergio's bed after coming over last night and practically undressing before we even said hello, then pushing a bewildered but totally agreeable Sergio onto the bed and throwing herself on top of him like a whore in heat. What am I turning into? And the bigger question, why?

The previous night, after apologizing profusely to the senator, Simone had tried to get a commitment out of him about the upcoming campaign. The staff needed an answer, something firm to say to the increasing speculation by the media as to why Senator Jefferson Davis had missed a pair of crucial votes in the Senate, and had not announced. The only answer he would give her was to wait a few more days and see what happens.

The only possibility that might resolve the problem was if the others found Gray and killed him. Then only time would tell if Montoya would release the girl as he said he would.

What do I do if the senator decides not to run?

She wanted something she could hold onto, returning again to the questions she needed answered concerning herself. Was she truly happy in what she was doing? She had thought so, certainly happier than many of her friends locked in marriages and child rearing, and having forsaken their career plans.

Sergio grunted and rolled over.

She shuddered, honestly confessing to rarely ever feeling truly happy, if there was such a state. Was she one of the countless people living day by day, in what Thoreau referred to as "quiet desperation"? She glanced at the naked back of the man beside her. Why not, she mused. Why not live a life of luxury and travel? Associate with those of a similar lifestyle. Worry about nothing except what country to visit next. Live on yachts comfortable enough to cruise the oceans of the world, to anchor in waters of the South Pacific, or the Mediterranean. Stay in five-star hotels or villas until the urge to move on overtook them.

This is what Sergio does with his time, or at least until he met me.

The dawn light crept up the wall, bringing into focus a picture hanging above the bed. She studied it, noting the play of light and shadows the artist had used to bring out the feeling he wanted to accomplish. With a rush she was back in California, in Conaire's studio, with the canvasses stacked against the walls, the coffee cans filled with brushes, rolled up tubes sitting on a paint-spattered table and a paper palette smeared with a profusion of colors where he had blended the hue he wanted. She could smell the heavy odor of linseed oil and paint. And the man in the apron, paint beneath his finger nails, a brush between his teeth, two more in his left hand, and the one he was working with poised like a rapier above the canvas in front of him, and her standing to one side and trying to envision the piece he was creating.

Simone closed her eyes and shuddered, fighting to bring herself back to reality.

Sergio woke and reached for her.

She slipped away from him and out of bed, pulling on his shirt as she did so.

"What is it?" he asked, rolling over and sitting up. "Are you leaving so soon?"

"I have to go back to my place before I go to the office, that's all."

He turned on the bedside light and clasped his hands behind his head. "Last night was…it was wonderful, yes. I wish you were always so, engaging?"

Simone stood at the edge of the bed with her back to him, feeling ashamed at the night's blatant act of sexuality. It was so unlike her, at least unlike anything recently.

"What is it?" he asked. "Have I perhaps offended you somehow or perhaps is it something to do with your trip?"

She shook her head. 'No, it's only me."

"I do not believe you. Since you're going to see this man in California, you are somehow different. Is it him?"

"Please, Sergio, I don't want to be interrogated at five in the morning. All right?"

"It is only that I would like to understand, Simone. You keep so much in yourself. It is not good."

"You're right. It's eating me up and I don't know where it's all leading."

"And this man you have been sent to see, I think you said his name was Gray. Will you need to return to see him again?"

"No, someone tried to kill him. He's gone now."

He reached to the bedside table for his cigarettes and lit one. "You cannot get in touch with him?"

Simone inhaled the smoke from his cigarette while she went over her last conversation with Gray. "I can, although I'm not sure he wants to talk to me."

"To run, people go to places they are familiar with, do they not? He has no family?"

"He has a grandfather somewhere on an Indian reservation up in Montana, I believe, but he didn't say he was going there." She rose from the bed and started for the shower.

Sergio stubbed out his cigarette. "I will come and wash your back, if you wish."

He sounded hopeful, but not now, she thought. Maybe later, or maybe not again. Oh, god, where was her life going. "I'm in a hurry. How long are you staying in Phoenix?" she asked before stepping into the shower.

He stood outside the shower door while she let the warm water cascade over her shoulders and back to wash away the scent of sex.

"I have not yet decided," he said. "I wished to speak to you about this."

"Why me?"

"Actually, I have not been completely honest with you. Yesterday I received a call from someone in my family. It would seem I must return home soon."

"Oh? How soon?"

"I am not positive of this, but when I go I would like you to come with me."

There it was. Not expected, or even hinted at. From the beginning of their relationship it was assumed it would run its course and they would walk away without regrets. But this would answer everything, wouldn't it, she thought. She could leave the senator and his troubles behind. Somehow she could deal with the Paris fiasco. All she had to do was say yes.

She open the door and took the towel he offered.

"Sergio, this is too sudden for me at this time. You'll have to give me time to think it over."

"But of course. I will not be leaving for a few days."

Why not? What do I have to lose? It might not be love, as some interpreted it, but it could be a comfortable life. Then why is it so difficult to put the decision off?

37

"Fuck. They missed. How could they miss?"

Castillo shrugged. "It is all he said. One of those sent is dead. The police have captured the others."

Miguel Zapata slammed his fist against the wall and cried out at his own stupidity as well as the pain he had caused himself. He cradled the bloodied hand, the one that the woman had bitten, under his armpit. Even this attempt to handle this situation for his father had failed.

Castillo shuffled through his notes and eased himself onto the plastic chair next to the broken television.

With his good hand Zapata poured himself a tumbler full of Jose Cuervo Familia Reserve and swallowed the tequila. "Who were these idiots?"

"They were some from Logan Heights in San Diego."

"Stupid fuckers. Have you sent others yet?"

Castillo lit a cigarette and crossed his legs. Zapata narrowed his eyes into a tight glare. *Soon, my friend, your day will come and I will rid myself of your counsel.*

"There is more," Castillo said.

"More? How can there be more?"

"The one who called with the information I have given you said he sent others to follow your orders. He apparently has someone who lives near Los Angeles he has contacted."

Zapata picked up the tequila bottle and took another drink. If nothing else it helped dull the pain. "So tell me what else you have that I will not like."

"Yes, well, he has said he sent the information to someone in a group that call themselves the *locos*. They are in the town called Norwalk, I think," Castillo said.

"I am not stupid. How were they to find this person?"

"I gave them the name of the man we have in their police department and he arranged it."

Zapata curled his lip and shouted, "Tell me. I cannot guess at what happened, but I know it is not good."

"Because of those that failed the night before, the man chose to leave in the early morning. They followed him on one of their main highways. They were waiting for the right opportunity."

Zapata looked at his injured hand. Some of the stitches had pulled loose. "But it never came. Am I right?"

"Miguel, I am giving you the only information the man had to give me. He said this man they were after seemed to know they were following him. He led them off this highway and into the mountains."

"And they killed him there. What is wrong with that?"

Castillo rubbed his face with both hands. "Miguel, listen to me. You must remember who this man is. He is not like one of these men who hang around you and carry their guns so everyone can see. This man is highly trained. Apparently, he set a trap for them."

"So when are you going to tell me they have killed him?"

Castillo shrugged. "I am afraid they have lost him."

Zapata groaned. "My god, tell me you know where we can find him again."

"No, Miguel, he has disappeared. I will have someone watch his house, but it is all we can do unless this man we have learns of where he has gone."

"Does he know?" Zapata said, pointing up at his father's house.

Castillo shook his head. "Not yet, but I must tell him."

"What will you tell him that will not get us killed, you fool? You said nothing would go wrong."

Castillo shrugged again. "It is too late to change what is done. I will convince him it was my idea to send those people. I will say I was under the impression he wished for me to take care of it."

Zapata's face twisted in a painful grin. "Good."

Castillo walked to the door, then turned back. "I will try to contact the one in the north to pressure him. Your father will want to know where this man has gone. And there is one more thing for you to think about, Miguel. Perhaps it is nothing."

"Then maybe you should keep it to yourself."

Castillo tilted his head. "Yes, perhaps, but this phone call I received. It was from that chief of police in Mexicali. He said he received a phone call from someone who wanted to know who he was."

"So, what is so important about this?"

"Thank about it, Miguel," Castillo said. "It was on that phone you gave him to use only for emergencies. How did this someone who called him get the number?"

A chill enveloped Miguel Zapata. The number had been written in the book.

38

Gray dropped the wet towel on the bathroom floor and began pulling on clean clothes. He checked the room to make certain he was leaving nothing behind and shouldered the backpack.

Dorn's Breakers Café sat on a cliff above the waterfront shops, overlooking the bay, although neither the landmark rock, nor the bay itself, could be seen through the thick layer of early morning fog.

He took a seat and ordered seafood benedict, with coffee. He lingered over his breakfast, letting the waitress refill his coffee and putting off for the moment the decision on where to run.

Back on the road, he followed the traffic up California Highway 1 until the stream of cars and motor homes turned into the parking areas for the Hearst Castle tours. The castle itself looked like a miniature dollhouse placed among the tall trees high up in the hills. The little community of San Simeon housed the warehouses where the eccentric millionaire had stored the artifacts he had collected from around the world.

Once past the tour lots, the highway reduced to two lanes of blacktop twisting through harrowing curves as it clung precariously to the edge of the North American continent.

A few miles below Big Sur he pulled into a turnout and parked the Jeep. He stuffed the backpack behind the driver's seat and locked the door, then stepped over the barrier and walked out to the edge of the cliff, stopping along the way to pick a handful of wildflowers. Forty feet below, the waves lashed the rocks, sending salt spray high into the air before the water receded and regrouped to gather strength for another assault. Gray tossed the flowers out and watched them float to the rocks below. The rocks where they had found her body.

She had never spoken of the demons that must have haunted her. He had been away at the time and returned to find a note that explained nothing. The note thanked him for the two years they had spent together at their easels and begged him to continue with the work she knew would guarantee him his place among Impressionistic artists in America. He owed her everything. She had come to understand what it was he sought. She took him into her life and taught him everything she knew about using paints and painter's tools to transfer images and moods onto canvas.

A few months later, a letter summoned him to an office in San Francisco, where an attorney read her will. She had left him the beautiful cottage overlooking the beaches and cypress of Carmel.

He walked back to the Jeep and drove north, through San Francisco, and across the Golden Gate Bridge. Highway 101 passed through green valleys and small communities before eventually working its way back to the coast and north, always north, and up the rugged coastline of Oregon, where little motels offered a haven for the night and a welcome shower.

He crossed the mighty Columbia River at Astoria, built by the fur-trading employees of John Jacob Astor. The phone lay on the seat beside the backpack. Occasionally he picked it up to see if it still worked. It never rang, which gave him no indication either way of where anything stood. He wanted to call, to hear her voice or find out the obvious, even if she had nothing new to report.

Cooler coastal temperatures prevailed as he drove through small towns, where rivers flowed out of mountains and fresh-cut logs floated in the water, waiting their turn for a ship to carry them to foreign markets. Seafood became a diet staple because he knew, without having to acknowledge it, that seafood was rare where he was going.

He stopped for lunch at the little resort community of Kalaloch, Washington, wedged between the crashing breakers of the Pacific and a rain forest. He sat in a bay window at a table with linen napkins and vowed to return someday to paint the storm-tossed driftwood stacked like children's play logs along an unfriendly beach, knowing that he could no longer work his way north.

The road turned eastward, winding along the Strait of Juan de Fuca, which separated the U.S. from Canada's Vancouver Island. On the ferry out of Port Townsend, Gray watched a mother holding a girl Carlie Kate's age in her arms and point out the silhouette of Mt. Olympus in the distance. What would he give to allow Carlie the same opportunity? What would he give to once more see her standing in front of his painting, her arms folded across her chest and her head tilted to one side, while he waited with breathless anticipation for her approval.

Leaving the western edge of the continent, he drove east, into the Cascade Mountains. At a place called Rainy Pass, he picked up two hikers, their packs laden with items, including a Christmas tree, and agreed to give them a ride to the nearest town for supplies. The girl punched her partner's arm and said, "trail magic," explaining to him it was a term hikers used to describe the help they often received from complete strangers.

On the east side of the mountains, Gray made the decision to forsake the easier route and take the road leading into the Colville Indian Reservation. He passed a sign that read "Nespelam 15," and slammed on the brakes. After checking to make sure no one was coming up behind him, he backed up and read the sign again.

"Son of a bitch," he said, fishing in the backpack and pulling out the mysterious notebook. He thumbed through the pages until he found it. Penciled in below the name were three Hispanic-sounding names and a phone number.

What did this little town in upper Washington State have in common with whoever murdered Bethany and left this book behind?

Nespelem advertised itself as a town of 236. Gray spotted a car, its engine running, parked beneath two large cottonwood trees, with the Colville Federated Tribe emblem on the side. He pulled alongside and got out. The car's sole occupant appeared to be sleeping when Gray tapped on the front fender and waited. The driver-side window opened slowly and a stream of cold air escaped.

"Nice day," Gray said, leaning against the fender and crossing his arms.

The man inside eyed him suspiciously, "Won't last."

"Probably right," Gray said. "Clouds building up over the mountains could mean rain."

"You have something you want? Or just passing through and feeling the need to talk? Grand Coulee's down the road the way you came, if that's what you're looking for."

Gray scratched an itchy scab beneath his beard. "Things quiet around here?"

The car door opened slowly and the figure emerging gradually stretched himself out to his full length, then adjusted his gun belt, dropping his cigarette butt in the dirt and crushing it with the toe of his cowboy boot. "Guess you're hard of hearing. Grand Coulee's down the road a piece. There ain't nothing for you here."

"Billie Little Bear over in Browning's a mite friendlier."

A slow grin split the leathery features of the man who had probably slept in his car in this spot for many years, while on duty. "How's that skinny beanpole doing these days?"

It was Gray's turn to grin. "Well, unless he's been run over by a steamroller, he's not the one I know."

"So you know him?"

Gray nodded. "Chased girls together before they shunted us off in different direction."

"Blood?"

"Quarter only. Grandfather is though."

The man held out his hand, "Charlie Fellows."

"Conaire Gray."

"So now you've got my interest up, what're you looking for here?"

Gray wasn't sure how much he wanted to reveal. "Actually, just passing through, but I heard some of the reservations were having trouble with pushers from down south. Wind River was mentioned. Meth problem, I understand."

The man spat in the dirt, took a crumbling pack of cigarettes from his shirt pocket, and shook one out. "We got our problems, no doubt there. We got meth, marijuana, alcohol of course. Unemployment's a problem. Gives our young bucks too much time on their hands. Some of them get high often enough, and they all get drunk most nights, and days, too, though beats me where they get the money. Keeps me and the others pretty busy when you consider there's only six of us looking after twenty three hundred square miles of reservation."

Gray said he would pass along Chief Fellows' greeting and got back in his Jeep. He crossed over the Columbia River at the Grand Coulee Dam and ran east again. He knew there was more going on in the reservation than Chief Fellows was ready to admit, blood or not.

East Glacier lay within the Blackfoot Indian reservation boundaries east of the Continental Divide and serviced visitors travelling to Glacier National Park. A few small privately owned motels and restaurants operated during the summer months on the narrow side streets. The few blocks of Main Street consisted of boarded-up businesses and local haunts, and the BNSF Railway Station.

Billie Little Bear had suggested meeting for dinner at Serrano's, a Mexican restaurant half a block off Main. When Gray pulled into a parking spot, his friend was sitting on a wooden bench beneath strings of red chili peppers, waiting for a table. A dozen other people stood chatting nearby.

A big grin greeted Gray.

"Billie, you look like you've lost weight."

"You tell my wife that. She keeps telling me I should do something about it."

Gray shook the man's hand, then wrapped his arms around the much shorter man. "By the way, a guy name of Charlie Fellows, over in Colville, says hello."

Billie Little Bear chuckled. "How is that old Nez Perce anyway?"

"Seems All right, though it appears he has his hands full up there."

"Don't we all? I had no idea how bad it could get till I took this job. Seems every night I get called out to take care of some dispute or other. Now we have this debate about fracking. They say there's oil under the reservation and oil means jobs and money. The old ones say we're desecrating our land; the young ones want the money and to hell with the land. Nobody cares about those that come after us, I guess."

A blonde waitress stuck her head out of the door and waved to him.

"Guess they have a table for us."

"You get here early?" Gray said, surveying the crowd waiting for a table.

"One of the many benefits of being the law in this area, money not being one of them."

As they made their way through the crowd, Gray couldn't help noticing that none of the servers appeared to be Native Americans. He mentioned it when they were seated.

Billie Little Bear sat with his back against the wall, facing the door. "If you check out most of the places in town, it's the same. Some of the help come all the way from Europe to work for the summer. Others come from all over the country. Come October, all the tourists leave. This whole town about closes up. Same thing down the road in Browning."

"Why so many outsiders? Can't imagine you don't have high unemployment, same as everyone else."

Gray received a shrug for an answer. After a minute, Little Bear called the waitress over and they ordered. When she had gone, he said, "Don't want to work for low wages, I guess. Government takes care of most of them. Got so they feel it's owed them."

They dipped tortilla chips into a large bowl of fresh salsa and waited for their cold beer. Most of the customers appeared to know each other, and a number of couples had gathered around a small bar in the corner where three choices of wine was offered, along with beer or margaritas.

Finally, Gray got around to asking, "You see my grandfather lately?"

"Saw him last week. Came into town to get some supplies. Didn't say much. You know what those old ones are like. Sometimes wonder if we all end up that way. I asked if he'd heard from you. He just grunted and shook his head. Didn't appear to think he'd be seeing you soon, either."

Gray toyed with a chip.

"You fixing to stop by, I hope?" Billie asked.

"Thought I would," Gray said.

"Why, if you don't mind me asking?"

Their plates of pork enchiladas and refried beans were placed in front of them, following by a warning about hot plates. It gave Gray a moment to decide what he would say.

"Need time to think. You know how it is, big cities and everything. Sometimes you need to get away."

Gray looked up into the depths of a pair of black eyes in a round face that had deceived people for years. Billie Little Bear used his short, fat stature, and slow-talking façade, to lure people into believing they were dealing with just another dumb Indian driving a new pickup and living on the Native American welfare system, while the family lived in little more than a wooden hovel surrounded by pickups from the past.

"Sometimes," Little Bear said. "And sometimes you have to leave."

Gray refused to take the bait. They finished their meal and, while sipping a second beer, talked about old friends and growing up on the reservation. Gray insisted on paying for the meal.

On the way out, Little Bear pocketed a couple of toothpicks and slipped one out of its wrapper while they stood on the porch fronting the restaurant. "Funny you showing up," he said, chewing on the end of the toothpick.

"Why's that?"

"Oh, just a day or so ago one of our young unemployed, and probably unemployable, fellows stopped by the office to shoot the bull. Never done it before. Ends up by mentioning your name and says he heard we were once friends, and then goes on a while about a bunch of crap, then says, "You ever hear from him?""

Gray felt a chill flow over him. "Say anything else?"

"Not much. I said you owed me money so I doubted you would get in touch. Fellow didn't seem to know what else to say so he left."

Half way to his car, Little Bear stopped and turned back. "It's a small world, Irish," he said, using a nickname given to Gray and referring to his grandmother's blood. "Let me know if I can help."

39

Gray spent the night in a tiny motel off the main road. In the morning he carefully shaved off the beard that had grown over the burn scabs, leaving blotched patches of skin.

Driving slowly down a road filled with memories, he crossed the Two Medicine River where the bluffs rose up to meet the gray-blue outline of the Rockies. A dirt road dropped away from the two-lane highway and followed the river west, toward its birth near the crest of the Continental Divide.

Each bend and curl of the river revealed places where he and his mother had sat, her with her easel and watercolors, and he lying in the grass beside her chair. Little had changed over the years.

The road swung to the left, and he saw the cabin nestled among the elm trees, the trees his mother had used in so many of her paintings. The paintings carefully placed in cheap frames bought in Cut Bank and sold in the souvenir shops in Browning to Glacier-bound tourists. He remembered her painstaking miniature depiction of an eagle on the corner of her pieces, along with "Peta," the name she used.

Two horses stood tail to nose in the pole corral by the barn, their tails keeping the flies in a constant state of distress. He coasted to a stop and sat. The old man had heard the approach of the car and turned, his pitchfork poised over a pile of hay.

The years seemed to have had little effect on the man. The checkered shirt still drew tight across the wide shoulders, the waist not what it might have been years before but still one of a man familiar with the labors of a small ranch. Maybe the braided hair beneath the wide-brimmed Stetson displayed more silver than Gray remembered.

Gray hoped he had not waited too long to return. He parked beside the Chevy pickup and got out, breathing in the smell of the old homestead, wood smoke spiraling out of the stone chimney, the rank odor of the corral, the sweet smell of fresh-cut hay, and the country itself, brought by the wind that swept down from the Canadian prairies to the north.

"You're looking good, Grampa."

The old man leaned the pitchfork against the corral fence and turned. Gray waited, unsure of what to expect.

His grandfather's eyes softened. "I see your mother in your face, and your grandmother. I am happy you have come back. They would be to."

Gray stepped forward into an awkward embrace, feeling the moisture in his eyes.

"Should have come sooner, but things got in the way."

"Some things should not come between us. There is no one else but us now."

"I know, and I'm sorry for that. All this time I felt you wouldn't understand," Gray said. "I could never tell you why."

His grandfather pointed to a bale of hay. "Put that in the corral and cut it loose. I have not had my breakfast yet and you look hungry. Your mother loved to watch you eat."

Gray grinned and dragged the hay through the gate, closing it behind him and cutting the strings binding the bale. Both horses pushed their noses in and pulled away a mouthful.

Over pancakes, eggs, and bacon and the strong boiled coffee his grandfather relished, they talked, nothing heavy, simple things like the weather. The old man said he saw Billie Little Bear the week before and Gray said he had heard.

"You mind if I stay a few days?" Gray asked.

The old man cleared off the table and sat back down. "This is your home. This land we sit on will be yours. You can stay forever if you wish. I would be happy."

"Maybe someday," Gray said, "but it's too soon. There are people who would like to find me. I don't want them coming here."

"I have not asked before, but if you wish to tell me I will listen. Your grandmother was very good at listening to me."

No one spoke for a while, both basking in each other's company without having to say anything. Then Gray said, "I wish I had known her. Ma talked about her often. You never said much but I couldn't help seeing how much you missed her. Hard to imagine a girl from Ireland coming out here and marrying into an Indian tribe."

The old man's eyes glistened. "Yes, we had young people they said needed to be educated, the government that is. They wanted us to live different from how we were living. She was a teacher, like your mother." He brushed crumbs off the table and gazed out the open window. "They did not like it when we married."

"No," Gray said, remembering arguments between his mother and father before his father left them. "Whenever we went to a new place to live, Dad always introduced Ma as someone from Europe. Then when he got drunk he would fly into a rage and call her a half-breed. She would say he knew that before he married her."

They sat over their coffee, Gray feeling the cabin memories return: the door down the short hallway that led to his old bedroom, the wood stove with the pile of firewood it had been his job to chop and stack, and above the door his grandfather's old Winchester carbine that Gray had used to hunt everything from the lightning-quick pronghorns to mule deer.

"You speak of your father. It was good he left. You did not think so at the time. Neither did your mother, but it was good."

"Why do you say that?"

The old man sipped his coffee, his eyes gazing out over his land, then said, "If he had not left, I would have killed him, for your sake, and your mother's. One day he would have killed her if he had not left. Maybe he saw that also."

Gray shook his head slowly. "I never knew that. All I remember is that one day he was no longer there."

On his second day back, they drove out the dusty road to the rocky patch of ground overlooking the Two Medicine River that had been used as a cemetery since the men in the black robes had come west to teach the Indians the ways of their religion. In his hand his grandfather clutched a handful of daisies they had picked in the field by the cabin.

The graves of his mother and grandmother lay side by side, outlined by a simple row of small stones; two small wooden crosses bore their names. Other graves, seemingly placed in no particular order, were marked with similar crosses, or with simple stone markers. Plastic and paper flowers in Mason jars, or simply held in place by a rock, competed with an occasional string of feathers draped over the cross to signify someone's visit. His grandfather knelt and placed the daisies between the graves.

"Your grandmother loved daisies. I think it was because they grew so near our house, and she could walk in them and bring them home."

"Ma would pick them and paint them. Not to sell though. No one wanted to buy a painting of daisies in the souvenir store."

They stood by the shallow depressions in the earth without speaking until the sun slipped behind the mountains.

"I hope you will see that this is where I will lie when my time has come. I hope to be with them again."

Gray could only nod, wondering who would see to his grandfather's request if anything happened to him. He then decided to tell the old man everything.

The next afternoon they sat on the porch, the sounds of the water rushing over rocks floating up the slope from the river. A lazy summer day with his grandfather speaking of the problems of the reservation, while inwardly Gray knew the old man was attempting to digest the story Gray had related.

"There is never enough for our young men to do," the old man said. "They say unemployment is around seventy percent, but now these oil companies are promising great things for us if we let them drill into our sacred land and take out something. Maybe it is our heart they want to take out. Some have already said that it is good; they like the money. But what about those that come after, when the money is gone and the land is empty?"

Gray's eyes picked up the two swirling clouds of dust on the road across the river as he half dosed, listening to his grandfather. They both sat, comfortable with each other and their thoughts. For the first time since the trouble began he felt a sense of peace. He dozed in the heat of the afternoon.

Then he bolted upright as something slammed into a wooden post, sending a shower of splinters onto his head. The crack of the rifle shot echoed across the river canyon. Gray heard a grunt and threw himself across his grandfather, driving him to the deck as more shots tore into the log wall above them.

He fought back the first signs of panic, quickly reverting to the memories of his training. Hell, this made three times in the last week or so. As more slugs ripped out pieces of the wall and deck railings, Gray judged that the shots came from two positions, one in the trees across the river, the others from a pile of rocks in a gravelly bend in the river somewhat below the level of the first shooter. Both positions covered the front of the cabin and the door leading into it. Using his elbows, Gray pulled himself to the back of the porch and up against the side of the house. His eyes swept over the line of willows and trees across the river, trying to locate the shooter's position.

"Damn it, concentrate," he muttered, realizing he was looking and not seeing. He chose a point to the right of where he thought the shots came from and began again. Almost immediately he saw movement. He shifted his focus to the bend in the river and realized that by pulling himself against the wall, the shooters in the riverbed could not see him.

"I can't see you and you can't see me either," he whispered, "and that gives me an advantage because you don't know I know this."

The old man lying beneath him groaned. That's when Gray saw the thin stream of blood seeping out from under his grandfather's body.

"Grampa, how bad you hurt? Do you know?"

"I do not know."

"Don't try to move. Just lie there. They can't see you where you are." He didn't know if it was true or not, but he knew movement of any kind would draw more fire and would only increase the bleeding.

Gray saw right away that if the shooter moved up the slope he could get a clear shot at anyone who tried to make it through the door and into the cabin. Gray braced himself. He would have precious seconds to make it. He rehearsed the moves in his head. Two or three steps and dive through. Once inside he would get a chance to grab the .30-.30 off the rack above the door.

His grandfather shifted slightly. Someone would pay. Whatever happened in the next few minutes, he knew no one could claim he was not within his rights to fight. No one could claim it was not self-defense.

His breathing slowed as dormant training returned. He went over the movements again.

Across the river a section of willows swayed, signaling the gunman was moving. Gray exploded off the porch, diving through the open doorway and rolling as soon as he hit the floor. Bullets flayed the door and the interior of the cabin. When the shooting stopped, Gray took it to mean the shooter needed to reload. He edged over to the wall by the door and reached up above his head, taking down the box of Winchester 150-grain ammunition. Thankfully, it still had a dozen rounds in it. All he needed was the carbine.

Seconds passed, with no following shots. He waited another moment, then eased himself up against the wall and reached above the door, lifting the old rifle out of its rack of horns. He levered it half open and saw it had a round in the chamber. He couldn't tell if the tubular magazine held more, but he doubted his grandfather would not have kept it full.

He jumped as a cavalcade of slugs shattered the windows on his right, followed by others systematically working through the other windows. He said a silent prayer for the thick log walls of the cabin. Anything else and the slugs from the high-powered rifles he figured they were using would come right through. He spun around when the window on the far side exploded in a burst of shattered glass. Either one of the shooters had moved or another had joined the fight. If that was the case, they could easily work their way in close and have him cornered.

Out here on the banks of the Two Medicine River, with no phones, it could be days before anyone shows up.

Gray's one chance lay in getting out of the cabin before they figured out he was cornered. If he could cross the space between the cabin and a shallow ditch beside the road, he would have the high ground on at least two of them. They wouldn't know where he was, and they wouldn't know about the rifle.

Through the open door he saw that the old man had pulled himself back to the protection of the wall. Gray called out, trying to reassure him. He didn't like the amount of blood on the deck. He knew he had a good chance to handle the situation over time, but time wasn't something he had in abundance.

He crawled to the far side of the house and pushed open the last unbroken window, climbing through and dropping to the ground. The fifty yards of open space to the ditch would leave him exposed as soon as he began to cross it. It would depend on how quickly they spotted him and how good they were. Scoped hunting rifles, in experienced hands, could kill as well as any weapon available; he knew that better than most. But he had surprise on his side, since they still thought they had him surrounded in the house.

A slug slammed into the window above his head. "Forget the surprise," Gray mumbled. "It's me and fifty yards of killing ground." He sprinted away from the house and raced across the open space, zigzagging as the puffs of dirt at his feet preceded the cracks of the rifles. Twenty-five feet and the number of shots increased as he came into view of all three shooters.

He grunted as something stung his arm. One of them had gotten lucky. Five yards to go and he veered off to his left, away from where they probably expected him to aim. It threw the shooters off for the precious seconds he needed. He crossed the last few feet and dove into the shallow, weed-filled ditch.

"Well," he muttered, "they know where I am and they know I have a rifle. But they don't know how well I can use it."

He flexed his left arm. The bullet had taken a slice out of the bicep but not enough to inhibit its use. For the moment the shooters held their fire. Gray tore off the sleeve of his shirt and tied it around his arm.

The shallow ditch ran alongside the road. He rolled over onto his stomach and began crawling, looking for a spot where he could get a clear view. He had forgotten about the culvert running under the road leading to his grandfather's small ranch. It had been a hiding place growing up, with only pretend enemies to fight. He wondered if he could still make it through.

He parted the weeds growing in the dried mud and gravel at the opening of the corrugated pipe and eased himself inside, remembering the first time he had attempted it. He pushed the Winchester out in front of him and inched his way through. At the far end, he dropped into a three-foot hole the water had carved out. From the end of the culvert the cabin blocked his view of the shooter across the river, but he could make out a figure crouched among the rocks in the riverbed below. The third shooter had to be somewhere along the road above him. Gray would have to get him to reveal his position so he could get a clear shot, which meant revealing his own.

He levered out the shells—seven of them—then slid one in and chambered it before returning the other six. He squatted down in the ditch to think about what he was about to do. People were about to die. They had already made it clear they intended to kill him. Still, the decision to kill others did not come easily. He knew his ability. The carbine in his hands might only be equipped with iron sights, but it was a familiar weapon and he could kill with it, even at that distance.

He pushed aside the brush and took a bead on a spot where the shooter in the rocks had tried to conceal himself. Three hundred yards separated them. He picked out a rock behind the shooter's position and fired.

His bullet chiseled chips of stone out of the rock an inch from where he aimed, sending the hidden shooter diving out into the open.

Gray adjusted for the wind coming across the river valley and held the man's chest in his sights, hesitating. The man lay helpless.

A slug clanged off the iron culvert a foot away. Gray scampered a few feet along the bottom of the ditch to a spot where the brush thinned. He saw the one in the riverbed scoping the area where he lay. Gray made his decision. He took a deep breath, bringing the carbine up in one fluid motion and finding the man in his sights. Without conscious thought, he adjusted for the wind and squeezed off the shot, then instinctively levered another round into the chamber.

The man staggered, his rifle sliding out of his hands, then dropped to his knees as he tried to take a step before falling face down in the river. Gray knew he would never get up.

As more shots searched the brush where he lay, Gray moved back to the mouth of the culvert and peered over the lip of gravel on the side of the road. A small grove of aspen and willows on the slope above his position drew his attention. Gray's eyes moved across the thicket and back until he found what he was looking for. His breathing slowed as he waited.

Leaves fluttered in the breeze. His eyes followed the natural sway of branches and the movement not caused by the wind. He began at a point to the right of the center of the small grove and systematically placed his shots. On the fourth shot, a figure fell through the willows onto the ground and lay in the short grass.

Gray waited a moment before moving out of the ditch and onto the road. Using the house to block his movement, he worked his way back to the window and around the side of the house until he could see the spot where the first shooter had been.

A cloud of dust on the road across the river indicated the last one had decided to beat a retreat.

His grandfather still lay in the same position. Gray gently rolled him over onto his back. Drying blood soaked the front of his shirt.

"We'll get you to town right away, Grampa. I think you'll be all right."

The old man's weathered face broke into a painful grin. "I hear you have decided to become a warrior again. Maybe it is not too late for you."

The sound of tires scrunching in the gravel froze Gray. He picked up the carbine and slipped around the corner as a car door slammed shut.

Billie Little Bear stood beside the dusty SUV bearing tribal insignia. Another figure wearing worn blue jeans and a blue shirt stepped out of the driver's side. Both had their hands on the butts of their side arms.

Gray leaned the Winchester up against the wall and stepped out. "Billie, it's me, Conaire. My grandfather's been shot. Can you radio in and get an ambulance out here?"

The squat figure of the chief motioned to his deputy, who climbed back in the SUV. "How bad?"

"Got him in the shoulder. He's lost a lot of blood."

Little Bear nodded. "Won't take them long to get here. Want to tell me what happened here?"

Gray went to check on his grandfather again before relating the attack and about the one that got away.

"Well, I don't think he did," Little Bear said. "We heard some talk and headed this way to check it out. Appears we didn't get here soon enough, but this other fellow passed us like his tail feathers were ablaze, so I had my deputy radio back to town to pick him up when he arrived."

"Know him?"

"Oh, yeah. Lived all his life here on the reservation. Not much good for anything except drinking and getting into trouble." Billie Little Bear walked away from Gray and looked down over the Two Medicine River for a few minutes before returning. His deputy rejoined him.

"Now you say there were three of them. We passed one up the road a ways who won't be going anywhere, except some hole in the ground, and there's that one that skedaddled. That's two."

"There's another down in the river bed by the big bend."

Little Bear said something to the deputy, who started across the pasture toward the river. "Well, if what we heard about you some years back is true I don't suppose that one will need any help either. Let's go see to your grandfather."

Gray led him to the front of the house.

Little Bear inspected the area where the bullet had entered. "Don't want to disturb it none. We'll let the experts do that. Expect they'll be coming soon,"

"What's next?" Gray asked.

"Well, that's a good question. Been some time since we had a shooting. Now I've got two bodies and a good-for-nothing to deal with. I knew the other night you were into something you didn't want to talk about."

40

A row of white plastic chairs sat against one wall, all occupied by those hoping to see one of the two doctors on duty at the small community hospital serving both tribal and non-tribal individuals. Gray stood by the bulletin board, rocking back and forth on his heels as he waited. When he had arrived two hours earlier, the receptionist informed him his grandfather was in surgery. No one could tell him about his condition. The same receptionist patiently assured those waiting that someone would see them soon.

He closed his eyes and replayed the events leading up to the attack. He recalled Little Bear's mentioning someone had inquired about him, and that's when he should have gotten in his car and gone in some other direction. He had brought his trouble to the reservation. If he had left, his grandfather wouldn't be in an operating room fighting for his life, and two more men he had never met wouldn't be dead. The signs were right in front of him, even the twin pillars of dust rising into a cloudless Montana sky that should have warned him something out of the ordinary was happening. One car alone on that back road was almost a traffic jam. Two cars together meant he should have gone on full alert immediately.

Gray moved aside as someone paused to read a notice on the bulletin board about a meeting to discuss the merits of allowing the big oil companies permission to tap into the heart of tribal land and suck out its juices. When he had read the same notice earlier, he couldn't help remembering the landscape of oil derricks and horsehead rigs dotting the landscape in Southern California.

He ran his hands over what was left of his hair and took a deep breath, his thoughts returning to those he had killed a few hours before, and the mounting list of deaths he was accountable for. How many more, he kept asking himself, and was Carlie Kate going to be another? If they finally caught up with him, would it end there? There was always the hope, slim but still there, that Montoya would turn her loose. The girl was the reason this whole affair was happening. Nom it wasn't. He was the reason these people had died, and he was the reason others would also, as long as he ran.

The glass door swung open and Billie Little Bear came in, nodding to the receptionist. He indicated he wanted Gray to follow him back outside.

"Anything?" Little Bear asked.

Gray shook his head.

"Well, he's one of the toughest old buzzards I know. If I were a betting man, I'd put my money on him."

"Hope you're right. I'd sure hate to lose him now."

"Listen, I took a few minutes to talk to the one we picked up. He was really cooperative after I told him his friends were dead and you were still on the loose." Little Bear laughed. "Made me promise I'd keep him till you were gone. Funny how some people will talk, and I didn't even need to persuade him."

"He tell you anything?"

"Not much. It appears whomever is their supplier passed on the information someone could score big time if they brought in your scalp. They figured they'd sashay out there and get rid of you and the old man, burn the cabin down, and nobody would ever know what happened."

"They didn't think you'd look into it?"

"Some of our local members aren't the swiftest antelope in the herd, and maybe their brains are a little scrambled from white man's feel-good powder."

"Any idea who this supplier is they're talking about?"

Little Bear shook his head. "No, all they had was a cell-phone number. Then some low-paid gopher brings in the stuff and collects the money."

Gray remained silent and Little Bear asked, "Doesn't it bother you so many people are looking for you?"

"They're not giving me enough time to worry," Gray replied. "Wherever I go, it seems they find me."

Little Bear waited for a young nurse coming on duty to pass. He opened the door for her, then turned back to Gray. "How do you figure they found you here so quick? In fact, that visit I got seemed to indicate they were expecting you to come here."

"Does, doesn't it?" Gray said. The same conclusion had come to him the moment he had time to think about it. "You figure on arresting me or what?"

"Well, I pretty much know what went down here, with the other fellow's confession and all. I may only be a dumb Indian, but I think if you stick around awhile I'll surely have more bodies to pick up and a whole lot of questions to answer."

"So, what are you saying, Billie?"

"I don't know why all this is happening to you, and I have a feeling I don't want to know." Little Bear leaned in close. "Get off my reservation, and the sooner the better. Today, in fact, would be just fine with me."

Gray sensed Little Bear wasn't joking. Their friendship only went so far. "What about my grandfather? He's going to need taken care of for a while."

"Don't worry. I've got a young lady took some nursing off the reservation and needs a job. She's lived on a farm, so feeding a couple of swayback horses won't be a problem for her. I figure you could help by giving her a job. Kind of a thank you to me for not keeping you around a spell."

"I can do that, soon as I know for sure he's going to be okay."

Half an hour later, both men worked on paper cups of machine-dispensed coffee and talked of their school days and the problems that plagued the reservation. Gray was about to mention his discovery in the Colville National Forest when the doctor strolled into the waiting room and headed for the machines in the back of the room. Gray and Little Bear rose.

"Looks like he's going to be fine," the man said before anyone asked.

"He's doing okay, then?" Gray said.

"Yes. He's lost a lot of blood, but the bullet went all the way through. And luckily it didn't hit anything vital."

"When can I see him?"

The young doctor grimaced at the first sip of coffee. "Damn, Chief, can't you guys bend a few reservation rules and get a Starbuck's in here? This stuff is going to poison someone one of these days." He turned to Gray. "I guess you're a relative, so it'll be okay to see him for a few minutes. You won't have long. I gave him something to make him sleep. He needs that more than anything else."

Little Bear waited for the doctor walk back down the hall before speaking. "You go in and say your goodbyes and then disappear. Don't go back to the cabin. I want to sleep peacefully tonight."

Gray nodded an acknowledgement. He exchanged phone numbers with Little Bear and was directed to the room at the end of the corridor.

The plastic blinds in the room let in enough light for Gray to see the loss of color in his grandfather's face. He took a deep breath and walked to the side of the bed. Tubes ran from a bag of solution hanging on a hook beside the bed and to the old man's arm. His eyes were closed.

Gray took the weathered hand in his own and held it. "You awake?"

The old man nodded, and Gray felt a small amount of pressure in his grip. "The doctor says you're going to be all right. Might have to stay here for a few days, though."

"The horses?"

"He'll send someone out there who'll look after you and the horses until you get back on your feet."

His grandfather's eyes opened. "What about you?"

"I can't stay. It's not safe for anybody as long as I'm around."

"Where will you go now?"

"I'm not certain. You might say I'm still working on it."

"There is always the hills."

Gray grinned. "You mean off the reservation hills, right?"

A slight smile creased the old man's face before his eyes closed again. Gray pulled a chair closer to the bed and sat down.

Half an hour later, Gray started to ease his hand out of his grandfather's grasp. The grip tightened. "I thought you were asleep. Doc says it's what you need right now."

"I will sleep later. But now I need to speak while I can."

"We can do that later, after things calm down some. I'll call you," Gray said.

"No, now. You have told me the story of what happened to you, and now I see that what you say is true. I have been thinking when you thought I slept."

"Don't talk. You need to rest."

"Soon, but first tell me. Do you think these people will stop looking for you?"

Gray looked down at the two hands clasped together. He placed his other hand over the two. "No, that's why I have to leave. I don't want to go and leave you like this, but I have to."

The old man seemed to summon a reservoir of strength. "No. It will happen again and others will die. You may be hurt, or die, and I do not want that to happen."

Gray held up his hand to stop him. He could see how much the effort was taking out of his grandfather.

"Not yet. I will finish," his grandfather said. "I have told you this, but you were not ready to listen. In your blood is the blood of the *Niitsitapi*. The white man chose to call us the Piegan. We were great warriors. Yours may be thinned by that of your father, but your grandmother's people across the seas I am told were also great warriors."

Gray waited a moment, thinking he was finished, then asked, "What are you trying to tell me?"

"If this child you speak of is still alive, she is waiting for someone to help her. She has no one else now but you. You must go after her. You are not afraid. I have seen this. You can die running or you can die fighting. You are all that is left of me. I do not want to see you die, but I do not want to die without knowing you will fight for what you believe is right."

The effort exhausted had him. Gray watched the tears seep out of his grandfather's eyes and flood the wrinkles in the weathered cheeks. He felt the grip loosen, and he, too, wept silently.

Gray knew what he had to do. Running wasn't solving the problem. He had already killed two men, and unless his pursuers did the same to him, or gave up looking for him, others would die. He had killed Emiliano Montoya's daughter and grandson, and Montoya was responsible for Bethany's death. In his own heart, Gray felt they were even, but he knew the drug lord's quest for further revenge would only end in his death. But until that happened, he wondered how many more would die and leave innocent families to mourn. As long as he ran, death would follow close behind. One way or the other, he had to put a stop to it.

He gripped his grandfather's hand again. "I'll go and find her, Grampa."

The old man's face softened. "I would like to meet this girl. Will you bring her to me?"

Gray felt a wave of emotion flow through him. It took a moment before he could speak, his voice barely a whisper. "She would like to meet you, too."

41

Montoya sensed someone at the door to his office and turned to see Castillo standing there.

"Emiliano, a moment of your time please," the man said.

Montoya motioned for him to enter. "You are here to give me good news, I hope."

Castillo shut the door behind him and took a chair in front of the desk. "I have a confession to make."

Montoya waited, then said, "Tell me."

"It is about Miguel. He begged me to find him a way to regain your respect. He somehow convinced me to let him take care of this problem in California for you."

Montoya knew by Castillo's demeanor that the problem had not been taken care of waved for him to continue.

"It would appear those he sent have failed."

"Then you send someone who is more reliable. You have been with me long enough to know better than to let him handle something like this. He has little ability other than running errands. You are the one who convinced me to send him in the first place."

"Emiliano, the fault is all mine. It is not that those sent failed so much as that the man has now disappeared."

"Disappeared?" Montoya slammed his hand on the top of his desk. "Disappeared. It has taken me eight years to find this man and now he has disappeared."

"We will find him again."

"Do you think he knows why he was attacked? Perhaps he will only hide for a few days and then return to his place."

Castillo shook his head. "No, I believe he was told. I cannot be sure, but my information is he was told who had taken the girl and why. We did not consider this when we gave our instruction to the senator."

"Very well. Have our people search for him. If he is located, do not give his location to Miguel. Is this understood?"

"Of course. I will do so immediately," Castillo said and rose from the chair.

Montoya still had not made up his mind, but this new information changed the balance of his decision. "There is one more thing before you go."

Castillo sat back down.

Montoya tattooed the desk with his fingers, then said, "What if you were to find a man, a man who knows where to look for people and what to do with them when he has found them. And, of course, someone with a great deal of discretion. Do you know of such a man?"

Castillo coughed and crossed his legs. "These men you are referring to, I think they are available."

"Do we have such a man?" Montoya asked.

"No, none that we could use for what you have in mind."

"Do you know where to find such a man?"

"I know of two who could be persuaded to take on this responsibility. I am sure there are more," Castillo said, drawing his words out carefully. "It is not always easy, as you can imagine, but I know how to proceed. One may be easier than the other."

Montoya opened a box on his desk and withdrew a cigar, then sat back in his chair. "Tell me about them."

"These men live on their reputations, you understand. Their failures are not advertised as are their successes. However, from what I have gathered, both men have built what you might call a portfolio of accomplishments. One is from Brazil, or at least that is his home country. He is known to work much in Europe and Asia, although I believe he has also taken employment in the U.S. at times.

His record is said to be unblemished. He is very expensive and not always available."

Montoya stripped the cellophane from the cigar and clipped the end. "And the other?"

"More of a man of this region. He has worked for a couple of your competitors, but was originally with Los Zeta. Then he decided to go independent."

"Los Zetas. How long ago was this?"

"It was before they decided to work for themselves."

"Then he was had military training?"

"Of course," Castillo said. "He was sent by the Panamanian army to America to train with their Special Forces. They call it the School of the Americas. Like others, when he returned, he abandoned the military and joined Los Zeta."

"So he is familiar with the north. That would be useful. How good is he, do you know?"

"From what I have learned," Castillo said, "he is very good. They say you must first get past his arrogance, but I imagine that assists all of them in believing they are superior to those they are sent after. I also understand his price is more reasonable."

Montoya rolled the cigar between his fingers while he digested the information. A thin smile spread across his face. "You have thought about our problem, it would seem."

Castillo tilted his head. "I thought it was an option needing exploration."

"Good. That is why you are sitting in that chair. Now, how can we be positive our hands will remain clean?"

"I have been assured it is vital to their reputations that they never divulge who their employers are. Rumors exist, of course, but that is unavoidable. The proof is elusive."

"And his price?"

"Less than the other. He has not yet reached the pinnacle of his chosen profession," Castillo said with a chuckle.

Montoya closed his eyes and squeezed the bridge of his nose. "How soon can you contact this person?"

"He is available immediately, I understand."

"I wish to meet him. How soon can it be arranged?"

Montoya saw the hesitation in Castillo's manner. "Is this not possible?"

"These men prefer to remain as, how shall I say, out of sight."

"Arrange it. Tell him who is requesting this meeting."

"Of course, I will arrange it," Castillo said.

"Of course, he will need something to begin with," Montoya said. "Put pressure on those who might know where this man who has disappeared will run."

Castillo rose from his chair. "And the child. What do you wish to do with her?"

"We might need persuasion of some sort. You know what must be done. Send Fuentes. We need to know the level of his reliability."

42

Gray returned to the cabin to pick up a few things, despite Little Bear's warning. He chuckled, remembering all the stories told to him by the tribe elders about the government's insistence on all members staying on the reservation land. Now he was being told to get out, although he couldn't blame Little Bear. The man was only trying to maintain the peace in a sometimes volatile land.

A sense of calm and purpose had settled over him since his decision. Still, he had to come up with some sort of a plan, although where to begin eluded him at the moment.

Gray parked the Jeep behind the cabin. He figured Billie Little Bear would probably send someone to make sure Gray stayed away. Gray didn't want to be around when he showed up.

He went to his old room and withdrew a small chest from beneath the narrow bed. If he intended to embrace his heritage, a good place to start was in the chest.

Underneath the odds and ends his mother had kept for him, he found the old Hudson's Bay Company long-bladed trade knife, its wooden handle wrapped with hide and sinew. He placed the knife and the beaded deer-skin sheath aside and picked up a small painting his mother had given him because he had not wanted her to sell it. He laid it on the floor, then grinned when he found the small beaded leather bag with drawstrings. In it were three pebbles from the base of Chief Mountain, or, as his grandfather called it, *Ninastako,* where the Blackfeet believed Thunder lived. The bag also contained a sprig from a shrub from the Sweet Grass Hills country south of Milk River. Hoping to instill in him reverence for his heritage, his grandfather had taken him to these places and explained their significance. Gray remembered feeling at the time they were nothing but foolish beliefs of the old people who refused to come out of the past. Gray placed the bag on the floor and put the painting back in the chest.

The last thing he did was put the Winchester back in its horn rack above the door. He would need something a little more familiar for what he hoped to do.

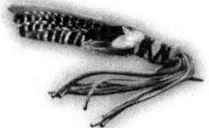

Highway 89 led south through land used for grazing and crop farming. He knew whatever plan he came up with would have a starting point somewhere in the south, in California or Arizona.

His cell phone beeped with a message signal. Gray hit the button and listened to two messages from Simone. Neither mentioned anything new on Carlie Kate, only that she was concerned because he hadn't contacted her. He deleted both and punched in Juarez's number.

Gray sensed the hesitancy in Juarez's voice when he answered.

"It's me," Gray said.

"I saw the number and figured it had to be you or whoever found the phone on your dead body."

"Yeah, well, no such luck, so don't go counting your inheritance yet."

"You okay, man?"

"So far. This guy Montoya seems to have cast a big net, or he's getting inside information. I'm hurting, friend. They shot my grandfather. Luckily, he's going to make it. But I had to kill two of the guys who came after me. Dumb reservation Indians someone fed with hopes of a big reward. It doesn't sit well, know what I mean?"

"Never does. You got to keep telling yourself it's them or you. You need to find some place better to hide. Who knows, maybe they'll get tired of looking."

Gray grunted. "Won't work. That's why I'm calling. I need your help. I want to hurt him. I want him to know that two can play this game. I'm hoping that somehow I can bring him out into the open."

"I hope you've thought this through. It may be the worst thing you can do. It would be like beating a piñata full of hornets. I know you, and many others will be hurt if you go to war with these people. Have you thought about the girl?"

"You said it yourself. There's a good chance that he's already gotten rid of her. My goal is to find out, one way or the other. If she's alive, I want to bring her back."

"All right, war it is. I have a few people who owe me. It'll take a day or two."

"There's another thing you may be able to help me with. I need to find someone with weapons to sell that won't ask too many questions. You know the kind I'm looking for. And I can't wait ten days for them to check my background."

"Then tell me where you are."

I'm in southern Montana, is that close enough?"

"Okay, for once in your life you're in luck. You're next door to Idaho, which probably has looser gun laws than Somalia."

Juarez gave Gray the address of a man in central Idaho and told him he would call ahead. Gray thanked him, figuring he would pick up an Idaho map at the next truck stop.

Gray pushed the Jeep down Highway 89 until Choteau, then followed 287, the highway that would take him west into Idaho. He recrossed the Continental Divide and drove along the Lewis and

Clark Highway until he met up with Idaho's north-south corridor, then followed the map to the address Juarez had given him.

Whoever built the house had failed Architecture 101. The house was clapboard, or looked as if that was the effect the builder desired. Moss carpeted the shingle roof. A thin column of smoke rose out of a stone chimney. Iron grills were securely bolted to the walls covering the windows.

Gray parked in the driveway, and surveyed the house and strange assortment of out buildings. A gravel path led to the wooden steps and the front door. He knocked.

A hand eased aside the corner of the curtain covering a small window. Gray felt himself being scrutinized before he heard the bolt being drawn. The door opened until a chain stopped it.

"My name's Gray. I believe someone called ahead to say I was coming."

"You the fellow looking for farm tools?" the man said. His week-old beard covered a face that showed nothing, but the eyes held Gray's and never wavered.

"Not exactly," Gray said. "A good friend said I might buy something I might hunt with."

"You a cop?"

Gray shook his head.

"Work for the government maybe? Bureau of Alcohol and Tobacco?"

"None of them and I'm not here to get you in any trouble. Just buy some things."

The man scratched the growth on his face and looked over Gray's shoulder as if expecting others to be waiting for his decision. Finally, he nodded and came out on the porch, and pulled the door shut, locking it with a key from a chain anchored to his belt. Without saying a word, he led Gray to a log building behind the house. Gray noted the heavy padlock on the door and the fact that the building had no windows.

They entered and man shut the door behind them, then turned on a bank of florescent lights. On one side of the building a long table made from exterior plywood and stud lumber took up most of the space. The table held an array of used cartridge brass, boxes of bullets and primers, along with a scale and dies. A self-loader sat on one end of the table, with rough shelving above for cans of gunpowder. The neatness and order of the equipment told Gray the man knew what he was doing, and did it well.

"Now over here I have a half dozen or so nice little pieces that are easy to handle and not very expensive, if that's what you're looking for," the man said, leading Gray to a bench on the other side of the narrow room.

Gray walked over to the display and worked his way down the bench, picking up and inspecting the assortment of handguns. He found what he wanted sitting away from the others.

"That CZ-75D is a bit more expensive."

Gray released the magazine of the 9mm and slid open the action to verify it was unloaded, then slid in the empty magazine and checked the gun for wear.

"It's only had a hundred rounds or so run through it. I have another model if you prefer a straight grip."

"No, I'm familiar with this one," Gray said.

"That is a workhorse, all right. Not too many people are familiar with them."

Gray handed it to the man and walked over to another table that held a rifle in a vise. "You mind?" he asked, reaching for it.

"Well, that particular piece is not your standard hunting rifle."

"I can see that," Gray said as he loosened the vise. He removed the rag that protected the stock and slid the bolt into place, turning the rifle over to look at the serial number. "Remington Model 700. Looks a lot like an M40A1 to me, especially with that scope on it."

The man nodded a time or two before he spoke. "This piece is somewhat special. I've spent some time refining it, you might say."

"You checked out what it'll do?" Gray asked.

"Oh, it's a long shooter all right, but before you go and get too comfortable with it, I don't want to sound like I'm pulling your chain but I would have to put a hefty price on it."

Gray pulled the bolt back and inspected the firing pin and slide. "Don't suppose you have anywhere to try it?"

It took a while to set up targets at five hundred yards and, at Gray's insistence, eight hundred yards. The man protested the waste of ammunition and the futility of shooting at anything that far away. In exasperation he handed Gray a box of 150-grain Nosler Match Grade ammunition.

Using two sand bags on a shooting table, Gray arranged himself while the man set up a spotting scope on an adjacent table.

The 10X Unertl scope had heavy scuffmarks from previous use, but the optics looked clear. Gray slid four cartridges into the magazine and sighted in on the five-hundred-yard target. After the four shots, he adjusted the elevation and made further adjustments for a slight breeze that moved across the target area. He loaded four more rounds and put the last two in the ten ring. By the time Gray had taken the last of his shots, his grouping in the eight-hundred-yard target could be covered with a pie tin.

The man stepped back from his scope and stared at Gray.

"Just where the hell did you learn to shoot like that?"

"Probably the same place you did." Gray had seen the tattoo on the man's arm when he answered the door.

"The Corps. I might have known when you called it an M40A1. Not many people would know that. I worked in the armory at Quantico. This is as close as I could come to the ones we built there." He placed his scope in its box and shook his head. "Well, shooting like that probably means Scout Sniper School, but sometimes we don't want to talk about some things, so I'm not going to ask what you want with this piece. Was there anything else you saw you might want?"

"No, I think these will do."

After settling up, Gray carried the guns to his Jeep, where he wrapped the Remington .308 in an old Hudson's Bay point blanket and set two plastic boxes of hand-loads next to it. He could pick up hollow points for the 9mm at any sporting goods store that handled firearms. The man's price put a dent in the backpack funds, but Gray felt he and Montoya were at war, and he needed serious firepower.

The question continued to haunt him as he drove from Idaho into Nevada. How did they know where to find him unless she had said something to the senator? She was the only one who knew his probable destination would be the reservation. Juarez had not asked; besides, Juarez would be the last person to betray him.

He drove most of the night and caught a few hours sleep in a rest stop before continuing on to Adelanto, a high-desert town in Southern California, halfway between Victorville and Riverside. He had arranged to meet Juarez at a Mexican restaurant tucked between a video rental store and an auto-body shop. He spotted Juarez's car and pulled in beside it, and sat watching the traffic in his mirror to see if anyone pulled off the highway. Satisfied, he picked up the backpack and entered the restaurant. Juarez had the last booth in the corner, his back to the wall and a beer in hand. A plastic basket tortilla chips and bowl of salsa sat on the table in front of him.

"Nice place," Gray said, sliding in to the booth.

"I only invite you to the best."

Gray grinned and reached for Juarez's beer.

"So, was my information helpful?" Juarez asked.

A middle-aged waitress dropped a menu on the table and took their order for two beers, managing to address both as "honey" in the same breath.

Gray dipped a tortilla chip into the salsa and munched it for a moment, then grabbed for Juarez's beer again. "God, how do you people eat this stuff? You could blister paint with it."

"Hey, this is no faux Mexican restaurant. This is the real thing," Juarez said with a chuckle. "You want something with less fire go up the road to one of those places you copy and put on every corner."

"Faux?" Gray said, shaking his head. He was going to comment further but Juarez's eyes moved to the front as another customer entered. Gray knew no one would take them by surprise. "To answer your question, yeah, the guy had everything I wanted, and more. Now it's your turn. What were you able to find out about this Montoya that might be helpful?"

"First off, you already know he's probably the most sophisticated drug guy in Mexico. This Hidalgo cartel of his is run like a first-class American corporation. The only difference is there are no other stockholders."

"We knew all of that. My question is, how do I get to him?"

"Depends on what you mean. You can't go to Michoacan like before; that road's closed. It would have to be something to do with his organization," Juarez said.

The waitress returned with the beers, and they ordered pork *carnitas* with refried beans and fried rice. Gray squeezed a slice of lime into his beer and said, "I agree, but how exactly? That's the question."

"You still have that book you found?"

Gray smiled. "I thought about that, too, after I came across a town highlighted in it." Gray pulled the book out of a pocket of the backpack. "It's on an Indian reservation in Washington."

Gray flipped through the book until he found what he wanted and turned it toward Juarez. "Look at the names on this page. I thought I had seen them somewhere recently. Just three common Hispanic names, but when you see them together like this you think there's got to be a connection."

Juarez furrowed his brow and nodded.

Gray leaned forward. "Talk to me, Mex. I'm listening."

"Happens I was following this guy's wife the other day. He thought she was putting out while he was at work. So I follow her in her little red Beemer into this town of Bell Heights. Now this is what you might call a low middle-class community about eighty percent Hispanic, and what do I see?" Juarez paused and took a sip of his beer, and dipped a tortilla chip into the salsa bowl.

Gray's eyes watered at the tablespoon full of salsa on Juarez's chip and reached for his beer while Juarez went back to the salsa bowl for seconds. Gray held up his hands. "How long you going to drag this out?"

"Yep, those same three names, right there in red, green, blue, and white, and printed on these cardboard signs and planted on the lawn, taped to telephone poles and hanging anywhere there was free space. All three of these guys are running for city council, and the one gets the most votes will be mayor.

"Son of a bitch, a city council."

"You got it. I did some checking around. You know me, being a licensed investigator and such. Well, they all appear to be well financed and are hoping to replace the current council."

"Any way to tell who's backing them?"

"Not yet, but it's too much to a coincidence. Our friend Montoya apparently wants a city council in his pocket."

For a moment Gray digested the latest item of information. "What would he do with it?"

Juarez used his beer bottle to push the crumbs from the tortilla chips into a pile. "City councils control a lot of what goes on and who has influence. If Montoya is looking to invest in a town and buy up some small businesses, what better place to start?"

"And you're thinking that this is what he's doing?"

"Small businesses that handle a lot of cash and little inventory are a great way to clean dirty money. He takes the proceeds from the drugs and runs it through various filters and buys these businesses and presto, nice clean cash. All you need is a willing city council to smooth out any problems with health or building permits, and a good accountant."

Gray turned the pages of the book until he came to the one he wanted. "Everything you say adds up, but blowing the whistle on these guys will take time, and we have no proof other than names in a book that we can't prove belongs to anyone. Whoever dropped the book obviously works for Montoya, but prove it. I think our answer might be right here," Gray said, pointing to an address.

"The storage unit in Azusa?"

"Exactly. There has to be something in there worth guarding. I'm thinking he's using it as a distribution center for his drugs. I want to get inside."

"What do you want to do with what you found up in that reservation?"

"You know anyone in the DEA?" Gray asked.

Juarez pulled out his cell phone and made a call, requesting an individual by name. After explaining the reason for the call, he handed to the phone to Gray, who spent thirty minutes telling the agent what he had found, without revealing the existence of the book. The agent said he had heard rumors and said he would pass the information on to the Seattle office, first thing.

Gray punched the End Call button and returned the phone to Juarez. "What have you been hearing lately? It would make my life easier if they were looking for me somewhere else."

"That's the funny thing. The word I hear is not to do anything but report if they find you. No more cowboy and Indian attacks."

Gray rolled the new information around in his head a moment, then said. "One thing is for certain. Once I hit that locker, things might change in a hurry, provided it's what we think it is. But, he needs to know it was me and not a random burglary."

"If it's what we suspect, I wouldn't worry. You say there are cameras covering every inch of the place. He'll be told pronto."

"Provided this place is a distribution point, then the rest of the information in here," Gray said, indicating the book. "Could hurt him badly. The names alone would shake up the Mexican judicial system for years. But I'll trade it for the girl. That's the information I want him to know."

"It has been a while now. What makes you believe he's kept her alive?"

"I think he will until he gets me. At least that's what I hope. It's all I can go on. Hopefully, I'm about to shake up his world."

Juarez looked skeptical. "After we turn over this locker and grin for the cameras, what happens next?"

"What do you mean, we?"

"Because you can't do this thing alone, and it will be easier to have a serious discussion with these *pendejos* if you speak their language."

"I don't like it. You have people depending on you, and it's me they're after. Why not leave now, Paco, and let me handle this one alone?"

Juarez grinned. "You need looking after sometimes, and I think this time is one of them."

43

Emiliano Montoya stepped into the circle. "Pull."
Immediately two round discs rose into the air and raced away in ever-increasing divergence. Effortlessly, he raised the side-by-side, 12-gauge shotgun to his shoulder and settled on the retreating target, squeezing off the first barrel before moving to cover the second clay pigeon.

Behind him a young boy stood with a second shotgun, loaded but still broken, ready to exchange for the one Montoya had fired. The boy's feet shifted nervously, having been told of the consequences of dropping either of the matched set of James Purdey & Sons custom-made shotguns.

Montoya turned toward the pad where his helicopter had deposited Castillo and another man. Montoya waved them over and used the moment to study the person with Castillo. The man was of average height, wearing a tight-fitting polo shirt that accentuated his muscular upper body. Several gold chains of varying lengths hung loosely around his neck. Montoya nodded to the boy, who handed him the loaded gun and took the empty one, breaking it and ejecting the spent casings.

Montoya ran off a string of a dozen hits while the two men stood to one side, waiting. He was pleased to note the patience displayed by this man whom he would possibly hire. Both men applauded when Montoya handed the empty gun to the boy and waved him off. He wiped his hands on a towel and seated himself at a table set up on the lawn, out of hearing of the household staff. He indicated to Castillo to proceed.

"Emiliano, this is the man we spoke of. He prefers to go only by the name of El Diablo. I am sure you can understand his reluctance to using his own name."

The man stepped forward. "Señor Montoya, it is an honor to be given this respect. I hope I can do it the justice it deserves."

Montoya nodded. "My friend here tells me of your skills. I assume he has given you some of the particulars?"

"I understand there is someone you wish to rid yourself of," the man said. "This person, he is in the north, yes?"

"Yes. Is this a place you are familiar with?"

"What do you know of him that will assist me in finding him?"

Montoya silenced him with his hand. "First, let me ask you. How certain are you of success?"

The man bowed his head and chuckled. "If I can find this person, they are already dead. Once I find them, they will not elude me."

"Understand my concern," Montoya said. "This man attempted to kill me, but instead murdered my daughter and my only grandson. I wish I could do this thing myself, but that is not possible, so I have had you brought here to me."

Montoya pulled a manila envelope forward and placed his hand on it. "All the information I have obtained is in here, but this report cannot be allowed to leave here. You may, however, have the photograph that was taken from his home."

"I will certainly read it, but what do you see as a problem? I understand others have tried and failed."

"Imbeciles. Incompetent fools, all of them. There should be no problem once he is located. He is nothing but a painter of pretty pictures, and this place where he lives, this Laguna something or other in California, is nothing but a place full of homosexuals, they tell me. They say he was seeing this woman, so maybe he is one of those who like both."

The man who called himself El Diablo grinned. "So, where do I find him?"

Castillo answered. "We hope to have information soon. Perhaps you should be in the north and be ready when it comes to us."

Montoya drummed his fingers on the folder, anxious to be rid of the man. His flashy demeanor repulsed him, as did the heavy scent of cologne the man must have considered attractive to women. He slid the folder across the table and sat back to observe the man's reaction to the information Castillo had managed to gather in the short time since they received his name.

The assassin opened the folder and took out the single sheet of paper, accompanied by the photograph taken from Gray's house. The photo fell to the grass at his feet. He ignored it and studied the report.

Montoya waited, his eyes never leaving the assassin's face. The man bent down and retrieved the picture, glancing at it before returning it to the folder, then slipping the picture back out and examining it closely.

"If this is the man who you say attempted to kill you, I cannot believe you are still alive."

Montoya shivered. "What do you mean?"

The assassin pulled a slim gold case from and pocket and took out a cigarette. His hand trembled.

Montoya shook his head when he saw Castillo react. If the man needed a cigarette at this time, Montoya planned to discover the reason.

"As you know, I was sent to America by my government to train at this School of the Americas. This training at their Fort Benning was conducted by instructors from their best Special Forces units. I was sent because I was already one of the best in our military. When we returned to our home countries, we were to be used to suppress organized opposition to our government. This, of course, was not what our American friends claimed was the purpose of our training, but that is what we were used for. Many of us found military opportunities less than what we could get elsewhere. I am sure you know this is how Los Zetas came into being."

"Please, I know all of this. What has it to do with this man?"

"I know this man. They called him Shadow. It was a name they used among themselves because of his ability to go anywhere he chose to, unheard and unseen. It was a joke, of course, a comic book name. His team partner they called Sunshine because he seldom smiled, and the two names together sounded funny. But take my word, there was nothing funny about them."

Montoya started to speak, but the assassin held up his hands. "One more moment, please, and you will understand. Along with this ability was what he could do with a rifle. We were sent against them in mock hunts. Now, in these games we played we never found them, and our teams were eliminated, always. No one ever bettered them. When we returned to our country, they were to go to Hawaii to be a part of their Marines' shooting team. I do not know if this happened."

"I believed you to be superior in what you do," Montoya chided. "Am I now to look elsewhere for someone who will not be afraid?"

"I said our team lost, but so did all the others. That you are alive today is a great mystery to me. How he failed is difficult to understand, if you were to know of his ability."

Montoya shuddered involuntarily. Had he begun something that would have been better left alone? Perhaps it would be better to close off all the loose ends before it was too late. "With what you are telling me, do you still choose to go ahead with this?"

The assassin said, "It would be known if I now turned down this assignment. I cannot let that happen."

"You do not fear to go in pursuit of him?"

"When the fish is swimming in the waters, he has no fear of the shark he does not see. Once I find him, you can begin counting out the money you will owe me."

44

A halo of light from a street lamp fell across the hood of the Jeep. Gray glanced at the dashboard clock. "If they're keeping to the schedule, someone will come out in ten minutes."

Juarez grunted. "Good of them to keep to a routine. Makes life easier."

Right on schedule, the door to the storage unit's office opened. One of the guards came out and slid into the golf cart parked by the door.

Gray and Juarez eased out of the car and closed the doors as quietly as possible. Both wore dark clothing, with low-top hiking boots and gloves. They worked their way down the fence line until they came to a spot the cameras didn't cover and squatted beside the wire fence to wait.

"Any time now," Gray whispered.

"Here he comes, right on schedule. Man, I love these guys," Juarez said.

The armed guard passed on the other side of the fence, the battery-powered cart making barely a whisper. Before it reached the end of the row of units, Gray climbed the fence and cut the three strands of barbed wire. He tossed a small satchel over the fence and jumped to the ground inside the enclosure. Juarez followed.

Neither saw any indication of an alarm system, or motion detectors, only the cameras mounted on the corners of the building near the front entrance. If the contents of the locker were what they thought, the police would be the last people notified in case of a break-in.

Gray checked his watch. "He should be at the end of the last row in three minutes."

They sprinted across the back edge of the three rows of buildings, hugging the walls as the reflected light of the cart's headlamps partially lit the pavement. Seconds later the cart rounded the corner to begin the return trip to the office.

Gray pulled his head away from the corner of the wall as the cart's lights lit the immediate area. He tapped the wall as a signal to Juarez waiting on the other side. The cart slowed, turning the corner between the last unit and a row of empty motor homes parked next to the fence.

Juarez stepped out of the shadow, the beam from his flashlight blinding the guard, and whispered a warning. The guard's right hand hung in the air above his holstered gun. Before he could make a decision, Gray wrapped his arm around the guard's neck and placed the 9mm against his cheek. Juarez spoke to him again, and the guard nodded in understanding.

Gray secured the guard's hands behind his back with a plastic electrical tie and covered the man's mouth with a six-inch strip of duct tape.

Juarez pushed the guard across the seat and took his place at the steering wheel.

The radio squawked. Gray shook his head and began to move.

Juarez held up a hand to stop him. He pulled the guard out of the cart and cut the ties. Gray shoved the muzzle of his pistol into guard's ribs, while Juarez stripped off the man's jacket and hat.

Gray chuckled and retied the man's hands. He walked him to the end of the unit closest to the office door, where he waited while Juarez parked the cart.

When Juarez returned, he rapped on the office door three times with his flashlight. Gray bunched the collar of the guard's shirt in his fist and again jammed his gun into the man's ribs.

A sliver of light appeared as the door opened. Gray pushed the guard into a run as Juarez struck the door with his shoulder, knocking down the man behind the door. Juarez rushed inside. Gray followed, pushing the first guard ahead of him and forcing him to the floor.

The looks of terror on the guards' faces confirmed Gray's suspicions that the storage unit held more than discarded furniture. He ripped the tape of the first guard's mouth while Juarez secured the hands of the other. Both guards screamed out obscenities and threats in Spanish.

Juarez shouted at them in their own language.

"What are they so excited about?" Gray asked.

"They say we don't know what we're doing, and we're dead men unless we leave now."

Juarez pointed at the second guard. *"Habla usted ingles?"*

"Si," the guard answered.

"Okay then," Gray said, "Tell us what's scaring the crap out of you?"

"He will kill you. You have made a mistake by being here. He will come for you."

"Well, in that case we had better hurry," Gray said. He pulled the man to his feet and pushed him out the door. Juarez followed with the other.

Another stream of threats followed when Gray found a chain on the back of the golf cart and wired it to the padlock of the unit they wanted to look into.

"Chances are the lock will hold but the door won't," Gray said. He wrapped the chain around the hitch on the back of the cart and climbed in.

The latch and part of the reinforced door came away with a loud screech, leaving a gap big enough to crawl through. Juarez slipped through the opening, carrying his flashlight, while Gray kept his 9mm on the two guards, sitting with their backs to the wall.

Gray glanced over his shoulder and asked, "What does it look like?"

Juarez grunted, the beam from the flashlight dancing around the interior. "Cardboard file boxes all taped up. Important to somebody but definitely not weed. Maybe it's coke or pills."

Gray felt let down. At this point he had no other method of attracting Montoya's attention. "Pull one of those boxes over here. Whatever's in them must be important or these two yoyos wouldn't be so nervous."

Juarez handed a heavily taped box through the opening, then crawled out and squatted beside it. Gray sliced through the tape and lifted off the cardboard top.

"Holly shit," Juarez exclaimed.

"You're right, definitely not weed." Gray lifted out a four-inch bundle of bills and thumbed through them. "Looks like mostly hundreds and twenties here. Any idea how much a bundle like this might have?"

"Sure, that's the way I always carry my money, all wrapped up in bundles."

"Okay, but if those other boxes are the same as this one, there's enough here to make a serious dent in the national debt. No wonder these guys are so nervous. Old man Montoya's going to fit these guys with flaming neck ties when he catches them, and that's only after he has removed their *cajones* with a rusty knife."

Gray went inside and tossed out two more boxes. Both held stacks of bills held together with paper bands. He picked up a bundle and approached the guards. "This money belong to Montoya?"

The two man exchanged questioning looks and shrugged.

Juarez shouted at them in Spanish.

"Montoya?" one said.

"Emiliano Montoya, Don Emiliano. You know, the guy you work for."

"Here, no. Not him, no," the other muttered.

Gray and Juarez looked at each other.

Juarez kicked one in the foot to get his attention. "Who are you working for?"

"Zapata, and he will kill you."

"Who?" Gray asked in disbelief.

"Miguel Zapata. *El Cabazon.*"

"Big Head," Juarez muttered. "Who is this guy?"

"He is Zapata, and he will kill you if you touch his money," one of the guards muttered as much to himself as anyone else. "He will kill all of us."

Gray tossed the bundle of bills into the box. "What do we do now? It sure as hell can't be legal."

"No way," Juarez said. "It's drug money. The problem is, we don't know whose it is, and if it belongs to someone like the Sinaloa or Gulf cartels, we're going to have every drug pusher in the Western Hemisphere looking to collect our scalps. Except yours of course, since you got so little hair left after your last scalping party."

"I still don't get it," Gray said. "Why was this address in a book dropped by someone sent up here by Montoya? There has to be a connection somewhere."

"Maybe they were thinking about raiding the other cartel's stash."

"No, there's something we're missing here. But we can toss that around later."

"What about all this stuff?" Juarez said. "I can't see taping the boxes up and leaving it. This is blood money from the hell they ship here."

"Okay," Gray said and picked up two packets of the cash and tossed them to Juarez. "I'm donating those to that group of yours that tries rehabilitating wayward Mexicans."

"Hispanics, wayward Hispanics," Juarez corrected. "You want a receipt for tax purposes?"

"All the same," Gray said, motioning to the two guards to get up. He picked up two more bundles of bills and headed toward the office. Juarez tossed the boxes back through the broken door and followed, herding the guards ahead of him. Gray went to the video recorder, pulled the cassette out, and pocketed it.

"What about these two?" Juarez said.

"You want them? I'd say they're prime candidates for rehabilitation. 'Course, they might not live long after whoever this belongs to finds out they screwed up. Just a waste of your time in that case."

"Too far gone. I think a guppy in a sharp tank has more chance than these two."

"You got that right." Gray cut the plastic ties on the wrists of both guards and tossed each a bundle of bills. "If I were you guys, I'd be out of town before the sun comes up. Now vamoose," he said, pointing toward the door.

One hit a switch to open the front gate before he ran after the other. The last Gray saw of them, they had climbed into a lowered Chevy with twin pipes and roared up the street.

"What now?"

"We can't just leave it. You know somebody you can call?"

Juarez grinned, pulling his cell phone out of his pocket. "Oh, yeah. I'm going to make this guy's day."

45

The news about the raid on the storage facility headlined every TV news station the following day. A scowling reporter stood in front of the empty unit interviewing the police chief, who was making every effort to convince the viewers how good police work by his department had brought about the previous night's raid.

Unaware that she was probably sabotaging her career, at least with this police department, the young reporter asked about a rumored anonymous call that sent a squad car to the location late at night.

Gray switched off the TV in his motel room and carried his cell phone outside. All his hopes had centered on attracting Montoya's attention by breaking into the storage locker. But he had gained nothing. And any hope he had for Carlie Kate grew dimmer by the day.

Remembering Juarez saying something about calling Detective Mondavi, Gray walked through the parking lot of the rundown motel and found a plastic chair beside an empty swimming pool. It took a few minutes to convince the Laguna Mesa Police Department he wasn't going to leave a message and he would hold.

When Mondavi took the call, he said with more than a hint of sarcasm, "You got my message apparently."

"I got it," Gray said.

"Look, I don't know what's going on, but I know this crap about national security I'm being told is bullshit. If you're interested, I might have something for you."

"I'm listening." Gray figured anything would be better than what he had at that point.

"This isn't something I can discuss over the phone. I got the impression talking to that friend of yours that you might be somewhere in the neighborhood."

Gray wondered how much Juarez had told him. "It's possible."

"Okay, let's quit playing games then. If you want what I have, it's face to face or it's nothing. What will it be?"

"Why do we have to meet?"

"What I have, I obtained in a manner not considered upright and kosher. It's only going from me to you, then I deny any knowledge of its existence, or even that we met."

"I'm about an hour away," Gray said. "Where do you want to meet?"

Two hours later Gray watched the people moving about the tiny park perched on the heights above Dana Point Harbor. Two women pushed strollers past a bench where an elderly man fed pigeons from a brown paper bag. A young couple took pictures of each other before persuading a passerby to stop and take one of both of them together. Detective Mondavi stood leaning against a metal railing, occasionally glancing at his watch.

Gray waited a few moments before approaching. "Where's the other one?"

"If you mean Detective Chavez, say so. I left him at the office."

"Did you ever find out why the surveillance on me wasn't pulled?"

Mondavi pointed down toward the strip of beach below. "Did you ever read the book *Two Years Before the Mast*? They say this is the spot Dana said they tossed the cowhides off to be taken out to the ships. Called them "California Banknotes" because they used them in place of money."

"Interesting, but you're not answering my question, which makes me nervous."

Mondavi smiled. "I'm putting in my application for police chief. I think I have a good chance, since our current chief resigned."

Gray turned to look at him. "Resigned?"

"Well, it was either that or be fired. People started asking embarrassing questions about his lifestyle and finances."

"What's all this got to do with me? It's not something you couldn't tell me on the phone."

"I'm getting to it," Mondavi said. "Anyway, there appeared to be an infusion of cash come to him that helped pay off a pile of debts. The city council looked at everything and decided to act. Either resign or they would look into it further."

Two sea gulls dove off excrement-covered pilings and fought over bait left by fishermen.

"Okay, here's that I have. The DNA samples from the scene and under Ms. Davis's fingernails just happened to be involved in an accident making them useless," Mondavi said. "So after checking the logs, and discovering it was our chief who ordered the continuing surveillance on you, I started to wonder. I took the liberty of calling a friend at the lab where we sent the samples. The accident destroyed any chain of evidence, so there was no reason to spend the money having the samples analyzed. But no one said anything about tossing them, so I took it on myself to have them run. This whole thing is costing me a lot of favors, but I figured to go all the way and sent the info to another friend in the San Diego PD.

Gray waited while Mondavi smiled at an old woman pushing an empty shopping cart through the park. "Well?" he said, holding his arms out for whatever it was Mondavi was trying to tell him.

"Bingo," Mondavi said, smiling. "Turns out they got a hit from an old case whose samples should have been tossed. It was a rape case and DNA was taken, but the woman wouldn't press charges.

Here's where we got lucky. The guy's lawyer should have requested that the records and tests be tossed, but it must have been his busy day and he overlooked it. Of course, none of this can be used in any court of law, but I thought you might like to know who killed Bethany Davis."

"This is for real?" Gray asked. "You know who did it?"

"Yeah, I know. Not that it'll do you any good."

"Who is this guy?"

"That's the interesting part. I ran his name past some guys I know in LAPD. He's heavy into dealing drugs down in Mexico. His name is Miguel Zapata."

"Zapata." Gray's head swiveled to face Mondavi. "Miguel Zapata, *El Cabezon*."

Mondavi frowned. "How the hell do you know that?"

Gray needed time to think. He jammed his hands into his pockets and walked to the railing, his back to Mondavi, trying to place the newest piece of information into the puzzle.

"I asked you a question," Mondavi said. "How did you know about Zapata?"

Gray took a deep breath. "First, I need to know if what I tell you can be held against me in any way?"

"I don't understand," Mondavi said. "Did you do something I should know about?"

If he was going to get anything out of Mondavi, he knew he needed to trade. "Did you hear about that bust in Azusa last night?"

"Come on Gray, I'm a cop. Of course, I heard about it. The guy in charge up there is making sure everybody hears about it."

"You hear anything about an anonymous tip?"

Mondavi nodded his head slowly. "Heard something, but it was retracted. Seems some new TV gal jumped the gun and didn't check her information. The chief claims they had been watching that locker for some time."

"Well, use this information as you see fit. Two guys who worked there, and I'm sure your compatriots can't locate them, claim they worked for Miguel Zapata, *El Cabezon*. Now isn't that a coincidence?"

Mondavi exhaled slowly. "I'm not going to ask you how you know all this. In fact, I don't want to know, since I'd probably have to arrest you. But this little piece of information is going to put a dump-truck load of favors back in my pocket. You have now become an unnamed source who cannot be identified."

"Now it's your turn. Who is this guy?"

"Miguel Zapata happens to be the bastard son of one Don Emiliano Montoya, drug lord of the Hidalgo Cartel in the state of Michoacan."

The pieces were falling into place. "So we have a connection. Zapata comes here, obviously on Montoya's orders, kills Bethany, and takes the girl."

Mondavi nodded. "You realize, of course, that I haven't had the opportunity to conduct a full-scale investigation, but from what I know, and what you're telling me, I would say there's a good chance Zapata's killing of Ms. Davis was an accident, and he took the girl instead. His reputation as a brutal womanizer with a violent temper has caused his father problems in the past. I would think maybe things got out of hand, and she fought him and he hit her. We'll never know, and if we did it wouldn't do us any good. But that still leaves us up in the air, doesn't it?"

"What do you mean?" Gray asked, although he had a pretty good hunch he knew what Mondavi was alluding to.

"The why, Gray, the why. You're not stupid, and I think you know the answer, but I'll spell it out. Why did Montoya send Miguel Zapata up here for the senator's daughter?"

Gray walked off to the side and said, more to himself than Mondavi, "And why did these guys say they didn't work for Montoya?"

Outside the breakwater a sloop dropped its jib and proceeded into the harbor under its reefed mainsail. Gray watched the boat come about and reach toward the green buoy, while he shuffled the information Mondavi had provided. "What do you make of it? You're the cop."

"If I were a cynical man, which is something all cops are, I'd say there's a good chance this Zapata is running something on his own, and if the dollar figure we hear from Azusa PD is correct, it's not a small organization."

"You mean something behind his father's back?"

"Wouldn't surprise me a bit. He knows who all the contacts are."

"I wonder what Montoya would say if he knew?" Gray said.

Mondavi grunted. "Now that's a good question, but I don't think I can help you there. However, if you're thinking about using it, I wish you luck. You seem to have had your share already but don't push it."

It wasn't much to go on, but at the moment it was all he had. As Mondavi prepared to leave, Gray asked him if he knew anyone in Bell Heights, and told him about the three running for city council.

"I'm not going to ask you where the hell you got all this information about the locker in Azusa, and now this, but if you come across any more, you could probably get me elected Orange County Sheriff.

Gray watched the detective make his way across the park toward the parking area. He knew who killed Bethany, and he knew why. *Now what?*

46

"The news is not good, Miguel. I have received a call from Tijuana. He is a judge and he is not happy. He threatened to speak with your father."

Miguel Zapata pushed aside his food, the flush of fear returning. "What did he want?"

"The same as the other, Castillo said. "He wanted to know who you have given his phone number to."

"Two times now. It is too many. Someone has found it. Have you told my father?"

"No, but if it happens again, he will hear about it. Then he will ask questions I cannot answer."

Zapata lit a cigarette. His hand shook. "How the fuck can we find out who has it? Castillo, figure it out. That's what you are paid to do. My father believes it is lost or destroyed. If he were ever to discover what is in that book, we are dead men."

"I know this, Miguel. I am as concerned as you, but what can we do?"

Zapata studied his father's counselor through the cloud of smoke from his cigarette. How much did he trust him? Was Castillo playing both sides, his and his father's, and who held the advantage? Castillo knew everything. In fact, he knew more than either Miguel or his father, and that made him a dangerous man.

"Thank about it," Zapata said. "There must be a way to trace these calls. Talk to that police chief. I am surprised he has not done that already."

Castillo stubbed out his own cigarette and pushed his chair back. "I have work to do, but I will call him."

"Good," Zapata said, then remembered something else he had meant to ask. "You brought someone to see my father. Who was it?"

"Oh, that was only a man who wished to do business with your father. It was nothing. What he had to offer was too little."

Zapata reached for the bottle of tequila. Had he noticed a hesitation in Castillo's response? And why had the man arrived in his father's helicopter? "You are sure of this?"

"Of course, Miguel," Castillo said, smiling. "We understood it to be a much greater offer than it was."

"You would not lie to me would you, my friend? You would not have to worry about what my father would do if he ever found out about Maria Consuela. I would kill you myself."

"Miguel, have I not protected you all this time?"

Zapata grinned. "Good. Are you still fucking her?"

"No, I believe she is offering her favors to someone else."

"Was it good, Castillo? Was it worth risking your life for?"

Castillo moved toward the door. "It was a mistake."

"Maybe I should try her." Zapata laughed.

Castillo turned, a tight smile creasing his face. "She would kill you herself, Miguel. You know this. And your father would do nothing."

"He is growing soft and careless. If his enemies do not destroy him, perhaps I will be forced to."

"And if he discovers what is in the book?" Castillo asked.

"Then I will be dead without warning. You will tell me if he learns anything, will you not?"

"Of course, Miguel. Why do you not trust me in this?"

Miguel Zapata again felt the cold wave flush of fear. He had no choice.

47

With Mondavi's information, Gray wondered if he was any closer to finding a way to get Carlie Kate back. The way he figured it, Montoya had sent Miguel Zapata up to take Bethany as a hostage, to force the senator to reveal his name and whereabouts. But Zapata took the girl instead, after he killed Bethany, and in the process Zapata loses this book in which he was recorded all the contacts, locations, and everything else he could think of, including what appeared to be his own operation. Gray shook his head at the stupidity. If this was the case, then the big question remained, did Emiliano Montoya know what Zapata was doing? For Miguel Zapata to accumulate that much cash, he had to have a pretty substantial network, or he was skimming off his father's. Gray wondered how he could use this information, or which one he should try to deal with?

His cell phone rang as he left San Juan Capistrano and took Ortega Highway.

He knew he couldn't put it off any longer. He would have to face it sooner or later, and there was always the possibility she had new information.

Her message said to call immediately. Gray pulled off the winding road and punched in her number.

"Damn it, Conaire. Why haven't you returned any of my calls?"

"I'm calling you now. What have you heard?"

"It's horrible."

His heart sank. "She's dead?"

"No, at least we don't think so, but they sent another message. This time with another photo. You need to see it."

"Tell me about it."

"I can't. You need to see it for yourself."

Gray didn't respond, wondering why she couldn't tell him.

"Conaire, are you still there?"

"What makes you think she's still alive?"

"It's her, and she's holding a newspaper from a couple of days ago."

"What does he want?"

"He wants us to find out where you are. He's giving us seventy-two hours to find you. That only gives us until the day after tomorrow."

"What's he saying, that he'll kill her if you don't find me?"

Simone's voice broke. "No, but maybe it's worse than that. You have to see what he sent."

Was the senator behind this? Or were both of them in on it? Gray balled his hands into fists. *How could she do it? I agreed to let Davis give Montoya my name and location before. Why am I angry if he's still trying to pin me down?* But it wasn't simply giving Montoya a location. It was having him come to a specific place at a specific time.

"All right, tomorrow afternoon."

"Can't we meet sooner?"

"No, and you have no idea where I am."

"All right, where?"

Gray had to think about a location. He wanted to choose the meeting ground. "I'll call you in the morning, but be ready to leave right away."

Would she relay the information to Davis? Was he at that moment passing it along to Montoya? It wouldn't give the drug lord much time, but with his resources time meant little. Right that minute instructions could be flowing out of Michocan to forces in Southern California.

"Conaire," she said. "I hope it's not too late."

For your sake, too, he thought.

48

After talking with Mondavi, Gray phoned Juarez and filled him in on what he intended to do, and waited for his friend to respond.

"Do you want back up?" Juarez asked.

"No, I can handle it. It's on my ground so I'll have a way out if it goes haywire." Gray wouldn't know for certain, but the maps he downloaded on a city library computer gave him a good idea about the spot he chose. If she didn't come alone, he could disappear.

Only after Juarez extracted a promise from him that he would back out if the forces against him made success impossible did Juarez consent to stay behind.

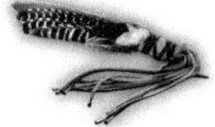

With dawn's first beginnings, Gray drove along the highway until he saw the sign for the turnoff. A big rig hugged one side of the off-ramp, its engine shut down and no light showing in the cab. Gray slowed at the end of the ramp and turned onto a narrow strip of pavement. A quarter mile later he passed through an open gate and onto an unmaintained dirt road.

He followed the road deep into a landscape of sandy hills held together by the water-seeking roots of chaparral. Twice he stopped to consult the map. He judged the road he sought to be roughly ten miles from where he left the interstate.

The track dipped down into a dry arroyo and climbed the sandy bank on the far side to come out at a crossroad of four-wheel trails. Gray swung the Jeep onto the northbound track and half an hour later topped a rise and saw the highway below. At that time of the morning, the rest stop remained filled with big rigs and motor homes.

Gray found a spot in the shade of an uprooted mesquite and settled in to watch.

He had called Simone before he left and gave her directions to the rest stop. He told her to time her arrival for one o'clock that afternoon and wait for new instructions.

With the sun past the noon hour, he turned his binoculars on the off-ramp leading to the rest stop. Fifteen minutes later her red car slowed and entered the parking area. For the next hour he examined the cars pulling in off the interstate, watching for one that stopped but no one got out to stretch their legs or use the restrooms.

Simone's car sat, its engine running to combat the heat of the high desert, until apparent impatience forced her out to stand and lean against the fender. Gray could tell she was angry, but so far she hadn't looked as if she was communicating with anyone. He waited another fifteen minutes before calling her on the satellite phone Juarez had forced on him.

After listening to her protests for making her wait in the heat of the Arizona desert, he gave her instructions to the next exit and told her to drive to an area beneath two trees where the pavement ended.

Gray waited until she parked before approaching, but stopped about twenty feet away.

"Okay, Conaire. What the hell is this all about? I sat in that stupid parking area for an hour. Have you any idea how many illiterate unshaven truck drivers asked me to join them in their cabs?"

Gray glanced back, along the road she had come. No cloud of dust rose from an approaching car. He listened, but the air was still; no thumping of a possible aircraft. How were they planning on doing it, he asked himself? He couldn't believe she would be his assassin.

"Gray, are you there?" she said. "Answer me or I'm getting in this car and leaving right now. This is ridiculous." She reached through the open window of her car and pulled out her phone.

Gray's hand hovered over the butt of the 9mm tucked beneath his shirt. "Turn it off." He moved closer, still searching the surrounding landscape for something that shouldn't be there. Was she carrying a weapon, or wearing some type of GPS that could pinpoint his exact location?

"Well, what is this? Why are we out here in this god-forsaken place?" she said. "Talk to me, Gray. Now, or I'm out of here."

"I do." He moved to within ten feet of her. "The problem is, Ms. St. Pierre, I think I know."

"You know what's happening? How?"

"Not about the girl, about me. They almost killed my grandfather, and you and Davis were the only ones who knew where I was going. I know what our agreement was, but it didn't include getting others killed."

He watched her mouth open and close without making a sound. She crossed her arms, shaking her head and turning her back to him. He felt the bitter loss of something he had felt for her, but he also knew the taste of betrayal that her presence caused him.

"So now you have me out here in the open. How are they planning on doing it, Simone? Or is it you I should worry about?" Would she deny it? Was he hoping none of it was true? How could she justify their treachery?

She spun around and pointed a finger at him. "How can you stand there and accuse me of this, you son of a bitch? What the hell do you take us for? Did anyone follow me? You should know or do you think someone's hiding in the back of my car, maybe in the trunk?"

Gray took a couple of steps to the side to look behind her. "I don't know, Ms. St. Pierre. Maybe you're carrying a GPS locator, or there's one in your phone that pinpoints this spot. There are ways to do it. All I know is, trouble follows soon after I see you, or talk to you. I told you I don't believe in coincidence."

"So your mind's made up. It's me then, and nothing I can say will change your mind. You really don't care if I brought information on the girl. Or maybe you think this whole thing is a hoax, and there isn't any new information?"

"I can't be sure it isn't."

"What was it you said, a locator of some kind? Here's my phone," she said, tossing it at his feet. "Or maybe it's in my pocket."

Gray picked up the phone and pulled the battery out of its slot, inspecting it to see if he could discern anything from it. "Turn around and lift up your shirt."

Simone stood with her hands on her hips, shaking her head. She spun around and pulled her blouse out of her slacks, and lifted it up as far as she could. "Where else could I hide this locator you're so worried about?" She turned back to face him and peeled her blouse off over her head, dropping it on the ground at her feet.

Before he could stop her she reached behind and unfastened her bra, tossing it on the ground along with her blouse. He couldn't take his eyes off her, the whiteness of her breasts against her tanned body. He held up his hand. "Okay, I'm sorry, please."

"Oh, no, you bastard, I'm not done. You stand there and accuse me of being an accomplice in all this and say you're sorry? No, you can have your fun," she said in a voice on the edge of breaking. "Maybe it's in my shorts." She unfastened her shorts and kicked them over toward him, standing naked except for a pair of bikini briefs. "You satisfied? Or do you want me to keep going?"

Gray picked up the clothing and shook off the dirt and held them out to her. "I said I was sorry. You have to remember how it looks."

She ripped the clothing from his grasp. "You sure you don't want to do a cavity search for your indicator? You might as well."

"Simone, please."

With a look of contempt, she picked up her clothing and turned her back while she dressed. Her shoulders shook with her sobs. As she buttoned her blouse, she walked over to the car and reached inside. Gray's hand moved to his back where the 9mm nestled under his belt.

Simone turned around with a Fed-Ex envelope and a small box in her hands. "This is what they sent," she said, passing him the two items.

Gray took the envelope out of her hands and opened it. He pulled out a sheet of paper and a black-and-white photo, recognized Carlie Kate immediately. The photo had been taken against the backdrop of a crumbling adobe wall, her hair unkempt and her face smudged from the tears tracking through the dirt on her face. She held a newspaper across her chest. One hand was heavily bandaged.

He recognized the name on the newspaper's header. It was a small town in Mexico, just across the Arizona border. She was close.

"It came two days ago, with the note. I tried to reach you then but you didn't answer my calls." She sobbed, then continued. "As you can see, there's not much time left."

Gray dropped the photo into the envelope and pulled out the note. Someone had handwritten the brief message on a piece of brown wrapping paper. It said simply, "Tell us where he is or more things will happen to her. Tell us this by three days after you receive this package."

"Okay, but what do they mean?"

She handed him the tiny box. "This," she said.

He took it out of her hand, a box used to hold jewelry, and lifted the lid. He froze, nausea beginning deep in his stomach and rushing up to his throat. On a piece of bloodstained cotton lay a child's wrinkled finger. He stared at the finger, remembering the bandages on her hand in the photo.

Simone took the box from him and placed the lid back on. "My god, Conaire, can they really mean they'll keep sending us pieces of her until they find you? You have to do something. You're the only one who can save her."

Without realizing what he had done, he folded her into his arms and buried his face in her hair.

Her body shook. "Can you do anything for her?"

"Yes I can. And I will."

49

Simone broke from Gray's embrace and pushed him away. "You think you can get away with what you had me do by saying you're sorry?"

She could have no idea the embarrassment he felt at seeing her standing there, stripping off her clothes, even though he had told her to stop long before she chose to drop her shorts. He couldn't let her know what affect the sight of her had on him. "What else do you want me to say?"

"You can start by telling me what gave you the idea that I led them to you. How could you think that? How could I do such a thing?"

"There has to have been a way. Wherever I went they found me. They were at my house only hours after you left.They were waiting for me at the reservation, I told you that. They shot my grandfather. What else do you want me to think? All my life people like your senator have been lying to me."

Simone reached over and touched his arm. "I am so sorry. Your grandfather, is he all right? Do you know?"

"He's doing okay. But I can't take the chance it'll happen again."

Simone wiped the perspiration off her forehead. "God, it's hot out here, Conaire. Do you suppose we could talk about this somewhere else?"

"All right, there's a town back a few miles. You can follow me."

The town of Quartzsite was nestled in a shallow valley between two arid mountain ranges. The only reason for its existence was the trailer parks, which filled to capacity during the winter months. Come fall, the population exploded, as snowbirds from Idaho to Michigan and Canada migrated south, looking for a warm place where their arthritis could be held at bay with less medication. In summer, the trailer parks served as temporary refuge for wind-driven sagebrush, looking and resembling deserted refugee camps after a crisis had been resolved. Storefronts showed cardboard signs advertising the fact they would reopen September 1. Only those businesses catering to the unfortunates left behind, to sit beneath their thumping air conditioning units and the occasional lost traveler, remained open.

Gray found a small restaurant wedged between Cactus Betty's Beauty Salon and the Desert Bliss Motel. The special of the day offered homemade pot roast with mashed potatoes. He and Simone ordered iced tea with the special.

"Okay, now tell me what happened," Simone said. She listened without interrupting. When he finished she asked, "Do you still think I had something to do with it?"

"I'll admit it's hard not to think that somehow you're not in the equation. It could have been something you said without realizing it. Can you think of anything better?"

The waitress placed two plates on the table and refilled their glasses. Simone pushed the mashed potatoes aside and forked a green bean. "Only the senator. He's the only one I've spoken to about you."

Gray raised his eyebrows.

"Oh, come on. There's no way it could have been him. There has to be another answer."

Neither spoke while they dealt with their thoughts. Gray discovered how hungry he was. The waitress slipped the bill under a water glass while Gray wiped up the last of the gravy with a piece of bread.

Her answer came out not much above a whisper. "Oh, god, no." Then much louder, almost a cry. "Sergio, you bastard."

Gray looked up. "What is it?"

"There was someone else, but I never…" her voice trailed off.

"Tell me, Simone. Who?"

She rolled her paper napkin into a ball and kneaded it with her fingers. "His name is Sergio del Mello, and he's someone I've been seeing."

"Just seeing or more than that?"

"All right, we've slept together. Is that what you wanted to know?"

Gray wasn't sure if what he felt was jealousy or envy, and a quick image of her standing in the desert after stripping off her clothes flashed through his mind. "Okay, I deserve that. It's none of my business what your relationship is. So tell me why you think it was him."

She described their meeting and how the relationship grew and his questioning her recently about the mysterious trips she had taken to California, and finally how she had broken down and told him as much as she dared.

Gray listened, his mind still wrestling with the facts of her intimacy with Sergio.

"And you think you mentioned the possibility I might go back to the reservation?" he said, breaking the silence.

She toyed with her glass a moment before nodding. "I think I might have. Yes, he asked me what I thought you might do."

"Does he know you were coming to see me today?"

She shook her head.

"Do you love him?"

She stared at him, wide-eyed, for a moment. He realized he was holding his breath.

"Why do you want to know that?"

He shrugged and waved the question off as if it were irrelevant.

"No, I'm not. At times I wished I was. Life would be easier, but it's not working out. It's not what I want. All this trouble, everything that's going on in my life, I don't know what I want."

"Everything passes eventually," Gray said. "You'll see. Then life should return to normal. I hope so, anyway."

She played with her mashed potatoes for a moment. "I wish that were true. Unfortunately, there are other issues."

"Like?"

"No," she said. She pushed the plate away and gazed out the window. "They're my problems and that's where they'll stay. But this is not solving the problem with this poor girl. Is there anything that can be done? I know why the senator can't do something. He wouldn't even discuss the possibility with me."

Gray had his own suspicions. "You know there's other factors involved. He's not working entirely on his own."

"What could possibly be so important that he refuses to do something? After all, she's their granddaughter."

"Put it away, Simone. It's too dangerous to go there."

A tow truck hauling a vintage station wagon pulled to the front of the restaurant and discharged a family of six. Gray watched them argue with the driver while he thought about the possibilities of Davis's involvement.

She broke into his thoughts. "There's not much time left, Conaire. What will you do?"

"I can trade, although I don't know whether I can pull it off and still have her come out alive."

"Trade what?"

"Me for her. That's what they want, isn't it?"

She looked stunned. "They'll kill you."

He wondered if he should tell her about the book. Could he trust her? But he knew he might need her help to pull it off. Outside, evening shadows spread across the street. He decided to take a chance. "I have a plan. It's not perfect, and it has a lot of ifs involved, but it's the best I can come up with."

"Can you tell me about it?"

He filled her in on the notebook, and what he had learned about the person who killed Bethany Davis, then said, "Look, it's getting late and you have a long way to go. Davis is probably waiting for you to report. It's better for him not to know everything. That way he can deny knowledge of possible deaths."

She pulled her phone out and shut it down. "I'm not going back tonight. I can't face him, or Sergio for that matter, and they'll both be waiting. What are you going to do?"

"I'm staying here tonight. I'll try to contact this Zapata in the morning."

"Can I stay here, too?"

It wasn't a question Gray expected. "Here? With me?"

"Don't get the wrong idea. Just spend the night. I don't want to be alone, and I'm definitely not looking for sex. I'll sleep in the chair if you like."

It felt the heat of embarrassment fill his face at the sight of the mischievous grin on her face. "All right."

The overworked air conditioning unit rattled at full capacity, sending a steady stream of cool air into the room. On the post outside their window, the thermometer hovered at 99 degrees. They sat on the bed and talked mostly about him and what had led to this moment. A couple of times he had asked her personal questions, but with a politician's ease she had maneuvered the question into a different area.

Finally, she asked. "What are you really going to do to get her back?"

He took a deep breath. "Whatever it takes. At this point caution is out of the question."

"Anything?"

"Three men are dead already, two of them by me. What does it matter if I have to do it again?"

Simone shook her head. "If you have to do this, and others die, will they come after you? The authorities, I mean?"

He hadn't gone beyond the thought of rescue, and whether he could pull it off. It would all depend on whether he could contact Zapata. Like the training missions, this one would be planned as it was taking place. "I don't know if I'll have a future to worry about, but if I do, to answer your question, probably."

She edged closer to him, and instinctively he put his arm around her shoulders. The occasional headlights of traffic on the nearby highway flickered through the thin curtain.

"When it's all over, will you go back to your painting?" she asked.

Gray leaned back and put his hands behind his head. Again it was a question he hadn't considered. "I guess. Right now I'm not thinking about a future. If I have one, yes, but maybe somewhere else. I think I'd go away. I doubt I could go back to my house now."

He stroked her neck and her bare shoulder and pressed his face against her back.

"Conaire," she said after a while. "I can sense you might think about me more than just as a friend. I hope it's not true. I don't want you to."

"Are you still thinking of him?"

She pulled away and sat with her knees drawn up to her chin. "A while ago, at the restaurant, I said something about other issues, remember? Well, something has come up recently that I have to face and I don't know how. It could affect any plans I had for continuing what I'm doing now; my whole life, actually. It could also affect what you think about me."

"What kind of issues?"

"Look, what I said about not getting too close to me. I don't want to make it a discussion. It's more like I'll tell you what it is, but I'm not looking for your help, agreed?"

He nodded, and she told him about her two years in Paris, and the recent demands of the former boyfriend. She said she knew he would keep up the pressure for more money once he realized she would pay, and she had to make a decision soon.

Gray did not interrupt and waited for her to finish. Her voice finally trailed off, and she looked up and shrugged.

"We do stupid things at times, believing we're in love," she said. "I did them. I'm not proud of them, obviously, but I can't erase them, either. So now you know."

"Why are you telling me this?"

"I wanted you to know who I am. I don't want you to fall in love with me. You can see why, can't you?"

He said nothing, not sure how to answer her.

Then she said, "If somehow you're able to save Carlie, I would only wish that you went back to your painting. I don't know what's going to happen to me. If the story gets out about my past, I'll never find another job in politics, but if I know you're out there working, I'll have something to fall back on. You'll be my strength."

The air conditioner shuddered and fell silent. They remained on the bed, apart. Gray watched her for some time before he spoke. "I don't know if I could ever feel at ease being in love with you. You're like that scene I see on a rare occasion when I'm alone in the mountains. That moment when light and shadow combine to form that perfect image, when everything is right, and you don't want to share it with anyone. You want it to be yours and only yours. To love you would mean sharing you with everyone. I don't know what the next two days will bring. I don't need to have you in my thoughts, confusing me at that moment when I might have to make the decision that means life or death. But you will be."

"I'm sorry I brought this all up. I thought it might make you think otherwise."

Gray rolled off the bed and tried unsuccessfully to restart the air conditioner.

Simone propped the pillows against the headboard and slipped off her blouse and shorts. Gray did the same and climbed into bed, curling her into the crook of his arm.

"When will I know?"

"I think forty-eight hours and it will be over, one way or another.

"Will you call me?"

Her hand lay across his chest. Would it be better to walk away? If, that was the question. "I don't know."

50

Conaire Gray walked out into the desert and stood for a moment, his breathing shallow. He had no idea what he would do if his plan didn't work. He opened the black notebook to the back page where he had copied the number given to him by one of the guards at the storage unit. They had been told to use it only in extreme emergencies. Gray wondered if the number led to Zapata or someone in the States.

Before daybreak, he and Simone had stood in the doorway of the motel and hugged briefly. He kissed her lightly on the lips, and she had taken his face in her hands and asked him to come back safe.

Before sleeping, they agreed she should give the senator as much information on what Gray planned to do as he had told her. All he wanted was twenty-four hours.

He knew Miguel Zapata might not accept a trade, or was not in a position to do so. He knew, somehow, Zapata needed to be convinced. He dialed the number.

The phone rang.

He waited.

It rang, each unanswered ring like a death knoll. He let it ring and ring, unable to break the connection.

"*Si*," the voice said, slurring, threatening, someone who did not want to be disturbed.

Gray took a deep breath. "Miguel Zapata?"

"*Quién?*"

"Is this Zapata?"

"*Mierda.*"

A chill coursed through Gray's body. He had the feeling he was speaking to the man who killed Bethany and took Carlie Kate. "If this is Zapata, I know you speak English, so listen carefully you piece of shit. My name is Conaire Gray, the man your father wants. Do you understand?"

He heard the sharp intake of breath. "Why the fuck you call me? It is my father who wants to kill you."

"No," Gray said. "It's you I'll deal with. I want to trade."

"What the fuck do you have to trade with, your life?" Zapata broke into a fit of laughter at his own humor. "You got nothing I want. Maybe that woman before she died I would have taken."

It apparently hadn't dawned on Zapata that Gray had somehow obtained his phone number. Gray fought back the rush of anger. He knew he would kill Zapata if he got the opportunity. "How about the book?"

"Book? What is this book you talk of?"

"The one you lost, remember? When you killed that woman. I have it, Zapata. I have the book. You want me to read it to you?"

Gray held his breath. He had no other plan. The background noise faded as if Zapata moved to another location. "So, you say you have something of mine. I think you are crazy. Soon you will be dead anyway."

"Then I guess I need to talk to your father. Maybe he lost it."

"Wait," Zapata muttered. "How do I know you have something you say is mine?"

"Have you heard about the money in California? Does your father know about it? You know the place, that storage locker, but maybe no one's told you yet. And that place where the Indians live, where you've got those guys growing marijuana. That will be gone soon, too. You want more?"

"*Cabron*, if this is something you say is mine, how much you want for it?"

"I don't want money. I want the girl."

"Shit, my father has this girl, not me."

"Then figure out how you're going to get her or I'm going to start calling some of these people in this book. Maybe I'll start with your father."

Gray sensed the hesitation. What if Zapata didn't take the offer? "Come on, Miguel," Gray muttered to himself. "You're my only hope."

He heard Zapata shout an order to somebody, then come back on the line. "You are a dead man. I know this because if nobody else kills you, I will."

"You've already tried that. Now, I don't have a lot of time before your father does something with the girl," Gray said. Then he remembered Carlie Kate's bandaged hand in the photo. "If that happens, I will bring vengeance down on you, wherever you hide. You won't have to find me. But maybe your father will already have taken care of you when these people in your book start asking why I'm calling them."

"All right, gringo, maybe we can do this thing."

Gray closed his eyes and let his breath out slowly. *Now to set it up. This is where the end begins.* Two trains now rushed toward each other and one, or both, would leave the tracks. "We meet. You bring the girl, and I bring the book, and we trade."

"And you have already made a copy of this book, I know."

"With the actual book nobody can be sure if I copied it or not. You have to take that chance. You need the one with your fingerprints all over it.

"And where will we do this trade?"

Gray had no idea where Zapata was, but he knew Carlie Kate was being held close across the border, and he knew Zapata could travel unrestricted in Mexico and he couldn't. He needed one more concession. "Anywhere, but it has to be on my side."

"Why is this?"

"Because any of your so called law enforcement *compadres* would be more than willing to grab me for the right price. So, where do we meet? You don't have much time to set it up. Twenty-four hours and I start making calls."

"Fucking gringo. I think I fuck this girl and give you her body. Do you know who I am?"

"They call you *El Cabezon*, I understand. If you touch that girl, I won't kill you Zapata, but I'll cut off your balls and make you eat them, raw, because that's who I am. Set this up and call me on this number and don't waste your time trying to have someone find me. Is that clear?"

"Fuck you, gringo."

Gray disconnected and leaned back in his seat. The wait began. Until he knew where the exchange would take place, he couldn't begin to put the plan together.

51

Emiliano Montoya knelt by the large crate sitting in the middle of his office. He pried up the last wooden slat and placed it alongside the others. He couldn't wait to view the latest addition to his collection of Aztec pottery, said to have come from the table of Montezuma himself. But he didn't want to spoil the experience, and he knew Castillo stood waiting with news. "What is it?" Montoya asked, rising and brushing away pieces of packing materials that clung to his clothing.

"I hesitate to bring this to you, Don Emiliano, but it is of grave importance. It is about Miguel."

"He is dead?" Montoya gasped.

"No, but it appears this book that he lost has been found."

"So," Montoya said, "Have we not taken precautions to minimize the damages if this should happen?"

"Yes, but there is something else. I have discovered that Miguel has been undermining you and has begun his own operation using many of your sources."

Montoya fell back into his desk chair. "No, there must be some mistake. I have given him everything. What more could he want? Are you sure of this?"

"Yes. It also appears Miguel has struck a deal with the man you seek, this Conaire Gray. Somehow this man has the book that Miguel lost."

Silence hung in the air as Montoya considered what this new information meant. "How is this possible when we do not know where to locate this man?"

Castillo placed his portfolio on the edge of the desk and opened it while Montoya waited. "What I have been told is that this man Gray has contacted Miguel."

Montoya's voice turned to ice. "And what is this deal, as you call it, that they have put together?"

"The girl in exchange for the book. I am told that a place Miguel used to store the money he had accumulated was discovered by the police. The information was given to them by Gray. Also, it was understood Miguel had people growing marijuana in a forest in a northern state, near Canada."

Montoya remained silent, gazing at the ceiling. He could not believe Miguel would have gone this far. If he would do this, there was no limit to what else he might do. "I cannot say you did not warn me." Montoya pushed his chair away from the desk and walked to the window overlooking the patio. "You are positive about this?"

"Everything points to it being so," Castillo said. "Our man in the home of the senator has confirmed much of it."

"Yes," Montoya said. "When this is all over, he should be dealt with, do you agree?"

"He will be a loose end."

Montoya struggled with the decision he had to make. "How is this to take place, this exchange?"

"Miguel has sent Fuentes to pick up the girl. They are to meet across the border from an Indian reservation in Arizona. It is a crossing point we had controlled."

"I see. And the American patrols?"

Castillo cleared his throat. Miguel has arranged for an episode to occur further east. It will draw the patrols away for a time."

Montoya thought about this new information. "It is obvious there is more in this book of his than he has told us. It would also explain his actions lately." He held his hands together behind his back and gazed out the window. "When is this to take place?"

"Tomorrow, sometime in the afternoon. Miguel took the plane and flew out an hour ago. He said to tell you it was an emergency," Castillo said.

"Very well, and this man you brought to me, where is he?"

Castillo nodded. "We are lucky. He has been waiting nearby, in Tucson. He is ready."

"Contact him immediately and give him his instructions. It has already gone on long enough."

"What is it you wish me to tell him?"

Montoya could see the confusion in Castillo's eyes. The man would earn his money this time. "I will leave that up to you, my friend. Whatever you decide I will agree to, but remember, if anything happens to Miguel, it will kill his mother. Perhaps there is a way to control him, but I will leave this in your hands. Tell him his fee will be doubled, but there can be no loose ends left for our enemies to pounce on. No loose ends whatsoever. Do you understand?"

"I will see to it."

"And make a note. When this man who has haunted me for so long is dead have that tree out there removed. It will no longer be needed as a reminder."

52

"It's all set up," Gray said into his phone.

"It's a trap," Juarez said. "Have you lost your mind?"

"Of course, it is," Gray said.

"Then why? You know he'll never let the girl live. Why do you want to give them your life as well?"

"Maybe not. There's always a chance they'll trade or make a mistake, and if they don't, I can always up the bargain."

"Are you crazy?"

"Seems that way doesn't it, but I can't live like this, Paco. It was bad enough before. You remember. But now, with Bethany dead, and if they kill Carlie Kate. Hell, if they don't kill me, I'd end up doing it for them."

"No way man. It can't be as bad as you say. You're supposed to be some super Indian. You can't do something like this."

Scattered sagebrush danced across the hot desert floor to impale itself on the wire fencing. Gray sat in the shade of an abandoned house trailer listening to a string of arguments by Juarez. When his friend had finished, Gray said, "It's like that guy who you're always quoting, Nietzsche, said: 'He who has a why to live can bear almost any how.' I've lost my why, Paco."

"Then let me go with you this time," Juarez pleaded.

"No. If it doesn't work out, the trade I mean, or they don't bring Carlie, I plan on taking out as many of them as I can before they take me. One way or the other, they're not leaving the place alive, and if by some miracle I pull it off where does that leave me? This is on our side of the border. Things are different here. You think they're going to find a bunch of dead bodies out there with holes in them and let it lie? No way. They'll have every politician in the Southwest looking for TV exposure demanding they find the party, or parties, responsible."

"You could drag their sorry asses back under the fence and let Mexico worry about it," Juarez said with a chuckle. "Far as I know they've never solved a murder yet."

Gray grimaced. "Wouldn't help none. I'd still have the nightmares if I can't bring her out."

"Man, you need back-up. You know this. You know this asshole. He won't come alone. From what I hear, he can't take a crap without someone to hand him the shit paper."

Gray nodded in silent agreement. "I'm counting on it. The place where we're meeting is on an Indian reservation. My kind of place. Four o'clock, tomorrow afternoon. I figure he'll send his people across a couple of hours earlier to set the trap. I plan on being in position by the time the sun comes up."

"So what do you want from me?"

"I mailed you something. It'll tell you what to do and who to contact if I don't come back. You're the only one I have, Paco."

"What about the girl?" Juarez asked.

"I can't see them letting her live regardless of what I'm saying here, but if they do, my only chance is in how many they send for me. If I make it, I'll bring her out. We used to talk about situations like this, remember?"

"That was different. We were young and indestructible then. Now we're older, and we're supposed to have more sense."

Gray said his goodbyes and tucked the phone back in his pocket. He had plenty of time before he to be at the spot, but why wait? It was an inhospitable spot, but like he had told Juarez, it was his kind of place.

53

The fence rose out of the stark landscape like an alien creature, separating the two countries. Gray lay in a shallow depression, surrounded by the dead branches of ancient mesquite and creosote bushes. His location overlooked an alluvial fan plain. He lifted his binoculars to his eyes and searched the monotonous land of gray-browns and gray-greens on both sides of the steel barrier that marked the border between the United States and Mexico.

He knew Miguel Zapata would send his storm troopers ahead to set up an ambush, but like those used to dealing with like entities, they would not figure their quarry would arrive before them.

Thankful for a three-quarter moon, Gray had parked the Jeep two miles back, a little after midnight, on the dirt track that others had used to approach this spot.

According to Zapata's instructions, they would meet about a hundred yards in, on the American side. Zapata said the Border Patrol would be following a tip about a shipment of drugs to be brought across by mules he promised to get into the U.S. These illegals would cross twenty miles farther east, right into the hands of the waiting authorities. They were expendable.

After leaving Juarez the previous afternoon, Gray had found an Army-Navy Surplus store and made some purchases. He had picked up a large nylon camouflage tarp to cover the Jeep. It wouldn't stand close inspection, but from a distance would fool anyone not looking for something too out of the ordinary. He also purchased a top and loose trousers in what the clerk described as desert camouflage, along with a few yards of netting and several tubes of face paint.

Before leaving the Jeep, he used the netting to fashion himself a reasonable ghillie suit, weaving pieces of cameo cloth through the netting and attaching it to the camo suit. To shield his head from the sun, he did the same with a wide-brimmed cotton campaign hat, tucking small sprigs of the desert growth into the netting. He had also found colored duct tape at a hardware store, what they called 100mph tape in the Corps, and wrapped strips around his rifle to break up its outline.

He pulled his beaded headband from his pocket and slipped it on before putting on his hat. Then he picked up the leather bag containing the three pebbles and sweet grass from the reservation.

He repeated a Blackfoot prayer and tucked the bag into his pocket, and, as a last act, took out the face paint and drew black and red chevrons on his cheeks. If he was going to war, he would do it as his ancestors had done it.

Lying under the mesquite, he would learn how invisible his camouflage would keep him from the untrained eye. Regardless, retreat was not an option.

Gray set down the binoculars and sucked a mouthful of water out of the tube leading to his camelback. The temperature at this time of the year might exceed 110 degrees by noon. He counted on this to make Zapata and his thugs less attentive.

He had forgotten the feel of the chase, the rush of knowing the hunt came down to them or him. His body hugged the hot sand and rock of the reservation land. He felt himself drift back to his former self, that of trained stalker and killer.

At noon the first thin trail of dust rose and curled into a punishing blue sky. Gray followed its slow progress as it approached the fence a mile from where he lay. He lost sight of the two SUVs as they pulled alongside the wall on the Mexican side.

Fifteen minutes later, four men wearing jeans, tight-fitting polo shirts, and baseball hats, and carrying automatic weapons, came through a hole in the fence, splitting into two groups, each carrying a plastic jug. They yelled insults at each other, pointing their weapons in mock threats, then laughing and heading off in different directions.

The meeting ground Zapata proposed was a small clearing surrounded by jagged rock formations that rose two or three hundred feet out of the desert floor. Numerous organ pipe cactus towered above their shadows, casting relief to any and all living things unlucky enough to live in this environment. Gray wondered who the Tohono O'odham Indians had pissed off to be awarded such a jewel as their reservation.

A spotted lizard slithered out from under a rock and froze within inches of Gray's face. Its protruding eyes scanned the object in front of it and, sensing no danger, scampered across Gray's hand and buried itself beneath a dead branch. Gray's head inched around to watch the first two men argue over the best spot to cover the track Gray was expected to follow to the clearing. They finally settled on a patch of thin shade in a shallow arroyo about eight hundred yards from where Gray lay. Both leaned back and pulled their hats over their eyes.

The second pair clambered through the jagged volcanic rocks, looking for a location that kept them in sight of the track but also provided some semblance of shade from the blistering rays of the desert sun.

Thirty minutes later, Gray watched the second group settle on a sandy flat between twin formations of rocky outcroppings. Both pairs were within a hundred yards of the rutted track, but a half-mile apart. Gray looked at his watch and reviewed his options. He knew they would have to be dealt with before Zapata arrived. He hadn't seen any indication they carried radios to keep in touch with each other, but if they had, it would be something else he would have to deal with.

Zapata had set the meeting time at four, which only gave Gray four hours to neutralize the ambushers. He had to decide which group to take out first and hope he didn't alert the other. But four hours, in such an open environment, wasn't enough time for him to move with any degree of caution.

From his position, Gray studied the routes to both sites. The one among the rocks would give him a superior position to take on the two men in the arroyo. He would need to move about thirty yards before he was out of their line of sight and hope they didn't look in his direction. So far they were content to sit back and smoke.

Gray figured on an hour to move across the two hundred yards of open desert to where they lay sprawled in the sand. He eased himself from beneath the branches and lay for a moment, picking out the route that offered the most natural protection. He fixed a number of way points in his mind and began the snail-like crawl to the first one, a long dead branch that lay across the shadow of a towering organ pipe Cactus. Gray slid the scoped rifle forward and began to move.

Thirty minutes later, he lay seventy yards from the first pair. From there the route he chose worked its way around behind them and across a fully exposed stretch.

A boot print in the sand startled him. It didn't belong; not a recent print, anyway. He saw others leading up a gentle slope to an area strewn with rocky outcroppings that appeared to grow out of the desert floor.

He forgot the tracks when movement caught his attention. Just a flicker, but there, and not caused by a breeze moving a branch, barely two feet away. He caught his breath and let it out slowly, while moving his head through a half arc, his eyes moving from the sand in front to a dead twig a few feet ahead. Half way back through the arc he saw it, its yellow and gray body streaked with pink and half buried in the sand. Gray froze, staring into the reptilian eyes of the sidewinder, the highly venomous pit viper not two feet away. His movement had disturbed the snake's effort to pass the heat of the day in inactivity. Gray figured it at about two and a half feet in length and able to strike two thirds of its body length. That left him only six inches out of range, if the so-called experts were right.

He searched for something to use to defend himself. Backing up was an option, but the movement might cause the snake to move closer. He wrapped his fingers around a dry branch, not more than eighteen inches long. Sliding the hand along the dirt, he brought the stick into his line of sight and pushed it toward the small cousin of the more venomous desert rattler. The snake might not carry the same punch, but it would definitely make a major impression on anyone it buried its fangs into.

Gray pushed the stick to a point between them and gently persuaded the snake to move away. Only after it moved off in its peculiar sideways movement did it warn him not to pursue. Gray took another shallow breath and continued creeping forward until he could crouch behind a small sand dune.

The two men he stalked sat within a circle of rocks, thin spirals of smoke marking their positions. His grandfather would have told him what the men had eaten for their last meal. For the last twenty minutes Gray's path had taken him out of their line of sight. With infinite caution he laid the rifle on the ground and removed his backpack and hydration bladder. He watched the two men while his fingers unclipped the top of the backpack and extracted the 9mmm. In his mind he rehearsed his approach, hoping to convince them in the first few seconds to drop their rifles without giving a warning or trying anything heroic.

As much as he hated the idea of having to kill them, he doubted their ability to think under the pressure, which usually led to doing something stupid.

When Gray stepped into the opening of their rocky bunker, both men reacted. One froze, with his canteen half way to his mouth. Seeing Gray crouched in front of him, a finger at his lips asking for silence, and a 9mm splitting the space between the two of them, he dropped the canteen and held his hands out in front, shaking his head. The other swore and scrambled for the rifle leaning against the rock.

Gray realized he had no choice and sent two hollow-point slugs into the man's chest.

"So much for silence," Gray muttered and quickly bound the smarter of the two with plastic ties and duct tape.

Gray stole out of the bunker area and moved back the way he came. He didn't know if the two hiding in the arroyo had his location in their line of sight, but they certainly would have been alerted. He crouched down and sprinted for a narrow enclosure among brush he had seen earlier, good cover, with some elevation gain, hoping he could look down on the other two of Zapata's paid killers. A frontal attack against two automatic weapons had not been part of his training. He knew he needed to eliminate them from a distance.

The yells from below to their companions went unanswered but gave away their exact position. Gray reached the spot he had chosen and pushed aside an accumulation of weathered growth. Blistering heat filtered through what meager shade the overhead branches provided, doing little to protect him from the sun as it approached its zenith. He glanced at the time. Zapata should arrive in about ninety minutes, unless he chose to wait for his four hit men to return in triumph.

A catclaw mesquite fifty feet away grew out of the desert floor, its roots having discovered an ample source of moisture deep below. This added source of nourishment kept the gray-green deciduous foliage thicker than its less fortunate neighbors. The location offered better concealment than where he lay. Gray began working his way across the few yards to the shelter of the twenty-foot tree. When he reached it, he dug his way under the hooked thorns that gave the bush the often-called wait-a-minute tree, a phrase used to tell other members of a party to wait-a-minute while they disentangled themselves from the thorns.

From beneath the branches, he watched one of the remaining two climb out on a rock and call out again to his companions. When he received no response, he started jogging toward their location.

Gray swore. Still unable to shoot someone without a warning, he held his fire. The man slowed to a walk three hundred yards off and called out again. Gray knew the bands of shade where he lay made him invisible to all but the minutest inspection. He scanned the area where he last saw the man's partner. Nothing showed. He placed the binoculars on top of the dead tree limb he lay behind and watched the shadows move away from his position as the sun continued its relentless arc toward the west. The decision to take out the two men had to be made soon.

The binoculars exploded into the air as the sound from a rifle shot reverberated through the surrounding hills. Gray buried himself behind the log. The shot had not come from an automatic rifle, especially one in the hands of one of the two waiting for him. Both were accounted for, and the shot had not come from either of their positions.

54

Gray peered out from under the branch, attempting to place the shooter's position. He had placed the binoculars a few inches above his head on the limb off to his left. They lay against the trunk of a cactus ten feet away, looking surprisingly intact. Then he noted the shattered lens. Whoever had fired the shot apparently assumed someone was looking through them at the time. Gray shuddered, knowing he had a very experienced shooter stalking him, and the shooter knew where Gray was.

For a moment he forgot about the one he had been watching. He picked him up again, kneeling in the sand and looking off in the direction the shot had come from. It appeared the attackers Zapata had sent were not expecting help. Zapata's man below began shuffling backward, his head swiveling in search of the shooter. Gray watched, knowing whoever had taken that lone shot couldn't be sure if he had hit his target.

Showing his impatience, another shot tore off a chunk of the dead limb Gray hid behind. He burrowed deeper in the dirt. How had he allowed himself to be trapped without a back-up position? Because he had underestimated the ability of the enemy. "Well, let's see how long you'll wait," Gray muttered.

Zapata's other attacker had scrambled back to his original position, drawing no response from the unknown sniper. Meaning, Gray concluded, he was the sole target.

Why would Zapata bring in another and not tell his own people? Unless someone else had hired him.

The temperature climbed, and Gray felt its strength on the parts of his body not protected by shade. If Zapata planned to keep the meeting, Gray figured he would see a vehicle approaching the fence in about an hour or less. The last thing he needed was more people with guns. He thought about Juarez's offer. He could use his own backup at that moment.

Gray closed his eyes and pictured his position. From where he lay, the two hiding in the arroyo posed no problem. The sniper, however, had Gray's location. It wasn't a matter of who could out wait whom. Gray needed to eliminate some of the opposition, and soon.

He eased his head around and peered out from under the lower branches of the bushy tree. Somewhere in the rocks above lay the shooter, and Gray figured his own position was under observation. He began his search at a point to the left of where he thought the shooter might be and worked his way to the right. On the third pass, movement above the area caught his eye. About six hundred yards away a bird broke from a dive toward an unseen object and beat back up into the sky. Gray concentrated on the spot below where it looked as if the bird had been heading.

A flicker of sunlight reflected off an object. He slowed his breathing. Could the reflection have come off of the lens of a scope? Pretty stupid using one in bright sunlight without a hood.

Gray needed a diversion, something to give him a second or two head-start. He reviewed what he had. The sniper lay among a low outcropping of rocks. slightly above him and close to a half mile away, well within killing range if the guy was any good. If his first shot were any indication, he certainly had the ability. Two more men with automatic weapons, but probably not too accurate with them, huddled in the arroyo below. Gray ran through a number of scenarios with little choice between them. He went back over the ground again, swearing softly at himself for being impatient. Again, he examined the landscape within his vision, noting particularly the play of shadows on the gray sand.

He closed his eyes and lowered his head a moment to clear his vision, then focused on a thin line of shadow twenty yards in front of him. A slight depression, probably caused by rain runoff over the years. He studied it, trying to determine the depth of the wash, then traced it up to where it veered off to the left behind a thick cover of dead brush. From that spot Gray drew a line to where his best estimate of the sniper's position was. Unless there was something he wasn't seeing, it looked as if the spot would be out of the line of fire. He didn't want to consider what would happen if it wasn't.

A dead limb beside Gray leaped into the air. He grunted as something buried itself in his upper thigh, the sound of the shot rolling over the arid landscape. He bit back the burning pain, not willing to shift his position to look at the damage. Another shot split apart a rock a few feet in front of where he lay, the impatience of the shooter becoming apparent, probably due to his exposure under a blistering sun. The spread of the shots indicated to Gray that the shooter was hoping for a response and an indication his first shot had not been a hit.

Gray realized his chances of making it to the shallow depression increased with the shooter's exasperation. He gritted his teeth at the pain in his leg, hoping it would hold up during the sprint. Then he could assess the damage. Using a finger, he explored the area on the leg and located a protruding object, wet with the blood seeping from the wound. It would have to wait. If he could make it to cover, the rules would change to what Juarez would say was, *mano a mano,* with both having equal firepower.

Gray looked at his watch, wanting to make the unseen shooter wait a little longer. Once he left the safety of his concealment, Gray knew he had only seconds to spare before an experienced shooter could pick him up again and bring his rifle into line. He tried flexing his leg, sending shafts of searing pain through his thigh. He gritted his teeth and counted down the seconds, taking a quick glance at the other two Zapata had sent. They still lay hunched down behind a mound of dirt.

A fist-size rock lay in the sand within reach. Gray eased his arm over to it and grasped it in his hand. With a last look over at his destination, he heaved the rock back over his shoulder, hearing it clatter against the rocks behind him. He burst out from under the branches, his leg screaming its opposition.

A tiny puff of dust exploded at his feet, followed by the crack of the rifle. The shallow depression seemed to be moving away as another shot whipped past his head. Time and the distance lengthened, Gray knowing that the next shot would take him. He waited for the hammer blow, wondering what it would feel like, and dove for the ground, crying out involuntarily as his injured thigh smacked the gravel bed of the shallow arroyo. For a moment he could do nothing but hold his leg with both hands and hope he had made it to a blind spot. Then, knowing he had to act quickly, he slipped his pack off his shoulders and inspected his leg. The blunt end of a wood splinter stuck out of his upper thigh. Gray dug in his pack for his first aid kit as slugs from the automatic weapons shredded the leaves and branches of the bush he lay beneath.

He swore and brought the rifle up to his shoulder, realizing he was exposed to the two men down below. He sat up quickly and found them in his scope, frantically attempting to reload after emptying their clips in their frenzy. One hurriedly reversed his magazine and chambered a round. As he brought the AK-47 to his shoulder, Gray's bullet ripped through his throat, blowing out the back of his neck and spraying blood and gore over his partner, who sprinted away, firing back across his body, obviously something he had seen actors do in the movies.

Gray wanted no part of another unseen enemy. He led the retreating man a couple of inches and fired. The man's legs gave out in mid-stride, his body slamming into the base of the thick cactus he had chosen for shelter and impaling himself on the jagged spines. The body hung for a moment before sliding to the ground at the plant's base.

Gray found the end of the tube to his water bladder and took a drink, then unzipped his first aid kit, taking out three large gauze pads and a roll of adhesive. The first thing he needed to do was remove the thick splinter in his thigh. He cut away his pant and gritted his teeth, grasping the stubby end of the splinter and easing it out of his leg. The two-inch piece came out clean, followed by a flow of blood. He let it bleed a moment, then clamped the gauze pads over the wound and bound it with the tape. He wiped his hands on his shirt and began crawling up the narrow defile in the desert floor, hoping he wasn't moving back into the sniper's vision. He could almost feel the rifle scope sweep across him in its search for movement.

A spot in shadow below the trunk of a petrified cactus offered protection. A minute before, he had spotted the thin spiral of dust climbing skyward a few miles south of the fence. Zapata intended on keeping his appointment. Gray said a silent prayer that Carlie Kate was in the car.

He put the approaching car out of his thoughts as he began his own search, asking only for the one shot he would need. He knew the rules of the game. Find your quarry before he finds you, and kill him. Prisoners were not an option.

Gray's heart missed a beat. A movement, five hundred yards plus, and off to his left. He took a deep breath and began a sweep of the bushes and shadows of the slightly elevated position, knowing whoever occupied it was doing the same. The dance of death went to the one who found his quarry first. There was no prize for second best. The stories went the rounds in sniper school of instances where both fired almost simultaneously, but only one lived to tell about it.

Again, a flutter of movement. Gray settled the cross hairs on it. Beneath a bent tree limb, the scope picked out what looked like the back of a hand and the circular form resembling the front end of a scope. He followed it forward until he saw the barrel of the rifle zeroing in on his position. He had to take the chance his estimate of distance and drop were accurate, and the effect the slight elevation gain would have on his bullet. He inched the cross hairs back across what he thought was a scope and hand, and hoped his bullet would find the sniper. He blew out his breath and caressed the trigger.

The rifle slammed back against his shoulder, and he refocused on the target area. Nothing remained in the narrow cleft of the rocks. He scanned the area on either side of where he first saw his target.

Nothing moved.

He waited.

Taking his eye from his scope for a second, he glanced over his shoulder. The cloud of dust drew closer. For a moment Gray fought off the thought. Then it festered in his mind. Why hadn't he thought of it before? If Zapata had not sent the sniper, could he also be a target? And what about Carlie Kate? Was Emiliano Montoya planning to clean house, closing out anything that could endanger his empire?

Gray found himself in the same position the shooter had been in earlier. He couldn't be sure his bullet had found its mark, and in order to find out he would have to take a chance and expose himself. He couldn't wait. A black Suburban pulled up near the fence and disappeared behind it. Once Zapata came through the opening in the fence, Gray might find himself caught between the two forces, if the sniper was still in play. He doubted Zapata would bring more firepower, figuring he already had four men in position.

Gray went back to studying the area above him. Still nothing. Bolts of pain shot through his thigh as he pulled his knees up and gathered himself to run up the slight slope to a rocky outcropping. He ruled out any attempt at trying to run a zigzag course, knowing his leg couldn't handle the extra pressure.

Using whatever bush or cactus shielded his movement he began moving up the slope, his eyes riveted on the slim opening in the rocks. Slowly the area came into view. It looked vacant. Could he have missed entirely? He felt a chill run through his body at the possibility the shooter had moved to another position and waited for a sure kill.

With twenty yards to go, Gray pulled out the 9mm, moving it side to side as he approached the opening. The area was deserted. A faint game trail led through a maze of rocks and brush, disappearing into a series of low hills. Then he saw the dark patch in the sand. He bent down and ran his fingers through it knowing immediately his bullet had found the shooter, but not enough to stop him.

Inspecting the faint trail again, he picked out more patches where the blood dampened the dirt. A scoped rifle lay in the gravel twenty yards up the slope. Gray whistled. His adversary had been supplied with a 7.62mm Russian Dragunov SVD sniper rifle. As deadly a weapon as there was.

Gray topped the low rise, the 9mm held with both hands pointing ahead. A body lay among the rocks, blood still dripping from a wound below its shoulder. He crept up and placed the automatic at the base of its neck, using his other hand to check for a pulse. Whoever Montoya had sent would not return to pick up his reward.

Four bodies now lay strewn over twenty acres of raw dirt, rock, and gravel, baking in a searing sun. The first Border Patrol car that came along would raise the alarm, and Gray knew he needed to be far away before that happened.

He heard a car horn. Zapata was summoning his assassins. Gray moved back through the rocks until he could see the fence and the narrow opening. Three figures stood looking across the small clearing and up the dirt track. Gray dropped to the ground and focused his scope on the group. A thick-bodied man with dark hair held a struggling child by the arm.

Carlie Kate was alive. Everything he had done to bring them all to this point seemed right. He could see her arm encased in a sling and held across her chest, her long blonde hair hanging loose and ragged. A few feet away, another man, taller and rail thin, stood looking up the track, searching for a sign of those Zapata had sent ahead.

Gray figured the short, thick-bodied one, holding the girl, was Miguel Zapata, the man responsible for Bethany's death, as well as the others who Gray had killed in his quest. As he watched through the scope, the man appeared to call out, becoming agitated when he received no answer. The thin man began working his way up the track of the flat-bottomed wash. Gray knew the man would soon see one of the bodies and shout a warning. He figured Zapata would not stick around if his back-up guns were silent and could easily slip back through the fence to the waiting car.

When the man came within hailing distance, Gray called out. "I'd stop right there if I were you."

The man halted in mid-stride when he saw the rifle in Gray's hands. Down by the fence, Zapata pulled the girl in front of him and wrapped his arm around her neck.

Then the man pointed up the wash at one of the bodies. "The others?"

"Them, too," Gray said. "There's one up in the rocks above me. But he can't help you either. The others..." Gray shrugged.

Zapata screamed a stream of obscenities.

The thin one called out Gray's news and waited.

Gray worked his way down the slope, keeping the man covered. He motioned for him to start back toward the fence.

Suddenly two shots rang out from below. With four hundred yards separating them, Gray doubted he was in any danger. He stopped when he saw Zapata tighten his grip on the girl and place the gun at her head.

Gray heard Zapata yelling but was still too far away to figure out what he wanted.

The thin man nodded in reply and shouted to Gray. "He says he will kill her unless you put down your gun."

The four hundred yards between them posed no problem. He could put six shots in the man's head at that distance. But paper targets remained motionless, and a child's life was the reward of failure. He didn't want to repeat that. Especially not with Carlie Kate.

"What's your name?"

"Fuentes."

"Well, Fuentes, tell him I can kill him from here. Let the girl go and I'll toss you the book, and we can all go home. That was the deal. If he hurts the girl, he'll never make it back through the fence."

Zapata dropped to the dirt, still holding the girl in front of him. He yelled what sounded like another string of obscenities and another demand.

Fuentes shuffled his feet in the sand and nodded. "He says he is a dead man anyway without the book. You give it to me first. He wants to be sure it is the one he lost."

Gray had little choice. If Zapata decided he had what he wanted and let Carlie Kate go it, would be over. If he didn't Gray, would kill him.

"Do you know what he did, Fuentes, to the girl's mother?"

Fuentes hesitated. "I know. It was not supposed to happen like that. He only wanted to find you. You killed his daughter and grandson. She was my wife."

Gray held his hands apart. "I am truly sorry for what I did. You have every right to hate me, but taking the life of this little girl will not bring them back." He pointed down the draw at Zapata. "Will he let her go if he gets what he wants?"

Fuentes shook his head slowly. "No, I do not think he will let her go."

"Why not, if I give him what he wants?"

"Because he is afraid of her, and who she is. He is afraid she will tell what she has seen, and they will come for him. Even his father could not save him if your government wants him."

Zapata squeezed off another two rounds in Gray's direction and called up again with more questions.

"He wants to know what we are saying. He says you have only a minute to decide or he will kill her."

"He's not going to do that yet. He doesn't have the book," Gray said.

"Throw it to me," Fuentes said.

Gray reached into the side pocket of his backpack and pulled out the frayed notebook, tossing it as far as he could in Fuentes' direction.

Fuentes walked forward and picked it up, thumbing through it quickly, then went down the slope a short distance and held it up, saying something to Zapata.

Gray couldn't hear what Zapata said in response.

"He wants me to bring it to him," Fuentes said. "Maybe I can convince him to let her go."

"Go," Gray said. "But tell him he will never make it through the fence if he tries to leave."

Fuentes approached Zapata, who maintained his grip on the girl. The two men began arguing before Zapata took a step backward toward the fence, dragging the girl with him. Fuentes held out his hands and continued to argue. Zapata checked behind him for the opening, fifteen feet away. Fuentes looked up to where Gray sat holding the rifle to his shoulder.

"No, please don't make me do this," Gray pleaded. He knew he had only seconds before Zapata reached the fence.

As if suddenly realizing his vulnerability, Zapata hunched down behind the girl and continued duck walking backward, dragging the girl.

Carlie Kate screamed.

Gray's right hand dropped to the 9mm in his belt. He drew it out and placed it on the ground as he knelt, the Remington carried to his shoulder in a measured movement, releasing the safety as he did so. The cross hairs on the scope passed over the tearstained face of Carlie Kate and rested on a spot on the side of Zapata's head, the only part of the man still visible. Gray knew if he missed and hit the girl, the chambered bullet in the 9mm would be for himself. He wanted no part of a life if he hurt her.

Zapata stumbled and Gray lost him for a second. Only five feet from the fence, Zapata sneered and brought his own gun up, placing it against Carlie Kate's head.

The rifle slammed against Gray's shoulder, and the echo of the .308 reverberated across the rocky hills. He couldn't remember regaining Zapata's image and calculating the adjustments before taking the shot. Both Carlie Kate and Zapata lay sprawled on the ground, Zapata falling with his heavy arm over the girl.

A scream formed in Gray's throat. He dropped the rifle and grasped the butt of the 9mm.

Down below Fuentes, rolled Zapata over and lifted the child up, placing her on her feet.

Gray raced down the slope to catch her in his arms and lift her off her feet.

Her first words came out among the sobs. "Conaire, I told them you would come. What took you so long?"

Gray held her tight, unable to answer while he carried her back to where Fuentes waited.

"So, you are the Indian she was expecting?"

Gray started to answer, then remembered her arm was no longer in the sling. He knelt down and took the heavily bandaged hand in his own. "Does it hurt?"

"Oh, no," she said. She unwrapped the bandage and held up her hand. "See? It's okay."

Fuentes looked at Gray and shrugged. "I could not do what they wanted. They do not know I have disobeyed them. There was a little girl in the village who had died. I paid for her funeral."

"*Si*, but that will not be for long."

Gray spun around. Zapata sat on the ground holding a gold-plated revolver in both hands. A thin trickle of blood ran down the side of his face from the shallow furrow Gray's bullet had caused. With only a few feet between them, Zapata could hardly miss. Gray could see the Colt's hammer at full cock and Zapata's finger on the trigger began to tighten.

Gray flinched, spinning the girl around behind him and reaching down for the gun he had dropped when he picked her up. He threw himself at Zapata, waiting for the heavy death-dealing slug to slam into his chest. The heavy concussion from the .45 going off beside his head stunned him, but instinct caused him to ram the 9mm into Zapata's side and fire it until the slide remained open.

Gray rose to his feet, the empty gun still clutched in his hand, unable to fathom how Zapata's shot had missed.

A voice made him look up.

"It is over now," Fuentes said, "Enough is enough!"

"What will you tell Montoya?"

Fuentes walked over and picked up the notebook, which had fallen in the dirt. He knocked the dust from it and put it in his pocket. "Don Emiliano will need this to repair the damage you have caused. He was certain you would make a copy, but if we know what it contains, precautions can be taken."

For a moment Gray considered the situation. He felt he owed Fuentes something. "Did you know about the other one? Not the four Zapata sent ahead."

"There was someone else?" Fuentes seemed surprised.

"I think your Don Emiliano wanted all the pieces taken care of. This one was not your ordinary clown. He was good. I wouldn't be surprised if you were on the list also."

Fuentes nodded. "I will find out about this. There was someone's name mentioned. I think he called himself *El Diablo*. When I tell Don Emiliano you have killed Miguel, he will continue to search for you until you are dead. This child here I could not see die for what has happened between us. Her mother is dead, and you saved my life. We are even, for the moment. Take her and go, and if we meet again, one of us will surely regret it."

"The notebook, I didn't make a copy. You tell Montoya it's over as far as I am concerned." He picked up Carlie Kate and started up the track toward the camouflaged Jeep. She put her arms around his neck.

"I miss my mom," she said.

"I do, too."

"Where will I go now?"

"There is a very nice lady who wants to meet you. She's your grandmother. She can't wait to meet Carlie Kate."

"Okay, but what happened to my cat?"

"She's waiting for you. There's also an old man I want you to meet. He's my grandfather."

"The Indian man?"

"Yes, the Indian man."

She reached up and ran her finger down his cheek. "You have paint on your face. Do all Indians paint their faces like that?"

He thought about his answer. Why had he done it? "Yes, Carlie, but only when we go to war."

He carried her up the draw toward the car. Some things still had to be resolved, including the leak in Senator Davis's household. And there was Simone. Would he call her? And what was he going to do? Carlie Kate was safe, and Miguel Zapata lay rotting in the heat of the desert sun. But it wasn't over. He knew it wouldn't ever be really over. There were more bodies to fill his dreams, to wake him in the night. He tilted his head down and kissed the top of Carlie's head.

ACKNOWLEDGEMENTS

I want to thank close family members for their patience and understanding while I researched and wrote this book. The grass didn't always get cut in time, the car often needed a good wash, and the to-do list grew, while the words s

lowly accumulated on the page.

Again, I need to thank Larry Edwards (larryedwards.com) for his invaluable help, and Tiffany Lynne at Gray Publishing Services (graypublishingservices.com) for the new cover and interior.

OTHER BOOKS BY E. PAUL BERGERON

IN THE SHADOW OF VARGAS
BOOK ONE OF A LAND IN TURMOIL SERIES
Available at: Amazon

When William MacLeod, a member of an American fur trapping party, is forced into Spanish New Mexico to seek help for a wounded companion, he finds love and encounters a vengeance that will test his power to fulfill the promises he made.

Maria de Cordero, the beautiful daughter of a wealthy hacienda owner, is promised in marriage to another, but she makes the fateful mistake of falling in love with the young American. When her secret visit to MacLeod's jail cell is discovered, the man who lustfully awaits their marriage, Miguel Griego, captain of the governor's own militia, seeks his revenge against this insult to his name.

Can MacLeod find a way to escape, and save Maria from what her family believes is a fate worse than death?

*****

THE SEARCH FOR DIEGO
BOOK TWO OF A LAND IN TURMOIL SERIES
Available at: Amazon

In the bowels of a hostile desert, a woman lay dying. As the last vestige of strength seeps from her body she passed the child into his hands. "Save him—for me. He is all I have to give you," were her final words.

Standing in his way is a fanatical priest who would take the child and save its soul instead. But the Frenchman, whose deadly reputation is built on the bodies of the men who challenged him, has other ideas. Filled with hatred for the man whose son it is, he takes the child from the woman paid to keep it, and passes it into the hands of a beautiful woman from the streets and slums of Vera Cruz.

It is 1823. Mexico has recently gained its independence, with little conception of how to govern this chaotic land. And in that far away place that is Alta California, leadership is based on the whims of the ignorant. It is here that William

MacLeod scours the land in search of his son, while the Church, and those in charge, struggle to banish this foreign intruder from their land.

Love, hate, treachery, and death stalk his path as he attempts to fulfill her dying request.

A thrilling historical novel in this Land in Turmoil Series.

ABOUT THE AUTHOR

You can contact E Paul Bergeron at: edpbergeron@cs.com

As I remember it, life began on top of a load of furniture in a sleigh drawn by a team of horses on a bitterly cold day. My mother was walking alongside in the snow when the moment arrived. She claims it was Valentine's Day, and of all people, she should know.

I attended a one-room schoolhouse outside of the French Canadian town of Mascouche, Quebec, and later in the metropolis of Montreal. At some point, an overworked schoolteacher wrote a note home to my mother to say that someday I would be a writer. The rest of the family laughed.

I spent long winter afternoons and nights reading, and acquired a love of history. I never realized the depth of this love until, years later, I stood on a street corner in old Montreal and read the inscription etched on a brass plaque attached to the cornerstone of a grey, brick building. It read simply, "Hudson's Bay Company." There stood the company synonymous with intrigue and adventure, and, being of French and Scottish heritage, the people behind those adventures were my ancestors. They were the French voyageurs, or coureur de bois, who traversed the mountains and forests, and paddled the streams and rivers, and the Scots who sent them out in search of the fur pelts, which led to the exploration of the North American continent.

I was sixteen when my father found an old farmhouse, badly in need of repair in West Bolton, Quebec. There I spent a year among people who would become lifelong friends. But my father passed away before he realized his vision for the house.

My mother took us back to Montreal, and I soon left school to find a job to help support the family. Then a Christmas phone call came from California, and the invitation to come west took us to North Hollywood, with palm trees and salt sea air--and word that I was too young to work. I returned to school.

I stood in the quad of North Hollywood High with a recent import from Australia, gazing at the parking lot and wondering how the school could have so many teachers. The Aussie informed me that it was the students' parking lot. Life had certainly changed.

I soon discovered California's lofty Sierra Nevada Mountains and streams filled with wild trout holding below the riffles, as if waiting for the dry fly attached to the end of my line. However, those towering, snow-capped peaks beckoned, and I could not care less if the trout were hungry. Life was wonderful.

With the early beginning of a writing life, and being married to an artist, our two beautiful daughters grew up in a home filled with artistic expression. Later, we moved down the coast to a town in Orange County, until it was time to sell a business and find a place to begin the work put on hold for so many years.

We settled in Hayden Lake, Idaho, with a beautiful home a few miles from the shores of Lake Coeur d'Alene. Now I load my Surly Long Haul Trucker bike on the back of the car and drive to the trail whose path winds its way along the Coeur d'Alene River. I find a spot beside a small lake to watch the ducks and geese feed among the lily pads, or sit in a small clearing beneath a canopy of leafy branches, and there work out the twists and turns of the stories I want to tell.

Visit him online at:

Website: http://www.epaulbergeron.com

Facebook: http://www.facebook.com/EPaulBergeron/

www.ingramcontent.com/pod-product-compliance
Lightning Source LLC
Chambersburg PA
CBHW070723280626
47159CB00023B/2347

* 9 780099 670132 7 *